Louisiana Family Mystery Series
Book 1

Running Home

SAMMY TIPPIT

Running Home
Copyright 2015 Sammy Tippit

Published by:
Sammy Tippit Books
P.O. Box 781767
San Antonio, Texas 78278

Cover created by: Dugan Design Group

Printed by CreateSpace

All Bible references are New English Translation
ISBN: 978-0-9864411-1-0
Printed in the United States of America

DEDICATION

To: Kirsta, Kendis, Kylla, Karin, and Lyn, who have been inspirational in their fight against human trafficking.

And

To: The 1965 graduating class of Istrouma High School.

CONTENTS

WHAT LEADERS SAY ABOUT *RUNNING HOME*

Radio Talk Show Host

"From the first paragraph, Sammy Tippit's new novel grabs you by the throat and refuses to let go. *Running Home* is a powerful story of redemption, revival and hope. "Riveting" has become a cliché for a literary piece, but it is absolutely appropriate for this wonderful book. It is literally difficult to stop reading as you are continually drawn into the story of a man's search for a place he can call home and the family he craves. You will be blessed, encouraged, challenged and convicted when you read *Running Home*!"

Bob Burney, Host – Bob Burney Live
President CrossPower Ministries

Elite Athlete

"By page three, I was very interested in continuing my journey into Win's life. The book had me dialed in early. It prompts you to push the pause button and ask, 'How am I living?' Sammy's passion for prayer, healing and revival demonstrates the transformative power that only God possesses."

Kevin L. Morning, M.S.
Masters Athlete of the Year on three occasions and two times World Record Holder at 200 meters for 45 – 49 year olds and 4 x 400 meter relay for 40 – 49 year olds.

Prayer Leader

"Running Home will keep you on the edge of your seat. It's a 'can't put it down until finished' story filled with drama and suspense. The best part, however, is the message of prayer, repentance, and revival that stirs your heart and soul. I highly recommend it; in fact, I'm going to read it again while I'm waiting for the next in the series!"

Glenn Sheppard, President
International Prayer Ministries

Writer

"Good stories hold your interest, but the best ones make you care. This one made me care—about the characters, their choices, and the true-to-life situations they encountered."

Tim Grissom, Senior Editor
FamilyLife Publishing

Family Leader

"Human trafficking and freedom, worldliness and holiness, sin and redemption, brokenness and reconciliation, rebellion and revival, desperation and prayer — Sammy Tippit sets it all in a gripping story about the real stuff of life that pulled me in from page one. In this age of godlessness, *Running Home* is a powerful reminder of what happens when sin meets grace. Sammy has given the body of Christ a suspenseful drama containing a much-needed biblical blueprint for revival in our broken world."

Rev. Buddy Smith, Senior Vice President
American Family Association

Pastor

"Running Home tells the compelling story of a man who returns home to make things right, but things go wrong. Sammy Tippit presents flawed characters, like us, who experience failure and redemption, brokenness and healing. Set against the backdrop of south Louisiana and competitive running, this book weaves together unique story elements that will challenge and inspire."

Dr. Brent Saathoff, Pastor
CityChurch West – San Antonio, Texas

Denominational Leader

"*Running Home* is a thrilling, page-turning story, juxtaposing multiple scenarios that lead into an amazing tale of redemption and the positive results impacting a number of unsuspecting people."

Dr. Wayne Sheppard, Executive Assistant to the Executive Director
Louisiana Baptist Convention

CHAPTER ONE

Win Bass took a deep breath and smiled as he drove toward the Houston airport. *I didn't think life could ever be this good.* As he passed the tall, east Texas pines, sentimentality welled within. This was the closest he'd been to his boyhood home in forty-four years.

A longing to return to Louisiana had been brewing since last September, when he won the World Masters Track and Field championships in Italy. Now he had fulfilled his dream to win the 2008 U. S. Championships in Houston, and the longing to go back home intensified.

The warm, muggy air reminded him of his days as a high school track star in Baton Rouge, but the weight on his soul was much greater. *Why not?* flashed through his mind. *I'll drop Calvin at the airport, hop on I-10, and be there in a few hours.* As Win dreamed about the possibility of returning to Baton Rouge, tears welled in his eyes and sweat appeared on his forehead.

Calvin's booming voice shook him from his daze. "A big truck stop ahead. Let's grab a sandwich before you drop me off at the airport."

"Sounds good." A sense of guilt rushed through Win. *How dumb can you be? You'll never be able to go home. It was that kind of impulsiveness that landed you in prison.* He tried to cast off those feelings by reminding himself that his ability to act quickly on unconventional ideas had also made him a multi-millionaire.

Win wondered if Calvin could sense his raging debate. He trusted Calvin — completely. He knew more about Win's past than anyone.

Should he share his thoughts with him?

Win missed the auto entrance to the truck stop and turned into the truck parking area. As they weaved back to the automobile side, Calvin pointed to a row of trucks. "That's strange."

"What's strange?"

"Between each row of trucks, there are girls walking around."

Win glanced and saw a couple of girls knocking on the doors of trucks. He lifted an eyebrow. "You thinkin' what I'm thinking?"

"Probably. Just keep moving. Once we're on the automobile side, it'll be all right."

After placing their order and being seated, Calvin looked at Win. "So, you're officially retired, and you've rented a beach house in Galveston for the next week." He lifted his eyebrows. "You planning to figure out what to do with the rest of your life?"

Win chuckled. "I'm thinking about returning to Baton Rouge."

"When did this come up?"

"It's been rolling around in my head for months, and being in Houston has reinforced my feelings." He sighed. "The weather, the trees, the bayous — they're so much like south Louisiana They bring back so many memories. Ever since I won in Italy, I've had a yearning to go home. Sometimes I feel this emptiness deep in my gut. It's like I don't know who I am. I start thinking about my family and my high school friends, and it turns into a raging fire."

Calvin shook his head. "I've told you there might come a time you need to deal with your past. Maybe this is it. Are you ready for what you'll face?"

Win looked at the table. "I don't know. I feel so guilty."

"Hey, man. You're not guilty." A smile crawled onto Calvin's face. "Stupid — yeah." His face resumed a somber expression. "You need to stop this guilty talk."

"But I feel so ashamed. I don't even know what I'm guilty of. Maybe it's my mom and dad, and what I did to them."

Calvin's voice deepened. "We've talked about this. You didn't kill them."

Win kept staring at the table. "I know, but I made a stupid mistake that killed them. I wish I could turn the clock back." Win turned away from Calvin. "Excuse me. I'll be back."

As Win headed toward the men's room, an African-American girl stood outside the women's door, her hands covering her face. "Are you all right?" When she took her hands from her face, Win couldn't believe what he saw. *She can't be more than fourteen.*

Mascara mixed with tears ran down the teen's face. She sniffled as she gave a nod.

"Are you sure?"

A dam burst, and she placed her hands over her mouth to try to stifle her sobs.

Win cleared his throat. "Where are your parents?"

The girl shrugged and tried to calm herself.

"You don't know?"

She shook her head and wrapped her arms around herself.

"Who brought you here?"

The girl's eyes darted down the hall.

Win stooped to look into her eyes. "Are you in trouble?"

Her lips trembled. She stretched to see around the corner. "I can't let Ginger see me."

"Ginger?"

"If she sees me talking, they'll beat me."

"Who'll beat you?"

She shook her head. "I can't talk."

Win took a step toward the corner and looked around the restaurant and store. A young woman talked with one of the store workers. Win pointed his head toward the woman. "Are you afraid of her?"

The girl shook her head. "Her man hit me when I said I couldn't do what he told me. They beat my friend really bad. If I don't do what they say, she's going to be really mad."

"How did this happen to you?"

The girl looked at the floor. "I'm afraid."

"Afraid of what?"

"They'll hurt me."

"Who? Who'll hurt you?"

She pointed toward the woman. "They kidnapped me."

"What?" Win wiped his brow. "When, where?"

The teenager placed her hands over her mouth to muffle the sobs. "A couple of weeks ago in Baton Rouge."

Fear, guilt, and desperation collided as Win took a deep breath. "Let me help you. I'll get you out of here."

The girl blew out air. "I can't. They'll find me. Th— they might kill me."

Win paced a few steps and pointed toward the woman. "Why don't you tell her there's a man who wants some action and that he has a room in the motel across the street? She might let you go with me. I'll bring you somewhere safe."

She rubbed her forehead. "I don't know."

"It's worth a try." Win pulled out his wallet and handed her a $100 bill. "Give her this, and tell her I promised another just like it."

The teenager sucked in air. "Okay."

Win's eyes pierced the girl's. "It's going to be all right. Go wash your face, then talk to her. I'll let my friend know what's going on." Her facial muscles twitched.

"Look into my eyes," Win said. "I know you don't know me. But, I *promise* I won't hurt you. I *promise* I'll help you."

She swallowed hard and walked into the restroom.

———◇◇———

Win sat silently, staring at Calvin. "Do you trust me?"

Calvin rubbed the back of his neck. "What?"

"I need you to do something, and I don't have time to explain."

Calvin leaned toward Win. "You know I trust you."

Win pulled out the car keys. "Take these and drive to the edge of the parking area so we can leave quickly. Then get in the backseat and wait. I'll be out in a few minutes." Win felt queasy. "Okay. I need to go. Are you with me?"

"What are you doing?"

"You said you trusted me."

"I trust you completely, but this is weird."

"I know it sounds crazy. But I need you to do this. I'll explain everything after I'm in the car."

Calvin rolled his eyes. "You definitely have a lot of explaining to do."

Win strolled into the convenience store and tapped the girl on the arm. "You ready to go, sweetheart?"

Her eyes gave a questioning look to the older girl, who nodded. The teenager gave a cursory smile. "Sure."

Win placed his arm around the girl and swaggered out. "Come on, baby. We've got a big night ahead of us."

The older girl yelled as they left. "LaKeisha, we'll see you in about an hour. Keep your cell phone on."

As Win and LaKeisha hopped in the car, he turned to Calvin. "Hang on. I'm headed to the back of the motel, then I'll circle around to the highway."

"What are you doing? Who is she?"

Win's eyes remained fixed on the road. "I'll explain once we're on the highway."

LaKeisha's body trembled as she gasped for air.

As Win headed north on I-45, Calvin shouted, "Man, what's going on!"

"We're headed to the airport." Win clutched the steering wheel. "She was kidnapped — in Baton Rouge. We need to take her somewhere safe."

As LaKeisha sobbed, Calvin grabbed Win's shoulder. "What! Are you . . ." Calvin paused. "No. We can't do that while she's in this condition. Do you realize how we'd look?"

"You have a better idea?"

"Let's head to Conroe. It's a little more than a half-hour. We'll be far enough from the truck stop that it should be safe to sort this out."

Ping. LaKeisha jolted as a text message dinged her phone. "Oh, no! What do I do?" She squeezed the phone.

Calvin grabbed her hands. "Give me the phone. Let me see what they're saying."

LaKeisha, where are you? We know you're not at the motel.

Calvin mumbled, "Oh, man. This is *not* good."

Win tilted his head toward Calvin. "What's wrong?"

"They're tracking her."

LaKeisha let out a scream. "They're going to kill me!"

Win glanced toward her. "I promised you'd be safe. Nothing's going to happen."

Calvin edged toward the back of Win's seat. "Head to the airport. Pull up to the curb, and I'll jump out. I'll go inside and drop the phone in a trash container. When I get back in the car, we head south — toward downtown. If they're tracking her, they'll think we brought her to the airport. They'll look for her here — or north of here. We'll head the opposite direction."

As Calvin strode into the airport, Win shot LaKeisha a sympathetic look. "You're going to be fine."

She sniffled. "Where are you taking me?"

"I don't know yet, but they won't be able to hurt you."

Win grabbed his phone as it buzzed. "Everything all right?"

Calvin's voice filled with tension. "I ditched the phone, but I wanted to talk to you while the girl's not able to hear."

"Hold on." Win glanced in the mirror. "A traffic cop is coming from behind. Let me circle the terminal, and you can talk while I'm driving." Win pulled away and made a loop around the terminal. "Okay, what's up?"

"How do we know she's telling the truth? How do we know she was kidnapped?"

Win glanced at LaKeisha, who continued staring out the window. "We don't, but I'm pretty sure . . ." He glanced toward LaKeisha.

"We need something that confirms what she's saying. A parent's name — a phone number. Anything. If we can confirm she was kidnapped, we need to take her immediately to a police station. If she's lying, we're in a heap of trouble."

"I'm coming up to the terminal. Are you outside?"

"I see you. I'm about fifty yards in front of you."

"I see you. There's a cop right behind you."

"No problem. I'll hop in quickly."

After Calvin climbed in the backseat, Win headed toward downtown. "LaKeisha."

She timidly murmured, "What?"

"We want to help, but there's some things we need to know. How do we contact your parents and let them know you're safe?"

She looked down. "I don't know."

"You don't know how to contact your parents?"

"My father left my mother two years ago. We haven't heard from him since."

"What about your mother?"

"She started living with a guy six months ago. After a couple of months, she told me I needed to find a place to live. They left Baton Rouge, and I haven't heard from her since."

Calvin leaned against the front seat. "LaKeisha, I grew up on the south side of Chicago — in an area filled with addicts, prostitutes, and gangs. I can't ever remember seeing my dad. My mom was a wonderful woman who believed in me. Everyone told me I'd live in the ghetto the rest of my life. But my mother felt differently. She said I could make something of myself. She was right. I've been successful, but there's one thing I know about escaping the hood.

You gotta shoot straight. Can't play games."

"I'm telling the truth." She crossed her arms. "You think I'm lying!"

"I didn't say that. We just need to know where your mother is. We need to get you to her."

LaKeisha stared out the window. "I already told you! I don't know."

Win cleared his throat. "Calm down. We just need someone to contact and let them know you're all right. Who were you staying with after your mom left?"

I stayed with a friend for a couple of weeks. Her parents told me I needed to find another place. I went to a different friend's place and stayed for a week. Her parents said I needed to find a more permanent place. They talked to Reverend Thomas Washington and his wife. They took me into their home and found a social worker to help me. I was living with them when I was kidnapped."

Win sighed. "Do you know his phone number?"

"Yes."

"We need to call him. You okay with that?"

LaKeisha nodded and called out the number.

CHAPTER TWO

Win's stomach churned as they pulled into the police station. "I don't know if I can do this."

Calvin grabbed his shoulder. "Hang on, man. There's no turning back now."

A perplexed look crept onto LaKeisha's face. "What's wrong?"

Calvin pursed his lips. "He'll be okay. He's just a little nervous." He turned to Win. "Let me do the talking. We haven't done anything wrong. I'll—"

Perspiration ran down Win's forehead. "That's the problem! We haven't done anything wrong. Nearly forty-four years ago, I didn't do anything wrong. If they look up my record, they'll think . . ."

"Listen to me! There's nothing to fear. That was a long time ago. It may not still be in the records." Calvin sighed. "We made a decision, and now we have to go through with it." He pulled out a handkerchief. "Dry your face."

Calvin turned to LaKeisha. "Let's go. Come on. Your pastor friend said he's on his way to Houston. He'll be here in a few hours. Once we're inside, I'll call him, and he can talk to the police. He said an alert was sent out the day you disappeared. The police should have all the records."

Chills crept up Win's spine as they entered the station. It was much different from what he remembered in Los Angeles. He stood sheepishly behind Calvin and LaKeisha while Calvin explained to the policewoman behind the glass barrier who they were and why they had come. The woman asked for identification. Win's hand trembled as he handed over his driver's license. Soon two detectives emerged from behind the glass.

The policewoman introduced the three to the detectives and pointed to Calvin, "Detective Stonewall will take your statement." She turned to Win. "Detective Ortiz will take yours." She gently smiled at LaKeisha. "We have someone from Juvie on her way over. She'll be here shortly. You can sit with me until she comes."

Win shuddered as he stepped into the interrogation room. Visions of his interview forty-four years earlier flashed through his mind. *Settle down. Get hold of yourself.*

Detective Ortiz pointed to a chair. "Let's start by giving me your name — where you live and work."

Win cleared his throat. "Winston Bass. I live in Seattle, Washington."

Ortiz tilted his head. "What brought you to Houston?"

"I ran in the Masters Track and Field Championships this week."

"I read about that in the paper." Ortiz paused and squinted. "Are you okay?"

Win tried to dry his palms on his pants. "I'm just a little nervous about being in a police station." He flashed a smile. "It's not something I do every day."

Ortiz nodded. "I understand. Now, tell me what happened."

Win told him about pulling into the truck stop and what happened afterward. He became more comfortable as he shared the story. Within a few minutes he quit slumping in his chair, and his voice strengthened. Ortiz took notes as he peppered Win with questions. After an hour of talking, Win finally had a chance to catch his breath. *I'm going to be all right. We'll help this kid.*

Ortiz pursed his lips. "Just relax for a little while. I need to process some things, and I'll be back."

⸺◇⸺

The longer Win sat by himself in the interrogation room, the more distraught he became. He remembered going through the same drill forty-four years earlier. He knew they were checking his statement — and his background. After half an hour, he paced the room. He prayed, then sighed, prayed more, and kept pacing. He looked at his watch and became more concerned. It had been nearly an hour.

Detective Stonewall strode in. "Take a seat, Mr. Bass."

Win swallowed. "Where's Detective Ortiz?"

"He's doing some follow up. I need to talk to you about some of what we've found." Stonewall's eyes pierced Win's. "There's some interesting details in the database of the National Crime Information Center. Did you have some kind of problem in California a number of years ago?"

Win's head dropped. It felt like an eternity before he could speak. He slowly lifted his head. "Yes. I had problems." Win squared his shoulders. "But that has nothing to do with this. That was forty-four years ago. I came in here to help a girl in trouble. I'd think you'd want to know about what's happened to this . . . this kid."

"We're checking that out. Don't you think it's a bit unusual that a man from Seattle who spent time in prison in California comes into a police station in Houston with a young girl from Louisiana who has been kidnapped?"

Win's voice firmed. "Don't you think it would be highly unusual for someone who kidnapped a child to walk into a police station with that same child and turn her over to you?"

"Everything about this is highly unusual. That's why I need some answers."

"You've talked to my friend. I'm sure he's verified what I'm saying."

"I need to hear the truth from you. Tell me. Have you had any contact with your drug dealers since you were released from prison?"

Win banged his fist on the table. "Wait a minute! I don't have drug dealers. I was a kid back then. They appointed an attorney to defend me, and he did a terrible job. But that's not my situation today, and that's not who I am. I don't know what you read, but not everything was true in my initial conviction." Win gritted his teeth. "I'm here to help." Win raised his eyebrows. "Understand?"

Stonewall stared at Win while tapping his pen on his palm.

Win wondered who would blink first. Finally Stonewall broke the silence. "I'll be back."

Another waiting game. The more Win paced, the more determined he became to be careful with his words. Old memories rushed anger into his heart. Nearly an hour passed before Detective Ortiz returned. Win's face flushed. He felt the heat rising in his body. "What kind of game is this?"

"Calm down, Mister Bass." Ortiz held the door open. "You're

free to go. We've checked out everything. The girl gave us details. They match what Baton Rouge police told us. You and your friend can leave."

"What about LaKeisha? What's going to happen to her?"

"The juvenile authorities are with her right now. We've talked with her pastor, and he should be here shortly. Juvie will sort things out. She'll be all right."

Win felt his body go limp. Calvin was waiting as he came out of the interrogation room. As the two walked out of the station, Ortiz held the door open. "We have your contact information. We may need to talk more."

Calvin smiled. "Feel free to call. We'll do what we can."

As Win drove toward the airport, he shook his head. "I can't believe what just happened. Man, I'm drained."

"It's okay. We did the right thing."

Win pursed his lips. "You missed your flight."

"Yeah. But I have an idea. There's a truck stop ahead. Why don't we get a bite to eat?"

Win jerked his head. "Are you crazy?"

Calvin roared with laughter. Then he said, "Let's get a couple of rooms at a hotel near the airport, and when we get up I'll try to catch a flight to Seattle."

Win and Calvin met in the restaurant after a short night's rest. Win held his coffee cup under his nose. "This is great. You never forget some smells."

"What do you mean?"

"Community Dark Roast, the best coffee in the world. Mom and Dad used to drink it every morning." The aroma seemed to transport him to another time. He looked out the window. "I miss them."

"I guess that means you're gonna visit Baton Rouge."

"I think I'll take a few days in Galveston, then head to the Red Stick."

"Are you sure you're ready?"

Win chuckled. "It's been nearly a half-century. How long does it take to get ready?"

"From what I saw last night, it's time for you to go home. But you realize, it probably won't be easy."

A deep calmness came over Win as he breathed deeply. "I know." His eyes pierced Calvin's. "I thought I'd dealt with all the negative feelings— until I was left alone in the interrogation room. The bitterness — the anger — rose like a tidal wave. I couldn't stop it." Win sipped his coffee. "That really bothers me. That's why I need a few days in Galveston — thinking and praying. I need to sort out my feelings."

"Would you ever want to move back to Baton Rouge?"

Win took a whiff of his coffee. "I'd seriously consider it. I didn't sleep much last night. I thought about that young girl . . . my life . . . my parents . . . and a lot of other people. If things feel right, I might look for a place to live, then make plans to return in January."

"Wow! Slow down, friend."

Win chuckled. "Impulsive me. That trait has made me a lot of money, but it sure has created a lot of problems." Win stared at the table, then glanced back at Calvin. "You don't know what it's like. It's impossible for you to understand."

"Understand what?"

"I have a beautiful house overlooking the lake. The view is one of the best in the world. But it's not home. At night, those walls don't talk to me. I'm alone. No family. I want a . . . I need a family."

"We've had this discussion before. You don't have a family in Baton Rouge. There's nothing you can do about that."

"The closest thing I have to family are the memories of forty-four years ago, and they're fading quickly. I don't want to lose them."

Win spent the next four days in Galveston, walking the beach, thinking, praying, and remembering. He had no choice —he had to return to Baton Rouge. As he made the four-hour drive to his hometown, emotions rose that he hadn't felt in decades. Guilt led him into a dark tunnel, while loneliness produced a sea of tears. But as he crossed the Atchafalaya River Basin, the beauty of the swamps mesmerized him. His heart burst with praise and admiration for the Creator of those swamps. He knew the chains that held him were about to be broken. But he knew there was a price to pay for his freedom, and he tried to shove it from his mind.

After Win settled into his hotel in Baton Rouge, he wanted to find his parents' gravesite. At the scenic cemetery just off Airline Highway, he stood silently for nearly five minutes, staring at his parents' names on the markers. Finally he mustered the courage to speak. His voice cracked. "Momma, Daddy." He continued with a whisper, "I'm home. I finally made it. I'm so sorry." Tears fell like a south Louisiana rainstorm.

Finally he gained his composure. "I didn't do it. I promise. I didn't do what they said." He placed a bouquet in the vase at the top of his mother's headstone. "I brought some dandelions because I knew they were your favorite. I put a red rose in the middle because I wanted you to know how much I love you. I'm so sorry, Momma, that I wasn't there when you needed me." He kissed his fingers and gently touched the flowers.

Win moved a few feet to his father's grave. "Daddy, I respect you so much. You were always there for me. I feel like I killed you. I'm so sorry. Sorry for everything. Sorry I didn't go to LSU. Sorry I didn't make the Olympic team. Sorry I let you down." The shower of tears became a downpour. "Last year, I ran in Italy — in the Masters World Track and Field Championships. I won the gold." He pulled a medal from his jogging suit. "When they put this around my neck, all I could think about was you. Daddy, this is for you."

He placed the gold medal in his father's vase. With a chuckle, he said, "You would have gotten a kick out of all those old men running. Some were pretty fast. A couple of guys hold world records. After the race, I kept looking at the medal and knew I needed to come home and give it to you. I love you, Daddy. Remember the last time I ran in Baton Rouge? At Catholic High, in the district championships. I heard you yelling as I came down the stretch. The look on your face after I won made me feel like a king. I don't know why I threw it all away." He wiped his eyes. "I'm going now. I hope you know how much I love you."

Win started to leave, then paused. "I'll be back. You're all I have."

CHAPTER THREE

Win spent the next few days in Baton Rouge looking for real estate. In Seattle he owned a historic home overlooking Green Lake. He loved living near the water and wanted a similar place in Baton Rouge. The lakes by LSU provided the perfect spot.

The Realtor said it would be a short sale. It wasn't just a great location, but also a familiar one. An old oak stood next to the lake in front of an elegant 5,000-square-foot home. Win inspected the house and liked what he saw.

Win asked the Realtor to excuse him as he walked to the old oak and rubbed its bark. "Hello, friend. It's been a long time. He circled the tree to survey the side that faced the lake and smiled. "I can't believe it. You kept my heart's secrets tucked in your trunk all these years. Never let them die."

Win returned to the Realtor. "I want the house. I'll pay cash."

"That — that's wonderful. Let's head back to the office and seal the deal."

As soon as he finalized the purchase, Win flew back to Seattle to prepare for the move.

Seattle had become home after he'd been released from the California prison. Right after he arrived, he met some guys who'd just started a tech company, and they offered him a job. It was mostly gopher work, but they saw his potential and taught him the business. He caught on quickly, and they gave him a huge pay raise and company stock. Win seemed to come up with crazy ideas that worked. The more he pursued his unique ideas, the more the company grew. When Dresdtech went public, Win became an instant millionaire."

Win had everything he could possibly want, but the emptiness in his heart kept him from enjoying all he acquired. After gaining a lot of weight, a group of runners at Dresdtech asked if he wanted to run with them. Wanting to shed the pounds, he agreed. That changed everything. After six months of training, Win lost seventy-five pounds and gained something very valuable.

After their workouts, Calvin led the group in a fifteen-minute Bible study. The studies intrigued Win because they were based on Bible verses that talked about running. Soon he was hooked. He learned not only about running, but also a lot about life. One day after the workout, Win placed his faith in Jesus to forgive and change him. Win often leaned on the group for counsel. Calvin had not only been Win's boss, but also his spiritual mentor. The toughest part of leaving Seattle was leaving those guys.

They met for breakfast the day in January that Win began his journey to Louisiana. Calvin reached to shake Win's hand. "If you get in trouble, call me." He pointed toward the sky. "If you can't get out of trouble, call on Him."

Win smiled and bumped Calvin's chest with his fist. "Thanks, man. I owe you, and I'll owe you for the rest of my life."

"You don't owe me anything. Jesus paid the price for your new life. You're a piece of His artwork. Don't ever forget it."

Each of the guys gave Win a bear hug. One exhorted him. "We don't want to see you seventy-five pounds heavier when you come back to visit. Keep running."

With a big grin, Win pointed at him. "Don't worry. I'll never allow you guys to outrun me. I've already signed up for an All Comers' meet the first Saturday after I arrive in Baton Rouge."

As Win hopped in his new 2009 Lexus convertible, Calvin called out. "Maybe you'll find a cute Cajun princess down there who likes red cars."

Win let out a hearty laugh. "You think they have cute, sixty-year-old princesses in Louisiana? And you think I'm a dreamer!"

***

Win had arranged for the Baton Rouge Realtor to have all his furniture moved into his home before he arrived. He wanted to spend his first few days contacting old friends. He was surprised his high school running partner, Todd Mayo, now pastored a mega church just outside the city. He was the first person Win contacted.

When Win introduced himself on the phone, there was a long silence. "You're kidding. Win? Win Bass? I can't believe it. I thought you were dead. Everyone thought . . ." He became silent again.

"I know this is a shock," Win said, "but I'm in town. In fact, I've moved back here. I'd like to get together and catch up."

"Su . . . sure. When? Where? Let's do it."

"After all these years, I'm still running the 400 meters. There's an All Comers' meet at Catholic High, Saturday morning. I'm planning to run in it and should be finished by 10:30. Is there a place where we can meet for coffee?"

"There's a CC's coffee shop on Airline Highway. I'll be there at 10:30."

Chip Thibodeaux's stomach churned as he prepared for the Baton Rouge All Comers' meet. The seventeen-year-old had been looking forward to it since the end of track season. With only two months left until the new season, he planned to make a statement: *I'm the fastest high-school runner in Baton Rouge and will contend for the state championship.* He felt nothing could stop him.

Chip's coach announced the final call for the 400 meters. "Let's get this show on the road. A storm is brewing." Chip was assigned lane four, and his best friend Jamie, lane five.

It was the perfect setup. Jamie would pace him for the first 200 meters, just like last year. Chip was stoked. His adrenaline ran high as he bounced to keep his muscles warm. When he saw a gray-haired guy stretching in lane three, he stifled a laugh. He looked like Grandpa Moses. *How did they let this guy in?*

Chip jogged to Jamie and nodded behind him. "What's he doing here?"

Jamie shrugged. "It's an All Comers' meet. But I saw a wheelchair at the 200-meter mark with his name on it." He thumped Chip's chest. "Remember, this is our race. You'll be first, and I'll be second. Nobody here can hang with us."

Chip wasn't amused. "Look at his eyes. I've only seen that look in one other runner: Dave O'Quinn. And he won state last year."

Chip had trained hard all summer and fall. He'd been at the track by 7:00 every morning during the summer, sweating and pounding the new rubberized track at Indian Heights High. Others had come for leisurely workouts. Not Chip and Jamie. They'd made it to the gym three times a week, pumping iron, doing pushups, pull-ups, and practicing running drills. They continually challenged one another to run faster, become stronger, and get better.

A spell of confidence had been cast on Chip after he'd taken third at the 2008 state championships. He'd been the only junior to place in the top five. Yet a cloud hung over everything — not just this race, but also his future. Winning state meant a scholarship to LSU. A gutsy runner, he didn't fear anyone or anything. Confident it would happen, he ran like a man on a mission.

Coach Landon shouted, "The clouds are rolling in. Let's get started. Runners, take your mark."

Each runner crouched in his starting blocks, except the old man. He didn't have any.

"Get set."

The runners stared at the track. *Boom.* The race was on.

When they came around the first curve, Jamie and Chip began passing the guys in lanes six through eight. The old dude held his own in lane three as they ran the straightaway. All three maintained relaxed but fast strides between 100 and 200 meters. Chip slowly caught Jamie, but heard someone's feet behind him at around 150 meters.

Who's that? It's impossible. There's no one in the first three lanes able to hang with me. Then he did the unthinkable. He couldn't help himself. He looked to the left. The old man was hot on his tail. By the time Jamie, the old dude, and Chip entered the second curve, they were nearly even. Jamie had a short lead, which he lost in the curve. Chip struggled to keep his lead over the old guy. At that point, he felt the lactic acid in his legs.

Chip lost his concentration. *What's the old dude doing here?* He glanced again to his left. By the end of the curve, the old man pulled alongside him — tied for the lead. Jamie fell two strides behind.

The last hundred meters were always a matter of mental toughness. The lactic acid made everyone's legs feel like lead. Chip trained for it and was prepared — except that he lost his focus. He tried to lift his knees, maintain his form, and pump his arms. The first thing to go was the passion in his eyes. They looked more like a question mark. *What's the old dude doing here?*

Chip again looked at the old man, then lost all power to lift his legs. His stride shortened. He lost his form as he leaned from the waist. The old guy passed him. Jamie pulled up on his right side. *What's going on?*

Jamie overtook Chip in the last thirty meters. That had never happened. They crossed the finish line, old dude first, Jamie second, and Chip third. His heart sank. As he bent, trying to regain his breath, he wondered what had happened.

Once Jamie was able to talk, he asked Chip. "Man, what happened out there?"

"I don't know." Chip gasped. "I just couldn't lift my legs. Nothing was there."

The old man walked up and stuck out his knuckles. "Good run."

Jamie returned the knuckles. "Thanks."

Chip looked at the old man, raised his lips in a sneer, and turned his head. He wasn't about to extend his hand.

Coach Landon interrupted the awkward moment. "Chip, what happened? You said you worked all summer and fall. Son, you died at the close of the second curve. You can't tell me you're in shape. At least, I hope you're not in shape. What the . . . ?"

"Run!" Jamie shouted. A downpour descended, and everyone scattered. Chip and Jamie were soaked to the bone by the time they reached Chip's car.

Chip and Jamie sat in the car shivering. Chip was so bewildered by the race, being wet and cold didn't affect him.

Jamie asked again, "What happened?"

Chip slammed his hands on the wheel. "I don't know! When I heard the old man's footsteps, I couldn't believe it. It was like everything fell apart." He looked Jamie in the eyes. "You know how hard I trained. You couldn't hang with me when we did 200- or 300-meter repeats. I don't understand how you beat me. What went wrong?"

They discussed every part of the race: coming out of the blocks, the straightaway, the final curve, and the last 100 meters — dissecting every detail and trying to understand what had happened. After about fifteen minutes, the rain eased, and Jamie said, "I forgot my sunglasses on the football field. I need to get them before we head home." He sprinted back to the field.

As he did, Chip kept rolling over in his mind each part of the race.

Jamie hopped in the car. "Okay, let's go. I found them. Can't do without these babies. They're my good luck charm — great luck today." Jamie's tone changed. "Isn't that Coach Landon's car? Who is the guy getting out? He doesn't look like one of coach's guys."

A guy with a scraggly beard, ponytail, and an arm full of tattoos left the coach's car and hopped in a truck. Jamie pointed at the man. "Look at that scar on his face. I wouldn't want to meet him in a dark alley."

"Maybe those rumors are true about Coach," Chip said. Maybe he does sell 'roids."

Jamie shook his head. "They're not for me."

"Me, either. When I was in the tenth grade, a runner told me that Coach sold him some gym candy, and it improved his race. But Coach made him stop taking them before the state championships. Didn't want him to get caught."

"You really think that stuff works?"

"I suppose," Chip said. "I don't care. I'm going to win state, but it won't be because of some junk I take. It'll be because I trained."

⎯⎯⎯⎯⎯◇◇⎯⎯⎯⎯⎯

Win waited for the rain to stop before heading to CC's coffee shop. He'd parked at the far end of the Catholic High parking lot, away from the main area. As he tried to pull out of the parking lot, an F-250 pickup overtook him and slammed on its brakes, forcing him to stop abruptly. A tall, well-dressed, but overweight man opened the door and walked toward the Lexus.

Win lowered his window. "Is there a problem?"

"Yeah. There's a problem. You!"

"What do you mean?"

"This race was for our kids. You on some kind of ego trip? You, with your fancy sports car? Those license tags say "Washington." We don't need no Yankee coming down here and messing with our boys. Understand?"

"Hey, man, I was just trying to . . ."

"Don't 'Hey, man' me!" He yanked open the door of the Lexus. "You want to explain to me? You step outside, and I'll make sure you never explain anything to anybody. Understand? I don't know who you are, but you just ruined my son's day. He would have won if you hadn't run. I don't want to ever see you in one of these meets again.

Got it?"

"I apologize for ruining your son's day. I'm going to close my door, leave, and act like none of this ever took place." Win didn't blink, and his stare called the stranger's bluff.

The man's hand trembled as he pointed at Win. The two stared at one another for several seconds, then the stranger looked away. "Don't ever think about running in one of these meets again!" He retreated to his truck and sped away.

CHAPTER FOUR

As Win pulled up to CC's coffee shop, he tried to process what had just happened—both the race and the angry stranger. Leaving Baton Rouge had been tumultuous, and it looked like returning could be just as hard. He toweled himself before going inside to meet Todd. Though shocked by the parking lot encounter, he felt good about how he had run.

It had been more than forty years since he'd seen Todd, and he wasn't sure he'd recognize him. Somehow, Todd had become a pastor. The last time they were together, right after graduation, they had gotten drunk. A pastor was the last thing Win thought Todd would become. This would be interesting. Both had a lot of catching up to do.

Win didn't see anyone who resembled the photo on the church's website. After ordering a large dark roast, he found a small, round table in the corner and waited. He reminisced about high school, especially his track days. Win and Todd had been stars their senior year, and both had track scholarships: Win to LSU and Todd to Louisiana Tech. But Win left for California and never returned. He'd forfeited the scholarship, left his friends and family, and never looked back — until the world championships.

Win breathed deeply, enjoying the aroma of south Louisiana coffee. *I love and miss this place.* Although Seattle was known for its coffee, it couldn't compare to the Community dark roast his mom had brewed every morning. The sign with red wooden slats and white letters above his table helped him forget about his encounter after the race. "Drink Community Coffee — a cup of Louisiana hospitality." He savored its smell and smiled. His lost sense of security returned as he contemplated his high school days in Baton Rouge. He wondered what had happened in Todd's life.

When his old friend walked in, Win recognized him immediately. "Todd."

"Win? I can't believe it." Oblivious to the other customers, they embraced.

"Get your coffee. I have a table."

When Todd sat down, they awkwardly stared at each other for several seconds. Todd broke the ice with a huge grin. "I can't believe it's you. I've wondered all these years what happened. And here you sit."

"It's amazing. I never would have dreamed I would be talking to Pastor Todd Mayo. I want to hear about that, but first tell me about your family. I read on your website that you married Elaine. I knew you were right for each other. How is she? You have kids?"

"We married during our senior year at Tech. We have three kids: two boys and a girl. What about you? Married? Kids?"

Win slumped as he briefly looked away. "No. I've been in several relationships, but never got married. No kids. Just me." With a smile, he said, "Old buddy, it's great to be back in Baton Rouge."

Todd chuckled. "That's fantastic. Where did you move from?"

"Seattle."

"How'd you get there?"

"That's a long story. What's important is that I'm home. Finally. And I needed to see my old bud. I was blown away when I heard you're a pastor — and Indian Heights Church. Wow! You must see a lot of our classmates. I understand that a lot of the Istrouma grads moved to Indian Heights. How did you become a pastor?"

"That's a long story, but the short of it is that while running at Louisiana Tech, the more success I experienced, the more I found myself feeling empty. Elaine attended a Bible study on campus. She told me we were headed two different directions. She became a Jesus follower and let me know if I wanted to see her, we needed to be going the same direction."

"So you did this for her?"

"No. It shook me up, though, and I began thinking about God. I'd never really thought about Jesus and a relationship with Him. But a few months later, I realized the emptiness in my life was a spiritual vacuum. Elaine and I prayed together. Jesus changed my life. I found peace and purpose. A year later, I decided I wanted to give my life to sharing this new purpose with the world. So here I am. Pastor Todd Mayo. That's the really short version. I didn't mean to preach to you, but that's my story. What about you? What happened? Why did you leave town?"

"Well, mine is a bad, sad, and ultimately happy story. I don't know, Todd." Win bit his bottom lip. "You remember the mid-'60s. I wanted to see the world, but I definitely wanted to miss a free trip to Vietnam. I thought I was in love with Grace, but didn't want to be committed. I was confused. So it was California or bust. It ended up being a little of both. I spent a little over four years there. Miserable the whole time. I decided California wasn't the place for me. So I moved to Seattle."

As Win told his story, Todd stroked the front of his neck. Win saw his doubts but continued. "I met some guys who needed a gopher. They started a company and needed cheap labor. I took a job with them. They gave me a chance and trained me — gave me a raise and stock in the new company when it went public. So I became the proud owner of stock in the upstart Dresdtech Corporation."

Todd's doubtful looks turned to a huge smile. "No way!" Todd slammed both hands on the table and roared with laughter. "You're kidding me!"

"No joke. Over the years, my stock grew in value. Before you knew it, I became very wealthy."

Todd shook his head, laughing. "Win, I can't believe this."

"It's true." He grinned as he leaned forward. "But here's the part I think you'll really like. I had money, friends, and parties . . . girls. But the same emptiness you mentioned filled my heart. I gained a lot of weight. There was a group of runners at Dresdtech about five years ago who asked if I wanted to run with them. I agreed, and that changed everything. They met for a Bible study. I learned about running, but most of all I learned about life. One day after the workout, I prayed exactly like you talked about and gave my life to Christ. It was like I really started living.

"The more I worked out with these guys, the more I wanted to do speed work. I started going to the track and practicing some of our old quarter-mile training regimens. Loved it. It seemed natural. I started competing in Masters Track and Field. It took me about two and a half years to get to where I could run to my full potential. When that happened, well . . ." He paused, looking sheepish, but with a twinkle in his eyes said, "I won the world championship."

"No. No way," Todd said with a huge smile. "You're putting me on." He paused. He slowly pronounced each word. "You're not putting me on."

"No. I couldn't believe it either. But it's why I'm here. I began thinking a lot about Baton Rouge and Istrouma High School. I thought about our mile relay team. It's hard to describe, but this immense desire to come home haunted me. I dreamed about it at night. I woke up thinking about it almost every night for the past year. Somehow I knew I needed to return to Baton Rouge. I don't know why, but I had to come back. I haven't had a real home for more than forty years. Todd, this is my home.

"I had all the money I'd ever need. I was in Houston for a meet and decided to visit Baton Rouge, then decided to retire and move here. I contacted a Realtor and bought a home on South Lakeshore Drive near L.S.U."

Todd stared at Win with widened eyes. "Wow. What can I say?"

"There's one other thing. Do you know a pastor named Thomas Washington?"

"Yes. Well, not really. I know of him. He's an African-American pastor down in our old neighborhood. I understand he has a good work with youth. How do you know him?"

"I don't. But I met someone in Houston . . ." Win took a deep breath. "I need to make contact with him. Can you help me?"

"I'll have my assistant contact him and put the two of you in touch." Todd shifted in his chair. "Man, I'm so happy for you — your success, your wealth, and especially your faith. I can't tell you how thrilled I am." Todd sighed, "Not everyone is going to be so excited and understanding. To be honest, I'm having a tough time with some things. Elaine had some pretty harsh words when I told her I was meeting you."

"Why?"

"I don't want to spoil your party, old friend. And remember what I just said. I'm excited about all that's happened in your life." Todd looked down as if struggling for words. "There were a lot of people who were very upset that you didn't show up for your dad's funeral.

You had only been gone for a year. How could you do that? I think at least a third of our class was there. We didn't want to ask your mother anything about you because she was so grief-stricken. His heart attack took everyone by surprise and . . ."

"I know. I know." Win buried his head in his hands. "I can't tell you how much it hurt not to be there, but I couldn't come. I just couldn't."

Todd's face flushed. "Why? What would keep you from your own dad's funeral?" He leaned forward, pointing at Win. "He was at every track meet. You were his pride and joy. He sacrificed for you. What was so important that you couldn't come to his funeral?"

"Nothing! Nothing!" Win felt like someone had punched him in the gut. "That's the greatest regret of my life. All I can say is that I couldn't be there. It's a long and complicated story. Maybe one day I can explain it. Just trust me. I couldn't come. That's all I can say."

Todd glared at Win. "Grace was there."

"How's she doing? I must have hurt her deeply."

After a very long pause, Todd said, "She brought your baby girl to the funeral. She wanted her to meet her dad."

Win slowly placed his hands on the table. Everything in the coffee shop seemed to be spinning. "What? What are you talking about?"

"Come on, Win. Don't give me that! After all these years, you didn't know Grace got pregnant on prom night?"

Win shook his head. "No. I swear. It can't be!"

For nearly a minute, the two old friends stared at each other.

Finally, Todd spoke. "Win, you're a dad. Your daughter is forty-three years old." He paused and quietly said, "And you're a grandfather."

Win's face dropped and his voice boomed, out of control. "Oh, God, help me. Oh, God, I'm so sorry."

Everyone at CC's stared at the two men. Todd quickly stood. "Come on. Let's go out to the car."

Win struggled to get out of his chair and walked past a sea of eyes staring at him. His head remained bent as he stumbled outside.

Win was limp by the time he took a seat in Todd's car. In the next fifteen minutes, more than four decades of pent-up guilt gushed forth. He sat silently. He moaned. He banged the dashboard. Finally Win was able to speak. "I want to see my daughter. And Grace? Is she married? My grandchild. Boy or girl?"

"Grace married an older guy about five years after you left. He was a great husband to Grace and wonderful father to your daughter."

"Was?"

"He died of cancer about two-and-a- half years ago."

"How can I find Grace? I want to meet my daughter. I have to see them."

"Hold on. You can't just walk back into their lives after forty-four years. It's not that simple. Look, you need to start with Grace. She and Hope go to our church. Let me try to set up a lunch date and see if she is open to meeting you. I can't promise she will. I'll give you a ring on the cell number you gave me."

"Hope. That's my daughter's name? Is she married?"

"She was married."

"Divorced?"

"Her husband was killed in Iraq — a car bomb in Fallujah."

Win groaned and looked upward. "I should have been there for her. Oh, God. I messed up so bad. I'm so sorry." He lifted his head. "What about my grandbaby? Boy or girl?"

"Boy. He's no baby. He's a high-school senior and a lot like you — a great runner."

CHAPTER FIVE

Win drove back to his house a broken man. He'd cried more that day than during the past thirty years. Win lived an isolated life with no family: a father and mother who'd passed before he'd turned twenty-one, no brothers or sisters, no wife or children. He'd accepted his situation, but it left him lonely and riddled with guilt. In one meeting, everything had changed, except the feelings of guilt. They'd only intensified.

After he pulled into the driveway of his all-white brick house on South Lakeshore Drive, he sat stunned and silent for about twenty minutes. He felt as though he'd run back-to-back 400-meter races. As he headed inside, his legs trembled.

Feeling brain-dead, Win put a meal in the microwave and sat on the couch in the living room, staring across the lake at the LSU campus. As he saw the university tower and the upper part of Tiger stadium, he wondered what life might have been if he hadn't made the decision to leave. *What if I had run track for LSU.? What if I'd never smoked pot? What if . . .?* The questions seemed endless and useless.

Although the view was fantastic, it did nothing to revive his heart. He would gladly trade his beautiful house, the prestigious neighborhood, and his sports car to have a family. Yet a ray of hope settled in his soul as he thought about meeting his daughter and grandson.

All the homes on South Lakeshore sat across the street from the lake. As the sun set, Win gazed toward the lake's bank, thirty feet from the street. The large, lakeside oak mesmerized him. The sunlight bounced off the lake and onto its leaves. Something about the oak captivated him. The tree stood strong with huge, twisted branches. It seemed immovable. A monument of strength and endurance, the oak had survived Katrina and a host of other storms, and it held Win's deep feelings for nearly a half-century.

A breeze began blowing the hanging moss, giving the appearance of someone waving, someone calling for an old friend to come visit. Like a magnet, the oak drew Win out of his home and across the street.

Win's heart fluttered as he approached the tree, reached out, and touched the rugged bark. *You didn't let go of my feelings for Grace, did you?* Win almost expected the tree to speak. He waited, rubbing the reddish brown bark. As he stared at the old oak, the wind gusted. A beautiful red leaf fell onto Win's head. As he reached to grab it, the wind sent it to the other side of the tree.

Win grabbed the leaf, and his hand landed on the bark. As he slid his hand around the edge of the tree, he saw the indentation in the bark. A ray of sunlight shone right on the spot. "Oh, God." He gasped and slid to his knees. The tree spoke, and he remembered his encounter with the old oak.

Today had been a wild ride. The race, the threat, and learning the consequences of his failures overwhelmed him. The oak stood strong and tall, but Win fell, bent and broken.

As Win knelt, he was overcome by a deep sense of repentance. He confessed disloyalty to his parents, sexual immorality with Grace, altering his mind with drugs, running from the truth, and a host of other things he'd hidden. He confessed wrong thoughts and deeds he'd experienced over the years. At last he stood, completely empty. The night was as dark and silent as his soul.

Win returned to his home and sat on a hard kitchen chair. Minutes turned into hours as he thought about his conversation with Todd. Occasionally, he whispered in bewilderment, "A father," then, "A grandfather." A groan and a plea followed. "Oh, God, I'm so sorry. I really messed up. Please, forgive me."

He walked toward the window, stared at the old oak, and cried to the Lord. "Oh, God. I'll do anything. I'll give up everything I own to have a relationship with my daughter and grandson. Please let me meet them. Whatever You want, it's Yours. I just want to know them. I need them, Father." Tears rolled down his cheeks.

Hours later, Win fell asleep on the couch. Once in a deep sleep, he sensed a presence in the room. He tried to rise, but couldn't. His arms seemed chained to the couch. He tried to speak but couldn't muster any words. He thought he was dying, having a heart attack.

A light filled the room, and peace swept over his soul. Whether he was conscious, he didn't know. In that moment, he only felt a peace that passed anything imaginable. The peace kept coming, like wind gusts, one after another. It seemed they would never end. The wind formed a tunnel, looked like a tornado, and descended. Panic rose in his heart, then peace again settled his soul. As the swirling cloud descended, nothing was destroyed. Instead, everything was placed in perfect order.

The light turned into shades of magnificent, sparkling colors: red, blue, purple, gold, silver, green, like nothing he had ever seen. The glorious radiance filled the room with a depth, width, breadth, and height of an effulgent light, but also displayed a dimension he'd never known. Win's mind could only describe it as perfect love. A face emerged from the colors, with bright, red blood rolling off the forehead and down the cheeks. It mingled with tears that poured from piercing eyes. An ugly crown full of thorns sat on the figure's head. Then silence. Absolute silence.

Win's heart raced. *Am I dreaming? Is this real? Why can't I move?* Then his thoughts were flooded with one name. *Jesus.*

A voice broke the silence and spoke powerfully, yet tenderly. "Father, forgive him." The words echoed, louder and louder until they roared like thunder. Then they came in a whisper: "Father, forgive him. Father, forgive him." More silence. The sense of His presence and the sound of His voice brought indescribable peace. It felt like a tornado of wonderful contradictions: compassionate thunder, tender authority, a whispering roar, and loving power.

As quickly as the face appeared, it left. Win awoke with his heart racing. He looked around. No one was there. At last his breathing returned to normal. He fell on the floor, crying, "I love You. I love You, Jesus. I love You so much." He didn't sleep the rest of the night.

At dawn, he picked himself up from the floor and stared at the old oak. *Was it a dream? Was it a vision? Was it really Jesus?* He glanced at his Bible on the coffee table. It was open to Acts 3:19, the place he'd read when the day had begun. "Therefore repent and be converted, that your sins may be wiped away, that times of refreshing may come from the presence of the Lord." After a sleepless night, all he could think was, *I'm forgiven — totally.* Waves of peace and joy flooded his heart. As he pondered those thoughts, he began to whisper, "I'm forgiven. Thank You, Father. I love You so much. Your love and grace are truly amazing."

CHAPTER SIX

Chip and Jamie had much in common, but also key differences. Both had grown up in homes where they'd lost their dads. Chip's father had been killed in Iraq, but Jamie's had left the family when he was fourteen. Jamie's dad was a businessman who supported his kids with a nice monthly stipend. Though he seldom spent time with them, he made sure he provided everything they needed.

Jamie had an older brother and a younger sister, but always felt like the family's black sheep. His siblings were outgoing and popular at school. Their dad's leaving didn't seem to affect them the way it affected him. Jamie was a follower, but secretly longed to be a leader. He never felt he could live up to his older brother's popularity. His dad spent time with his brother, but made little effort to get together with Jamie. So Jamie became a loner who couldn't figure out why he was so shy.

Chip was a natural leader and quick to express his opinions. He was an only child whose dad had been killed about the same time Jamie's dad had left. Chip loved running because he was gifted, but also because it cleared his mind of the lingering hurt from his dad's death.

Jamie was taller than Chip. Both were thin, but Chip was more muscular. Jamie loved running because it took him into a world where his family problems seemed far away. While Chip was driven by his running, for Jamie, it was more recreational. Because Chip was always faster, Jamie occasionally thought about winning, but accepted that he would probably be second to Chip throughout high school.

After Jamie and Chip finished working out Monday afternoon, they discussed the race. Jamie looked at Chip, "The best thing about the All Comers' meet was that dad came. It was the first time he's come to anything I've done since I started high school." He looked down. "He probably thinks I have a chance at a scholarship and wanted to see if it was true."

Jamie told Chip he'd received a note in his English class saying Coach Landon wanted him to come to his office Tuesday morning. That wasn't good. Usually when Coach called in people, it was to chew them out. Jamie wanted to get it over with, so he went to school early Tuesday morning and headed directly to Coach's office.

Chip normally didn't work out in the mornings, but mostly ran after school. But he decided that day to work out while Jamie met with Coach Landon. If Coach had a problem with Jamie, then he and Jamie could talk about it after his workout.

Chip went with Jamie to the locker room, changed his clothes and headed to the track. Once he got there, he realized he'd left his running watch in his backpack. He returned to the locker room and heard Jamie and Coach Landon talking, and Coach mentioned his name. He decided to hang around discreetly and listen.

"I was really impressed with your run Saturday."

"Thank you, sir. I don't know what happened to Chip, but . . ."

"I didn't bring you here to talk about Chip. I want to talk about you — your dreams, your goals. On Saturday, you showed me something I've never seen. You were gutsy — hungry for victory."

"I was, but I never thought I could beat Chip."

"But you did. That's the point. That doesn't happen by accident. It takes determination, willpower. It takes courage. All of that was present Saturday. Son, I think you have potential."

"You do?"

"I think you can win the state championship."

Chip's jaw dropped. He edged closer to the office, but made sure he couldn't be seen.

"Whoa, Coach. I beat Chip Saturday, but that was a fluke . . ."

"Now, son, do you want to be a winner or a whiner?"

"A winner, Coach."

"Then listen. I saw it in you. I saw the champion. You just need to work hard and apply the basics. I know you have the work ethic, but you need to concentrate more on the basics. I've never seen a champion perform without having mastered them. If you'll work on those things, you can be a champion." He raised his voice. "Do you want to be a champion?"

"Yes, sir. Of course. But which basics am I missing?"

"It's real simple. Intake. Output. Good nutrition. Hard training. That's it."

Jamie stammered, "I don't understand. I eat right — well, most of the time. And you just said I work hard. So what am I missing?"

"Look at you, Jamie. You're tall and thin. Decent muscular structure. Now think about Chip. He's a couple of inches shorter but much more muscular. That produces power, which translates into speed. He's faster than you because he has more power. When he takes off, he gains at least three meters before you come out of the first curve. You run with him through the middle of the race. Then he takes you at the end. He has more left in his engine." He smiled. "I want to put some high octane in your engine."

"But how, Coach? I'm doing everything I know. Chip and I work out together, and we're doing the same things."

"Like I said, nutrition. The right kind of stuff will build your muscular system. You need the right intake. You can build muscles and easily become stronger and faster than Chip. You do that, and you're headed to LSU on a track scholarship. What do you think, Jamie? You want it? You hungry for the state championship?"

"Sure, Coach. I want it. What do I do?"

"I'm a distributor of a supplement that has a proven record of building muscle power. It's a little expensive, but it works. Within a couple of months you'll see a noticeable difference in your training and performance. You interested?"

Chip's discussion with Jamie about the gym candy flashed through his mind. Chip couldn't believe Jamie might be going along with Coach.

"Is it legal?" Jamie asked.

"Look, Jamie," Coach said with a stern voice. "Not everything is black and white. There are some gray areas. There have been many athletes falsely accused of substance abuse. I certainly wouldn't give you anything that would hurt you. But if you want the championship, I can help you get there. Because this is a gray area, you'll need to keep this between you and me. If you're okay with it, I'll meet with you once a week between now and track season and give you training tips. You probably shouldn't train with Chip. I'll train you. It comes down to this: Are you really hungry for the championship?"

"I'm in, Coach."

Chip breathed deeply. He forced himself not to punch the locker.

"Great. Can you come up with $150 a month?"

"Whoa. That's expensive." After a short pause, Jamie said, "Yeah, I've got money in a fund that Mom doesn't have anything to do with. I can take it from there, but are you sure this is okay?"

"Positive. Trust me, you're headed to LSU. That's what you want, isn't it?"

"Yes, sir."

Jamie walked out and saw Chip standing by the lockers.

Chip placed his finger over his lips.

Jamie nodded and motioned for Chip to slip out. Chip tiptoed out of the locker room and waited for Jamie.

Todd arranged Win's lunch meeting with Grace. At exactly 11:30 on Tuesday, Win pulled into the parking lot of Mike Anderson's Cajun restaurant near LSU. Though Cajun food was Win's favorite, it was the last thing on his mind. He thumped the steering wheel with his finger so many times, he almost caused a blister. Yet underneath his edginess, a deep sense of peace rested in his heart. As he entered, a five-foot six-inch, elegant lady waited inside. He paused, trying to see if it was Grace.

The well-dressed, slender woman with slightly graying hair spoke. "Win?"

His stomach turned over a few times. "Grace?" He started to hug her, then pulled back.

Grace saw his awkwardness and extended her hand with a smile. "It's been a long time."

He nodded. "Yes. It has."

A waitress came to seat them. Win quickly asked, "Can we have a quiet spot in a corner?"

After being seated, Win took a deep breath. "It's so good to see you. You look great."

Grace stared at him for a few seconds. Her face radiated a calm strength and a rare, inward beauty. "It's funny. I've thought about this moment for years — decades. I wanted to give you a well-prepared speech. Now that we're here, I don't know what to say."

"Me, too. I spent the whole morning rehearsing what I'd say, but none of it seems appropriate." Win stared at Grace. "You're so beauti—"

Grace's expression changed. "Don't go there, Win. I don't want to be schmoozed. I'm only here because I need some answers. So let's get right to it. Why did you leave? Why . . . ?"

The waitress walked up. "Excuse me. Can I take your order?"

Win was relieved by the intrusion. Grace Johnson hadn't agreed to meet Win for some nice chitchat. Her calm strength had quickly turned to burning rage. She'd come with questions he'd have to answer.

After they ordered, Grace looked sternly at Win. "Do I need to continue, or would you like to begin with your explanation?"

"Grace, I swear, I didn't know you were pregnant when I left."

"And I guess you didn't know if you loved me, either. How many times did you tell me you loved me? How many, Win?"

Win sat in shamed silence.

"Was it a lie? Something easy to say so you could have sex with me?" Her voice became firmer. With fire in her eyes, she asked, "What was it, Win?"

"It was the truth. I did love you, and I never stopped loving you."

Grace rolled her eyes.

"But I was confused. The war in Nam. I was drinking a lot. My mind was messed up. I felt like I was in love with you, and I wanted to marry you. But I was immature. I didn't know what I wanted. I freaked out. Didn't know what to do." Win lowered his eyes to avoid Grace's accusing stare. "California seemed like a great escape. After graduation, I got drunk and just took off."

"I wish I could say I understand, but I can't. I don't understand why you left, why you didn't come back. You broke your mom and dad's hearts when you left. Why didn't you return for their funerals? They loved you so much. How *could* you?"

"I know, I know. It was stupid. I got involved with the wrong kinds of people in California. Became involved with drugs. I messed up big time. I wish I could apologize to Mom and Dad. I wish I could do it all over. I wish—"

Grace leaned toward Win. "Your mom. She loved you. When I asked her about you, she wouldn't say much, just to pray for you because you were very confused. All of our friends showed up at your dad's funeral, expecting to see you. We were shocked when you didn't show. But when your mom died of cancer a year later, no one could believe you were so cold-hearted that you wouldn't come back." Grace shook her head. "She died a broken woman."

"Oh, God. I'm so sorry." Tears filled Win's eyes. He wanted to tell Grace about what happened Saturday night, but wasn't willing to risk it. "I wish I could turn the clock back. I'll have to carry that burden to my grave."

"Burden. Don't tell me about your burdens, Win. Do you know what it was like to have a baby and not know where her father was, if he was dead or alive? Do you know how hard it was to tell her that her real father just vanished? Do you want to know what a burden is?" Grace's voice was quiet but emphatic. "I'll tell you what a burden is."

"You're right, I don't know. I don't know what Mom or Dad went through. I don't know what you felt. I wish I could ask their forgiveness. I ask your forgiveness — right now. I know I don't deserve it, and I understand if you can't give it. But, I know . . ." He paused and looked her in the eye. "God has forgiven me. I've made it right with Him, and I want to make it right with you."

"I forgave you a long time ago. At first, the hurt was too much. Then the bitterness ate me up. I felt like I was going crazy." Grace's voice began to soften. "Todd and Elaine helped me so much. They taught me how to forgive and how to move forward with my life. I've done that, but one thing I learned is that forgiveness doesn't mean there's no accountability. I've forgiven you, Win Bass, but there's still a lot of questions that need answering."

"I know. You deserve answers. I'll try to provide them. There may be some things I can't answer because I don't understand them myself, but I'll try." Win shifted in his chair. "What about our daughter? What's she like?"

"She's beautiful. Smart. She's got a great head on her shoulders."

"Not like her dad?"

"No. Not like her biological dad. But like her real dad, the one who raised her, took care of her, and taught her how to handle life. His name was Rick Johnson.

Grace's words shot like an arrow through Win's heart. "I'm glad you found a good man," he said. "You deserved that. Todd told me he died of cancer a couple of years ago. I'm sorry."

"He was a great guy. He loved me, and he loved Hope."

"Do you think I could meet Hope sometime? I know it would be awkward, but it would mean so much if I could see her."

"Like I said, Win. I've forgiven you. I refuse to do anything out of bitterness. But I also won't do anything or allow anyone to hurt that young woman."

Win smiled. "You're a good mom, Grace. I understand. I just want a chance. It might be good for Hope as well. She might have some questions that need answering."

"I'm sorry, Win, but you're going to have to prove yourself. I don't know you. I thought I knew you in high school, but obviously I didn't. You show up forty-four years later and want to walk back into our lives like nothing ever happened. Well, I want to know who you are. I'm not going to feed my daughter and grandson to a wolf in sheep's clothing. Just because you say you've changed and you're sorry, that doesn't mean much. I want to see how you live. I need answers. And I need to see that you are who you say you are." Grace paused. "So, Win, who are you?"

After their meal was served, Win told Grace most of his story, leaving out key details about California. He emphasized how he'd moved to Seattle and worked odd jobs for a couple of years. He explained how he'd become involved with Dresdtech when it was a start-up company. He told her how he'd begun running with some colleagues after work five years ago. He shared about the Bible studies, his newfound faith in Christ, and how he'd felt he needed to return to Baton Rouge.

"I'm glad you've gotten your life together," Grace said with a sarcastic tone. "I hope it's true. But I still don't feel I can introduce you to Hope yet. I want proof that you've really changed."

"Whatever it takes to prove it, I'll do it. You just tell me what I need to do."

"I have to think about it. But I do know this. It will take time."

"How much time?"

"I don't know. I just know it will take some time."

"Fair enough. It'll be hard, but I'll wait." Win smiled. "Now tell me about my grandson. What's he like? Todd said he's a runner. Is he good?"

"Yes, he's a good runner. But you need to leave him alone. He doesn't know anything about you." Grace's voice became stern.

"Promise me you won't try to meet them until I've said it's okay. I need to take this slow. Promise you won't try to find them on the Internet. Promise you'll not do *anything* . . ." Her voice rose. "Anything to make contact with them until I've decided it's okay. If everything works out, I want to make sure this is done the right way. I need to prepare them. They're the most important people in my life."

"I understand, and I promise. Tell me what to do, and I'll do it."

"Give me some time to think about this. I need to go. Call me in a week, and I'll have an idea where we go from here."

"Before you go, there's one last thing I need to ask. Do you know what happened to my parents' belongings? Is there anything left that I could see?"

"I don't know. A lot of things were given away. Others sold. But do you remember Sandra Long?"

"Yes, I remember her."

"She and your mom were very close before your mom died. She might know."

"Miss Sandra's still alive? Where can I find her?"

"She's in the Indian Heights Assisted Living facility. She's eighty-nine, but still in good health."

"Thanks."

Grace forced a smile and excused herself. Win stared at her until she turned the corner. *I can't believe I walked away from her forty-four years ago. How stupid can you be, Win Bass?* Win left a generous tip and headed home.

<hr>

After Jamie's meeting with Coach Landon, everything changed. Until then, Jamie and Chip viewed themselves as teammates, not opponents. "This will make both of us better runners," Jamie said. "Maybe both of us can get a scholarship to LSU." Jamie smiled. "Dad came to the meet Saturday. Maybe he'll start coming to all of them. That will make it worth everything. You need to understand, Chip."

"Understand what? That you're going to be doing drugs?"

"Wait a minute. I'm not going to take drugs. You heard Coach. They're nutritional supplements."

"Sure. I don't believe that, and neither do you." With a snarl, Chip said, "So you're going to be a doper."

Jamie lost it. He jumped on Chip and wrestled him to the ground. After a few minutes of wrestling, Chip hit Jamie in the nose, and it started bleeding. Once the blood flowed, they stopped.

Chip got in Jamie's face. "Our next match will be on the track. I'll leave you in the dust. Then you can ask Coach why the supplements didn't work."

Chip walked away angry and confused. It seemed his whole world had collapsed. *I lost a race I should have won easily. Now I've lost my best friend. What else can go wrong?*

CHAPTER SEVEN

Win didn't sleep well Friday night. He kept thinking about Miss Sandra. He paced the kitchen, then the family room, stopping occasionally to drink some coffee. He didn't know whether it was the coffee that gave him the jitters or the thought of meeting Miss Sandra. Finally, he decided to work out the next morning before going to the assisted living facility to talk with her.

Though the high school was a long drive from Win's lakeside home, it was worth the trip. Indian Heights had a latex-surfaced track with an Astroturf football field — a great surface for an old man's knees. It had quickly become his best place to work out. He arrived around 8:00 a.m. He normally started with a fast walk for a lap or two, followed by a couple of laps of jogging. As Win began his second lap, Hope Thibodeaux dropped Chip at the track.

<hr />

Chip's clunker needed repairs, so he and his mom had taken it to a garage before going to the track. Hope told Chip she'd pick him up in about an hour and a half, enough time for him to get a decent workout. As Chip left the parking lot and walked to the track, he spotted the old dude. His blood boiled, and he turned to see if he could catch his mother before she left. Too late. She was already on the road, heading for breakfast with her mother. Chip was stuck for the next hour and a half.

Soon after Chip began jogging, Win caught up and greeted him. Chip just nodded, turned his head, and kept his slow warm-up pace.

Win had become an expert at eating humble pie since his arrival in Baton Rouge. "Look, I'm sorry I messed things up for you. I'm new in town. Didn't know the All Comers' meet was designed for high-school guys. I run Masters Track and Field, and I picked up an advertisement about the meet in a local running store. I thought it would be good motivation for me to keep training. So, I'm sorry."

"No problem." Chip began softening. "It doesn't matter anyway."

"Sure it does. The race was yours. You should have beaten me. I ran my best, but you still had more left. You lost focus. That's all. With focus, I would have been at least ten meters behind you at the finish line."

"You don't have to try to be nice. It doesn't change anything."

"It was just a fun meet! Right? So what needs changing besides your focus?"

"It doesn't matter. I just need to improve."

"Maybe I can push you today. Let's stretch together and do some strides. Maybe I can help a little."

Chip considered the offer. He didn't like running alone. Since Jamie would no longer be with him, he agreed. "Okay. Maybe we can do a few things together."

As they walked onto the football field, Win introduced himself. Chip began to let go of his anger and was finally able to shake hands. While stretching, Chip asked, "Do you really think I could have taken you by ten meters, or were you just trying to be nice?"

"There's no doubt you could have taken me by that much. I'm running right now close to my potential, but not you. It's amazing what focus does. One of the first lessons I learned when I started running again was to place my focus on the finish line and never lose sight. That's what makes people successful in running — and in life."

"What do you mean that you started running again?"

"I ran the 400 meters in high school, except we called it the 440-yard dash or the quarter mile back in the day. After I graduated, I quit. But I took it up again about five years ago with a group of guys in Seattle. We'd run, then have a Bible study about running. I learned more about running and life in that Bible study than I ever learned during high school track."

"So you're a Jesus freak?"

"No." Win laughed. "Hardly. Just an old guy who started running and living in a fresh way and enjoying every minute of it. You ready for some strides?"

"Yeah. What kind of pace do you run?"

"I start slow and progressively speed up. Let's do between six and eight."

After completing a half-dozen strides, they ran ten 200-meter repeats. With every repeat, the barriers fell between Chip and Win. The unspoken comradeship that often exists between runners emerged. After completing the repeats, they took a fifteen-minute break, warmed up again with a half-mile jog, then ran a couple of 400 meters at three-fourths speed.

As they jogged to cool down, Win continued encouraging Chip. "Not only could you have beaten me, but you have much more potential than beating me by just ten meters."

"Why do you say that?"

"You have decent form, great strength, and you're in tremendous shape. But I noticed today you have some basic mechanics that need tweaking. Once you get those down, you'll be flying around this track."

Chip looked at Win skeptically. "Do you really think I can run lots faster?"

"I know you can. But you'll have to be patient. It takes time to develop the proper mechanics. You may even run slower at first, but once you have them down, running will be much more natural. You'll be running at maximum potential. I can help you, if you want. Do you run here every Saturday morning?"

"Yeah, but normally a little later. My car broke down yesterday and Mom dropped me off on her way to a breakfast meeting."

"You name the time, and let's plan on getting together."

After dropping Chip at the track, Hope met her mom for breakfast. They had seldom talked about her real father. When Hope was a child, Grace had tried to explain why she didn't have a dad before she married Rick. But Rick was such a good father, he had filled the void in Hope's life. She and Rick were very close, and his death was almost as difficult for Hope as for Grace. After his death, thoughts about her biological father had occasionally flown through her mind, but they never found a runway to land.

She and Grace enjoyed meeting for breakfast on Saturday mornings at a little French bakery near Interstate 10. They loved the baked goods, and the atmosphere enabled them to talk privately.

Grace felt she needed to feel out Hope about Win, and she needed to do it soon. She didn't trust him — or want him to be the one to introduce himself. After some small talk, Hope asked, "What's up, Mom?"

Grace wrinkled her nose and took a deep breath. "Have you ever thought that you wanted to meet your biological father?"

"Not in a long time. When I was little, I did. But that was so long ago. God gave me a daddy, a great one. So I haven't really thought much about it. Why are you asking?"

"I was just wondering. We've never really talked about it, and I was just thinking this week . . ."

"Mom, I don't think so. You don't just come up with things like this. What's going on?"

Grace twisted the napkin around her hand and looked at the table. "I don't know. I was just wondering if you had the opportunity to meet your biological dad, would that be something you would want to do?"

"I thought you said you didn't know where he was or if he was even alive." Her eyes caught her mother's, and her words burst out. "Is he alive? Do you know where he is?"

"Yes, he's alive, and I do know where he is. I just found out. I didn't know what to do. If Rick were alive, I would have asked him. He was so wise. But I didn't have anyone to talk to. I decided I'd better talk to you."

Hope looked at the ceiling, then at her mother. "Wow. I don't know what to say. This is the last thing I would have imagined. Do you want to meet him, Mom? I'll go with you."

Grace's napkin-twisting became more deliberate. "I met him earlier this week."

"What? Where? How did . . .?"

"I don't know." Grace began to cry. "He just showed up."

Hope reached out and grabbed her hand.

"I don't know what to do. I feel so angry. I thought I forgave him, but when I saw him, this rage came out of nowhere. I wanted to slap him." She looked at Hope with fire in her eyes. "Hard. I wanted to hit him hard."

"It's okay, Mom." Hope squeezed her hand and smiled. "If I do meet him, I want the first punch."

Grace smiled through her tears. "Maybe we'll give him a one-two punch. Me first, then you."

"Mom, it's okay. Don't worry about me. I just need to think about this. I don't know anything about him. All you ever told me was his first name." Hope paused and restarted her rapid-fire questions. "Does he live here? Where has he been all this time? When would we meet? Where would I meet him? What's the best situation for a meeting?"

"Slow down. He'll have to answer some of those questions. But he is in Baton Rouge right now, and he does want to meet you."

Hope sighed and shook her head. "This certainly isn't what I expected this morning." A shy look came across her face. "Mom, is he a little . . . You know . . .?"

"Know what?"

Hope looked up, then down. "Heavy like me?"

"Hope, what are you talking about? You're not heavy. Where did you get that idea?"

"Come on, Mom. Look at you. You're so thin. And Chip is so muscular. I'm the only one in this family who is a little overweight. I've sometimes wondered if my struggle with weight came from my biological dad."

"Oh, honey, you're not overweight. Every woman puts on a little weight after having a baby. And you've been through so much. With work, you hardly have time for yourself. It's just natural." Grace placed her hands on Hope's. "No, your biological father is not overweight. He's just the opposite. He has broad shoulders, very muscular."

"Is he cute?"

Grace's face turned red and she looked away with a sly grin. "Nobody over sixty is cute. But he's kind of."

Hope pulled up Grace's chin and looked at her directly. "Mom, I see something in your eyes. Do you still have a little something for him?"

"Absolutely not," Grace said sternly. "Now, what about Chip?"

"I don't know, Mom. Chip's going through some tough times with his running. I don't think this is a good time for any big surprises. I need to think through this. If there is a meeting, it probably needs to be just me and not with Chip. But give me some time to think."

After their post-workout stretches, Win and Chip walked to the parking lot. "What kind of workouts does your coach have you doing?"

Chip had a disappointed look. "None."

"He doesn't have you on a preseason training program?"

"He's working with my friend, Jamie. I think he lost confidence in me after the race last week."

"That's not very smart. I'll tell you what. I caused your problem. If you want, I'll work with you. I'll train you."

"I don't mean to be rude, but you're not a coach."

"No, but I know how to train and run the 400. I've done pretty well in Masters Track and Field."

"How well?"

"I represented the USA in the World Championships in Italy a little over a year ago."

"I'm impressed. How'd you do?"

"Won my age division."

"No way. Why haven't I heard of you?"

Win laughed. "You will never hear of old codgers like me, and like I said, I just moved here. Some of the old timers know me. I ran at Istrouma over forty years ago. We had a pretty mean mile relay team back then." Win paused. "It's just an offer. No problem if you don't want to do it."

"Sounds good. I'll go for it. I don't have anything to lose. Let's do it."

"Okay, but next week I'll need some information from you. I'll need to assess where you're at and where you want to be when track season begins in March. I need to know your fastest time for 400 meters, your goals, and how you've been training. That will help me to develop a plan. Then we can talk about it, and I'll begin to show you some basic mechanics."

"Sure, I'll have that for you. Oh, here comes my mom."

Hope pulled up, and Chip opened the passenger door. "Mom, this is Mr. Bass. He's the guy I told you about last week. We worked out together." He smiled. "He's not as bad as I said last week."

"Pleasure to meet you, Mr. Bass."

"My pleasure, Ms.?"

"Thibodeaux."

"Ms. Thibodeaux, you've got a fine son. Great runner. He has tremendous potential."

"Thank you. Well, Good bye."

"See you next week, Chip."

CHAPTER EIGHT

As Hope and Chip pulled away, she looked at Chip. "I thought you hated the guy. What changed? And what did he mean, 'Next week?'"

"He's going to show me some stuff. Coach isn't going to work with me until track season begins. He wants to train Jamie privately. So Mr. Bass said he would set me up with a training plan that will have me in top shape for track season. He knows tons about running."

"Your attitude sure changed."

"It'll be interesting. He thinks I can run much faster than right now. I'm pumped about that. I lost faith in myself last week because of this guy. Now I can feel it. My confidence is coming back." He thrust his fist in the air. "Yes. Chip Thibodeaux. The next Louisiana state 400-meter champion."

Hope smiled. She didn't know who the new guy was, but was happy to see Chip back to his old self.

From the track, Win went directly to the Indian Heights nursing facility. He asked at the front desk where he could find Sandra Long and was directed to the recreation room, where four elderly ladies played Scrabble. The ladies stopped abruptly and looked at Win. One asked, "Can we help you?"

"I'm looking for Miss Sandra Long. I was told she was in here."

"Tell us who it is that's askin', and we'll tell you if she's here."

"I'm Win Bass. Miss Long was a friend of my mother."

One of the ladies who'd been silent spoke. "Well, Win Bass. I can't believe it."

"Miss Long?"

"Come here, son, and let me look at you."

Win walked to her wheelchair, knelt, and took her hand.

"Now, aren't you a sight. You don't look a bit like you used to." She laughed. "You're old."

Win smiled. "Yes, ma'am. I guess I am old. Could I talk to you alone for a few minutes?"

"Sure, son."

Win wheeled Miss Long outside to a well-manicured, shaded area. "Miss Long. I've heard that you and Mom were close before she died." Win looked away and began stammering. "I couldn't be here when Mom and Dad died. I wanted to, but I couldn't."

"Son, I know. Your mother told me everything. She made me swear not to tell anyone what was happening to you. I've not told a soul. And she didn't, either. Don't know why she told me, but I've kept the secret all these years."

Win was glad someone knew the truth. "I need to know a lot of things. Was there anything Mom or Dad wanted me to know? Is there anything they left behind that I could have as a memory? Anything at all?"

"You were their pride and joy. They loved you very much. That's what they wanted you to know — that they never stopped loving you. When you got into your predicament, they didn't want anyone to know. They wanted everyone to remember you as the young star from Istrouma High School. When your mom became ill, it was clear she would never see you again. She gave me a letter she wrote for you. She said to give it to you when you came home. She didn't tell you about your baby girl while you were in . . ." She looked sympathetically at Win. "You know, that awful place. She was afraid you wouldn't be able to handle it, with all that you were going through."

"Do you have the letter?"

"It's in my room. I thought I would take that letter to my grave. Then, you walk in here. Ain't that somethin'?"

Win pushed Miss Sandra's wheelchair to her room, and she handed him a sealed envelope. His hands trembled.

"Are you going to open it?"

"Not right now," he said with a shaky voice. "I want to bring it home. I'll read it there."

<hr />

Sunday afternoon, Win called Todd, inviting him and Elaine to his home for lunch on Thursday. Win's situation with Grace was very complex. He desperately needed advice. Elaine might have some suggestions about redeveloping his relationship with Grace — and beginning to connect with his daughter and grandson.

As Win waited outside for Todd and Elaine, he enjoyed the great view of L.S.U. Todd and Elaine got out of their Mercedes, and Win greeted them with a big smile. He gave Todd a hug, then turned to Elaine. A petite woman of about five foot two, she was dressed immaculately and attempting to hide her graying hair. "It's so good to see you," Win said. "It's been a long time. You look great. This old boy must have treated you really well for the past forty years."

Elaine gave a cold smile, "Thank you. It's good to see you, too."

As they entered the family room that overlooked the lake, Todd was taken aback. The dark wood floors, the leather furniture, and the beautiful accessories gave a sense of comfort and wealth. The openness of the family room with its accompanying view caused him to breathe deeply. "This must be the best view in all of Baton Rouge. They must have given you a lot of stock at Dresdtech."

Win's face flushed. Though it was true, Todd's statement made him uncomfortable. "Have a seat. I ordered some food. Since you like the view so much, let's eat in here."

While they ate, Todd talked about Win's home. "You've done well for a north Baton Rouge boy. God's blessed you, Win. This is fantastic."

"Yes, He has. But this means very little. I'd really like to start a foundation for children in poverty. I've received so much. Now I want to give back. Since we talked, I've thought about going to the old neighborhood and tutoring kids after school."

"That's great," Todd said. "God loves a cheerful giver. You give to Him, and He'll give back a hundred-fold."

"I don't know about the getting back part, but I do know that a radical change has taken place in my heart." He gestured toward the fine leather furniture. "This lifestyle is all I desired for so many years. Now it means nothing. I just want to do what's right in every part of my life. That's why I asked you over today. I want to do the right thing, and I desperately need your advice."

Win told them about the dream or vision the evening he'd met Todd at the coffee shop. "I know I don't deserve it, but I know that I'm forgiven. Completely."

"That's tremendous," Todd asked.

Elaine sat silent, with the aura of an iceberg.

With a soft voice, Win said, "Elaine, you seem skeptical."

"To be honest. I have a real problem."

Todd flinched as Elaine began telling Win how terrible it was for him to run off and not return for his parents' funerals. She blasted him for using Grace for his own gratification, then disappearing.

Win listened intently. "I agree with you, Elaine. Everything you've said is true. I deserve everything you've dished out and even more. That's one reason I wanted you to come with Todd. I wanted to hear a woman's perspective — an honest one. Yet, I know God has forgiven me. I really do want to do the right thing. I met with Grace and she's struggling with it all." Win explained where he and Grace were in their talks.

Todd placed his hand on Win's shoulder. "Look, my friend, I'll do what I can to help, but you've got to give it some time. Let Grace work through this. I'll talk to her and see what she's thinking. She may be further along than you think."

"Win," Elaine said, "do you believe in miracles?"

"Yes. I do."

"It will take a genuine miracle for me to forgive you." Elaine caught the stern look from Todd but continued. "You said you wanted a woman's perspective. Here it is. You are despicable, and what you did to Grace and your parents was horrible. I'm glad you think God has forgiven you, but I'm not God. It's going to take more than a story about some dream to convince me you've truly changed. So, there it is. You wanted honesty. Now you have it."

"Thanks. It's difficult to hear, but I'm trying to understand. I really am. I accept the fact you're struggling with this. There's one more thing you need to know. I visited Miss Sandra Long last weekend. She had a letter that my mom wrote just a few weeks before she died. It explained a lot of things."

"Like what?" Todd said.

"The letter was about Hope. She told me I was the father of a beautiful baby girl. She didn't want me to know until . . ." Win looked down.

"Until what?" Todd asked.

"Nothing, nothing." Win shook his head. "She asked Miss Sandra to give me the letter when I returned to Baton Rouge." He looked up at Todd. "She's had it all these years. Todd . . ." He looked at Elaine, "Several months ago in Seattle, I was spending some time reading the Bible and praying. This intense desire to return to Baton Rouge swept over me. I couldn't shake it. When I woke up each morning, that desire burned deep within. I'd go to sleep at night, and those thoughts flooded my mind. I'd run with my friends, and it was still there. Then last month I was in Houston for the U.S. Masters Track and Field Championships and ran into a young girl who had been kidnapped."

Todd shook his head. "What?"

Elaine rolled her eyes.

"She was from Baton Rouge. That's why I asked you about Pastor Washington. He was taking care of her when it happened."

"I read about it in *The Advocate*."

"My friend and I brought her to the police station, and I think she's probably back in Baton Rouge. When that took place, I knew I needed to return home. I knew it would be tough, but I didn't know it would be this difficult. Todd, even if you hadn't told me about Grace, I would have learned it from Miss Sandra. I'm just glad I have a friend in town who is willing to walk with me through this. I am so anxious to meet Hope and my grandson."

Todd looked sympathetic. "You have to be patient. Give Grace some room, and she'll do the right thing."

Win looked at Elaine. "I'm so sorry about my actions. I've asked Grace to forgive me. I'm so sorry for all the people I hurt, including you. I hope you can find it in your heart to forgive me. I don't expect it to happen right away. But forgive me, please."

Win saw the struggle on her face. He figured she didn't know if he had become a con man — or if he had sincerely changed.

With a half smile, Elaine said, "You and Grace were our best friends in high school. Because of that, I'll try. But it won't be easy."

"I understand."

Todd let Win know they needed to leave, and Win reminded him he needed Pastor Washington's phone number.

"Sure. I forgot to mention it to my assistant. I'll send her a text right now. You should have it within an hour." Todd patted Win's shoulder. "When we have more time, I need to talk to you about some business decisions. Maybe I can help you with your family life, and you can help me with my financial decisions." Todd and Elaine excused themselves and returned to their Mercedes.

CHAPTER NINE

When Win was growing up, the Istrouma district on the north side of town consisted mostly of families of white plant workers at industries near the Mississippi River. In the late '60s after Istrouma High School was forced to integrate, white families started moving out. The Istrouma district slowly became a predominantly African-American neighborhood.

Win phoned Pastor Washington as soon as he received his number from Todd's assistant. The pastor recognized Win's name and thanked him for helping LaKeisha. He told Win he looked forward to their meeting.

Before Win met with the pastor, he drove through the old neighborhood, thinking about his childhood. Most of his classmates' parents had moved to Baton Rouge after World War II, and they formed a tightly knit community. They were reared with a strong work ethic and deep-seated belief that they could do anything they set their minds to, though they'd grown up in a time of great change. The Vietnam War and racial tensions had transformed the social landscape.

The small, wood-framed home on Dalton Street looked the same, but the theater a few blocks away had been torn down. He smiled as he drove by the house. For a moment, he forgot all his confusion. He remembered only the good times. He recalled track meets in the middle of the street during the summer in his preteen years. He thought about the bamboo cane pole he'd made for pole-vaulting. His dad had taught him new vaulting techniques, but it was running that made him the neighborhood hero. No one could ever stay close to him when they ran their dashes in the middle of the street.

Win sat in his Lexus in front of the house, soaking in the sweet memories, until a middle-aged black man stepped out on the porch and looked at him suspiciously. Win started his engine, drove down Dalton, across Plank Road, and toward the church. He saw the houses of his classmates and thought, *I've come so far. Todd was right. God has truly blessed me.* He considered the kids now living in the neighborhood. He wanted them to have the same opportunities. An excitement grew in his heart. His shoulders relaxed as he took a deep breath. *I'd like to give back to the old neighborhood. Maybe Pastor Washington will know how I can help.*

When Win pulled up to the Mount Calvary Missionary Baptist Church, children were playing in the parking lot. Others were entering the church with their backpacks. It appeared the church had an afternoon tutoring program. Win took a deep breath and walked into the church.

"You must be Win Bass." A booming voice spoke as Win entered the sanctuary. A tall, slender African-American man with grayish hair stretched out his hand. "Welcome to Mount Calvary." Sensing Win's uneasiness, the pastor laughed. "I'm Thomas Washington. And it's okay. We don't bite." He pointed to a door near the platform. "Let's go into my office."

"I'm sorry," Win said as they walked into his office. "I've never been anyplace where I was the only white guy."

"Well, congratulations." Washington chuckled. "You're here now. Have a seat."

The small office contained only a desk and chair for the pastor and two folding guest chairs. Bookshelves, every one of them filled, covered the walls. A beautiful painting of what appeared to be slaves being baptized hung behind Pastor Washington's desk. "I want to thank you for rescuing LaKeisha," Washington said. "We were so worried. We had . . ."

Win turned from the books and toward Pastor Washington. "In a certain sense . . . she rescued me." He gazed downward. "I'd like to do whatever I can to help her. How is she doing?"

"She is just fine."

"I was hoping I could see her."

Pastor Washington pressed his lips together. "I don't think that will be possible."

"Why?"

"What happened to LaKeisha is unusual. We've had problems with trafficking in the neighborhood. It's mostly been on a local level. A girl meets a nice looking, older guy at a party. He slowly makes her feel she owes him something. Before you know it, he puts her on the streets as a prostitute. But each year it gets more sophisticated. A young girl meets a guy on the Internet. He's slick and takes it real slow. After a few months, the guy sets up a meeting — at a coffee shop or a mall. The guy slowly pulls the girl into his web. The average age of these girls is thirteen."

Win's eyes widened. "Thirteen!"

"Yes. And there's about 100,000 American children each year that enter the commercial sex trade." He tapped his hand on his desk. "But it's very unusual for someone to be kidnapped. That gives us even greater concern about our community."

"What do you mean?"

"Since Hurricane Katrina, we've had lots of people from New Orleans move into the neighborhood. Many are very needy. We've tried to help. But some have connections to gangs and even the mafia."

"The mafia! I thought they went away when Carlos Marcello was put in prison."

Pastor Washington shook his head. "Evil people will always be stalking in darkness. They're experts. They don't go away. They just reorganize wherever the darkness appears."

"You think organized crime might have something to do with LaKeisha's kidnapping?"

"We don't know. My opinion is that the gangs are working with the mob. They put out feelers. They find the most susceptible people. They knew LaKeisha was vulnerable. I can't prove they had anything to do with it, but we've not detected the level of sophistication as seen with her kidnapping." He lowered his voice. "We felt it would be too dangerous for her to stay in the neighborhood. There's a ministry near Denham Springs that has a place for girls who've been trafficked. She's staying out there until we can get to the bottom of what happened. It's a safe place. But we can't allow you to go out there."

"I've never had contact with human trafficking before. Just read about it." Win shook his head. "Look, I'm from Baton Rouge. This is my old neighborhood. I haven't been here in more than forty years. I've been afraid to . . ." He paused. "When I found LaKeisha, I knew I had to come home. I wanted to help her and to give back to the community. This is horrible. What can I do?"

Pastor Washington rubbed his chin. "I don't really know you. So that's difficult to answer. But I'll tell you this. It begins with men acting in a responsible manner." His jaw stiffened. "If you are buying pornography, you may be financing these criminals. If you buy child pornography, you are participating in trafficking."

"Wait a minute. You don't think . . ."

Pastor Washington raised his hand. "No, I didn't say *you* were. I said, *if* you're purchasing it. I'm not accusing you." The pastor nodded toward the painting of the slaves. "This is modern-day slavery, and the first step in stopping this evil begins with men. I've heard many men say their pornography addiction didn't hurt anyone else. That's absurd. It hurts their family. A lot of Internet porn helps to finance these thugs. We've got to educate the public, and we need to help kids understand the dangers lurking on the Internet."

"I'm not into pornography — of any kind." Win felt a deep ache in his heart. "But I don't believe it's an accident that I found LaKeisha. I want to help her and others like her."

"How do you think you can help?"

Win told his story — from Seattle to his move back to Baton Rouge. He spoke of his newfound faith and desire to help people. He said he thought he could raise funds to help educate the community about the trafficking problem. "If we could save one kid, it would be worth it."

Pastor Washington stroked his chin. "When I spoke with the police in Houston, they seemed a little wary of you. Why would that be?"

Win lifted his eyebrows. "They told you I'd been in trouble?"

"They didn't tell me anything. But I work with all kinds of people, and I've learned to read body language. I could tell there was something about you they didn't trust."

Win sighed. "When I graduated from Istrouma, I headed to California. Got into trouble. I messed up big time. But I also know God has forgiven me. I was a kid, and that's all behind me now." Win told Pastor Washington about his experience when he started running and how he knew he needed to return to Baton Rouge. He told about the experience that night in his living room.

"When I sensed God's presence and His forgiveness, an immense desire filled me to give back to the community. It's because of His love that I want to do this. I don't have a complicated answer. That's all I know. I've been forgiven of so much, and my heart is full of thanksgiving. I just want to give back some of the love He's given me."

"That's quite a story. Todd Mayo is a very well known pastor. I assume he will vouch for you?"

"I'm sure he would."

"And you say you're a runner."

"Yes, sir."

Pastor Washington's eyes narrowed. "I'm pretty sure Todd Mayo wouldn't have some crazy guy hanging around. You mind if I call him later to verify what you've said?"

"No problem."

"Okay, I'll give you a chance. Let's start small and see how things go. I have a young man I'm working with. He's a great kid — loves the Lord and is really sharp. His father left his mother when he was a baby. He needs a good male role model. Maybe you can work with him for a few weeks, and we'll see how you do and if he can relate to you. He's a junior and ran track last year. Did decent, but not great. I've watched him run, and I think he has potential. Maybe enough to get a scholarship. Would you be willing to train him?"

"I'd love to."

"Just a minute." Thomas Washington stood and opened the door. "Melissa, get Isaiah for me, please."

In a few minutes, a five foot nine, athletic African-American boy walked into Pastor Washington's office. "You need me, Pastor?"

"Yes, Isaiah. I want you to meet Win Bass. Mr. Bass is here because . . ."

Isaiah's eyes opened wide.

"Isaiah, is something wrong?"

The kid had a sense of awe written across his face. "*The* Win Bass?"

Win responded slowly. "I'm Win Bass. I'm not sure who *The* Win Bass is."

Isaiah answered quickly. "The runner."

"I am a runner, but how did you know that?"

"You hold the state record in the quarter mile. Your mile relay team won the 1965 state championship. There's never been a mile relay team at Istrouma like that one. During track season last year, every day our coach would say to the 400-meter guys, 'Win Bass — 440 yards in 47.2 seconds. Don't ever forget that name, that time.'

"Then he would thrust his fist in the air with his finger pointing upward, saying, 'Until you've beaten it and the name of Win Bass is erased from the records of Istrouma track.' Then he'd ask. 'What's the name?' We would shout, 'Win Bass.' And then he'd say, 'What's the time?' '47.2 seconds.' Then he'd yell, 'Okay. Let's go to work to make that a distant memory.' He did that every day. It was like a ritual."

Win was stunned, while Pastor Washington looked impressed. "Well, I guess you'll be open to what I have to share. Mr. Bass has agreed to train you for a few weeks. How does that sound?"

"How does that sound? Every Monday morning, I go by the trophy case, look at the mile relay trophy from 1965, and whisper, 'Win Bass, my name is going to be on a trophy one day, and the track coach is going to be shouting my name, not yours.' I can't believe that Win Bass is here wanting to train me. This is so cool. When do we start?"

"What about it, Mr. Bass?" Pastor Washington smiled. "When do you start?"

"Give me a minute." Win gathered his thoughts. "Look, I'm supposed to start training a young man, Chip Thibodeaux, at Indian Heights High School on Saturday. Maybe we could all work out together."

"I don't know about that," Pastor Washington said. "There's only white folk in Indian Heights. Isaiah may not feel comfortable."

"Pastor, it's okay. Having Win Bass train me would be great. And Chip Thibodeaux is the best 400-meter runner in Baton Rouge. It couldn't get any better than that. Besides, I won't have to train on the old cinder track here at Istrouma. They have a new rubberized track at Indian Heights."

"Okay, we'll try it for a week and see how it goes. Now you get back to your studies while I make the arrangements with Mr. Bass."

Isaiah left with a huge smile, and Win sighed with relief.

"So you're *The* Win Bass." Pastor Washington laughed, then

became serious. "Well, The Win Bass, I'm telling you that you had better not let anything happen to that boy."

"Pastor, thanks for giving me a chance. I promise you, I'll set up some good, solid workout routines for him. That's all. Then I'll bring him back here. I'll need to pick him up around 7:30 Saturday morning."

"I'll be honest. I'm a little nervous about this. It seems strange that a guy of your caliber would come here and want to help. This doesn't happen every day. Is there anything you're not telling me? If you're going to work with our kids, I need to know everything. So don't lie about anything." Pastor Washington looked straight into Win's eyes, and his voice became firm. "And I mean anything."

Win froze, not knowing how much more he should say.

When Washington saw Win's reaction, he looked with suspicion. One of Win's weaknesses — as well as strong points — was that he was very easy to read. No secrets with him. If he was happy, everyone knew it. If he was discouraged, everyone knew that, too.

Win knew that every person with whom he shared his heart in Baton Rouge sensed he was hiding something. Only Pastor Washington had the courage to confront him.

Win had an important decision. Miss Sandra was the only one in Baton Rouge who knew the truth — well, most of it. Though he had just met Pastor Washington, he sensed a genuine faith and love for others, and somehow felt he could trust him.

"Pastor, I have a letter from my mother I'd like you to read. I think it will explain everything."

"You want me to read a recommendation from your momma? A man your age? What kind of game is this?"

"It's no game. The letter was written over forty years ago, just before my mother died. I think it will help you understand what I've gone through and why I want to help. I can bring it Saturday morning when I pick up Isaiah."

Pastor Washington shook his head. "Okay. This ought to be interesting. But if I find out you're not forthright with me, it's all over. I'm not taking any chances with Isaiah."

"No problem. I'll see you Saturday."

"One more thing." Pastor Washington pointed at the red Lexus convertible. "That will call attention to your wealth. It could cause problems, but I'm mostly concerned about people asking about you.

If the word gets on the street that you're the one who rescued LaKeisha, it could be very dangerous."

"Thanks. I'll be careful."

CHAPTER TEN

On Saturday morning, Win spent time reading the Bible before picking up Isaiah. The sun was shining and the temperature in the mid-70s. The lake glistened. *This is going to be a great day,* Win thought. *Perfect weather. Perfect everything. This is the first day of a new season in my life.* Win took a deep breath and started singing. Hopping in his Lexus, he headed down Stanford Avenue and onto the Acadian Thruway to pick up Isaiah.

When he arrived at the Mount Calvary Missionary Baptist Church, Pastor Washington and Isaiah were outside talking. A big smile crossed Isaiah's face when he saw the red Lexus. Win hopped out and stretched his arm toward Isaiah, giving him a fist bump. "It's a great day. Good morning, gentlemen."

"Morning," Washington said.

Win handed Thomas Washington an envelope with his mother's letter. "We can talk about it when I get back."

"When do you expect that to be?"

"The workout will probably take an hour and a half. Then I thought I'd pick up some things from a health food store for the guys. They need to put some healthy food in their bodies, not the junk a lot of kids are getting. I want to see what the store has and get some things for them. Then we'll come straight here. Is that okay?"

"Sure. We can talk about your momma's letter then."

Isaiah climbed into the Lexus and headed to Indian Heights with The Win Bass.

There couldn't have been a more beautiful day for Grace and Hope to meet, but the sunshine didn't ease Hope's nerves. She needed to make a decision, but she still wasn't sure. Because Chip's car wasn't ready yet, Hope planned to drive Chip to the track, then head to the French bakery to meet her mom.

Hope pulled into the track's parking lot the same time as Win and Isaiah. As Win pulled up next to Hope's car, Chip got out and began explaining to Win about his car situation.

"Ms. Thibodeaux," Win said, "why don't you let me bring Chip home? I need to stop by a health food store as soon as our workout is done. Then I'll bring Chip directly home."

Hope felt a little uneasy. "I don't know. I'll . . ."

Chip interrupted and insisted.

With a half-hearted smile, she agreed. "But call me on your cell when you finish your workout. I'll head home and meet you there."

As the three walked to the track, Win introduced Isaiah and Chip. He explained he was going to train Isaiah and thought it would be good for them to work out together.

Chip responded positively. Isaiah was a year younger than Chip, and it would give him someone near his age to work out with. Since Jamie was no longer training with him, it sounded like a great idea.

Win noticed both boys had worn, cheap running shoes. "Guys, I'll make you a deal. If you are faithful to the workouts, I'll buy each of you a new pair of running shoes. We can go to Varsity Sports near LSU. They've got a great selection."

Isaiah smiled broadly. "Man, this is going to be better than I thought."

"That's great," Chip said.

"Before we start our workout, I need to let you know a principle of training that you'll never get at school. It's the first principle I learned when I started running five years ago. It's probably the best thing I ever learned about running and about life."

Isaiah and Chip listened attentively.

"Isaiah, you're named after one of the great prophets in the Bible. He wrote a great truth about running. He wrote, 'But those who wait upon the LORD shall renew their strength; they shall mount up with wings as eagles, they shall run and not be weary, and they shall walk and not faint.' I know this may seem odd, but I believe that verse of Scripture is true and have put it into practice when I run. I'm not trying to be pushy. It's just what I do when I work out. I like to start with a prayer and commit the workout to God. Are you okay with that?"

Isaiah responded first. "No problem with me."

Chip didn't seem so enthusiastic but went along. "Fine with me."

Win led the boys in a word of prayer and asked God to protect them, enable them to train at their full potential, and renew them when they became tired. After prayer, they jogged a slow mile, then stretched. Win explained the type of workouts they would be doing the next few weeks. He asked Chip if he'd brought the information Win needed. He explained to Isaiah that he needed to assess his level of conditioning and racing times.

———————————⟨><⟩———————————

Grace had a corner table for Hope when she arrived at the bakery. They embraced, and Hope told Grace she was a little concerned about leaving Chip at the track with an older guy and a young black man.

Grace assured her that everything would be okay, and she would go with Hope to their home to meet Chip when they finished.

Hope looked at the small figurines placed throughout the restaurant and the pictures of scenes from Paris. "There's something very secure about this place. It feels so homey." She sipped her coffee and nibbled on a muffin. "I'm not sure what I should do about meeting my biological father. I'm leaning toward it, but I don't think it would be good for Chip to meet him yet. Maybe I could meet him in the next couple of weeks and see how it goes. If it's positive, I'll feel Chip out, and we can take it from there. What do you think?"

"I think that's a great way to go about this. I'll do whatever you want."

"Mom," Hope said nervously, "You don't have to answer this if you don't want. But what happened? Why did he leave you?"

"That's the mystery. I don't know. He left before I knew I was pregnant. He just vanished. He never came back, not even for his parents' funerals. It wasn't like him. He was always considerate. Then he showed up two weeks ago, asking forgiveness. I'm baffled."

"Maybe he'll give me some answers to your questions. Is he nice? What's he like?"

"He seems nice, but I don't trust him — not after what he did. I'm not going to let him hurt me, or you or Chip. The pain was so great back then. Sometimes I still feel the hurt. Rick was God's healing medicine for me. His love did something extraordinary. I thought I was completely over the hurt — until Win showed up. Since then it's been a huge struggle."

They spent most of the next hour talking about Grace's concerns. Grace couldn't remember a time they'd had such a profound talk. She shared with Hope her fears, hurts, and memories from her youth. Hope proved a good listener.

After an hour and a half, Hope's phone rang. Chip was calling to let her know they had finished the workout and were headed to the health food store for some protein powder. They would head home and make the drink there.

"Let me follow you to the house," Grace said. "I'll stay there with you until Chip's friends leave."

CHAPTER ELEVEN

Win drove Isaiah and Chip to a local health food store and took them to the protein powder section. "You want to make sure your protein drink doesn't have a lot of additives. You don't need junk in your body. You need protein to rebuild muscles that have been torn down by your workout. Now, which flavors do you like?"

Each picked a large container — vanilla for Chip and strawberry for Isaiah.

"We won't be able to do this today," Win said, "but you need to try to drink your protein within fifteen to thirty minutes after completing your workout. Your body will be able to absorb it more easily."

Win sensed something troubling Isaiah. "What's wrong?"

"How do you mix this stuff?"

"With a blender." Win realized Isaiah probably didn't have one. "Before I take you home, I'll stop by a store and we'll buy a new blender." Isaiah perked up. Win picked up some Almond milk and headed to Chip's house to mix it with their protein drink.

At Chip's small ranch-style house, they went directly to the kitchen. Win started mixing the protein drink, showing Isaiah and Chip how to measure and make it.

When Grace and Hope walked into the house, Chip stuck his head around the kitchen wall. "Hey, Mom; Hi, Mimi."

As Isaiah walked around the wall and saw the two women, Hope said, "I see you made it home okay. Who's your friend?"

"This is Isaiah. He's training with us. Mr. Bass is making a protein drink for us."

Grace froze. She slowly said, "Bass. Did you say Mr. Bass?"

"Yeah, just a second." Chip walked back into the kitchen where the blender buzzed loudly. "Mr. Bass, you've met my mom. I want you to meet my grandmother. She's in the living room."

———⋈———

When Win walked around the corner, the first person he saw was Hope, who had a smile on her face and her hand extended to shake his. Then he saw Grace.

Her face turned red. Her muscles tensed, and her eyes filled with rage.

Win's mouth dropped. Everything in his body went limp.

Chip and Isaiah looked perplexed.

Hope didn't understand why he stood there like a thief caught in the act.

Grace walked toward Win and stood six inches in front of him. She slammed her right hand across the left side of Win's face.

Hope and Chip gasped.

Isaiah's jaw dropped.

"Liar. You rotten, filthy liar. How could you?"

Hope grabbed her mother's arm. "Mom, what's going on?"

Win couldn't move, couldn't speak. He just stared at Grace.

Grace looked at Hope and bawled. Between sobs, she said, "This is . . . your father."

Hope looked at Win, walked up to him, and with her left hand, slapped the right side of his face. She walked to Grace and wrapped her arms around her.

Chip stood in disbelief. "Mom, what? Who?"

Isaiah looked toward the ceiling and whispered, "Oh, dear Jesus, Pastor Washington isn't gonna believe this."

Win finally snapped out of his shock. "Grace, I didn't know." His voice cracked. "This is Hope?" He turned and looked at Chip. "Chip, you're my grand . . ." He was once again speechless.

"What? Mom, what's this all about?" Chip walked over to his mother. "What's going on?"

Between sobs, Grace said, "Chip, this is your grandfather. He wasn't supposed to make contact with you until I gave him the okay. I'm sorry. He lied to me. He . . ."

"My grandfather? Do you mean like . . . like Mom's dad?"

Win took a deep breath. "Grace, Hope, Chip, I'm so sorry. I had no idea. I didn't know when I ran against you in the race or when we decided to train. I promise. I didn't know any of this. I'm so happy to meet you. But I told Grace that I wouldn't . . ."

Grace shouted, "Stop it! I don't want to hear another lie. That's enough."

Win's phone rang. He glanced and saw it was Pastor Washington. He handed the phone to Isaiah and asked him to tell Pastor Washington he'd call him back.

Hope started crying again, and Grace continued yelling at Win. "I trusted you, and you lied again. No more phony stories. I want you out of here. Right now."

Isaiah took the phone and whispered, "Dear Jesus, help me." Then he answered. "Pastor, this is Isaiah. It's crazy here. They hit Mr. Bass on the left side, then the right side. Oh, man. I can't believe it. I gotta go. When we're in the car, I'll call you back."

CHAPTER TWELVE

Emotions were so high, all reason disappeared. Grace again told Win to leave.

Hope said, "I'm going to call the police if you don't leave right now."

"Okay, I'm going. I'm sorry. Come on, Isaiah."

Isaiah grabbed his protein powder, and the two started toward the door.

Chip stepped between them and the door. "Wait a minute. Do I get a say in this? We need to sit down and talk. I have a lot of questions. We can't just kick them out of the house. We . . ."

"I'm sorry, Chip, but they have to go." Hope turned to Win with squared shoulders and a shaky voice and pointed to the door. "Now, get out."

Win and Isaiah left. When they climbed into the Lexus, Win put his hands on the steering wheel and let out a big sigh.

Isaiah sat silently, staring at Win.

Finally Win started the engine. "I'm sorry, Isaiah, that you had to see this. I really didn't know that Chip's my grandson. I'm as shocked as everyone."

For ten minutes as Win drove, neither uttered a word. Once they reached the Airline Highway, Isaiah finally spoke. "Do you mind if I ask you a question?"

"Go ahead."

"When they hit you, why didn't you push them back or do something to make them stop? You just stood there and let them do it."

"Isaiah, I would never do anything to hurt them. They're my family."

"My dad would have laid them out."

"Isaiah, listen to me closely. Never . . ." He repeated himself for emphasis, "Never hit a woman. No matter how angry you are, you never hit a woman. Understand?"

"Yeah."

"And when someone hits you, it takes a bigger man to turn the other cheek than it does to fight back."

"You sure did good turning the other cheek."

Win laughed. "I guess I did one thing right." Win remembered the call from Thomas Washington. "Isaiah, what did Pastor Washington say?"

Isaiah told Win the essence of the conversation, and then remembered. "Oh, I told him I'd call back."

Win handed Isaiah his phone. "Go ahead. Call him now."

Isaiah quickly dialed. "Pastor, we're on our way to the church. We'll be there in five minutes."

Pastor Washington asked Isaiah if he was okay and what was happening.

"Everything's cool. Don't worry. We're just about at the church."

———◇◇◇———

Grace and Hope sat on the couch, emotionally exhausted. Chip gave them no time to recover. He wanted answers.

Grace placed her hand on the seat next to her. "Sit down, and I'll try to explain. She told him the story of how she and Win had been high school sweethearts and how he had disappeared before he knew she was pregnant. She told Chip about meeting him again a few weeks ago and how he'd promised not to make contact with the family until she had prepared them.

"Mimi, I don't know about all the stuff that happened between you and him," Chip said. "But I really don't believe he knew I was his grandson when we ran in the race or when we met at the track last week." He shrugged. "I think I would have sensed something. How would he have known I work out on Saturday mornings? And how would he have known that Jamie wasn't training with me anymore? And why would he bring Isaiah with him if he thought I was his grandson? It doesn't make sense."

Grace was aghast. "Oh, no! I can't believe I hit him. I've never hit anyone in my life."

"Me, either, Mom. I can't believe I did that." Hope spoke with concern in her voice. "We joked about it last week, but I can't believe we actually did it."

"I was pretty shocked." Chip laughed. "I'm glad you never did that to me when I messed up."

"Oh, Chip, I'm sorry you saw that," Grace said. "I've never done anything like that, and I'll never do it again. Forget you ever saw it."

"Forget!" He laughed. "How can I ever forget the knockout punch from Mimi Tyson and Mom Holyfield?"

Grace and Hope both asked, "Who?"

Chip smiled. "Never mind."

"Mom," Hope asked, "where do we go from here?"

"I don't know, but I think we need to talk to Todd. Are you going to church tomorrow?"

"Yes."

"Let's talk to Todd after the service. Maybe he and Elaine can tell us what to do."

Hope looked at Chip with a plea in her eyes. "It's been a long time since you've been to church. Would you go with us and talk with Todd."

"Sure, Mom. I'll go." He paused for a second. "For you, I'll go. This is hard for all of us. But I have to tell Pastor Todd that I believe Mr. Bass didn't know anything." With a perplexed look, he said, "Do I call him, Mr. Bass, or what? This is weird."

Thomas Washington was waiting outside of the Mount Calvary Missionary Baptist Church when Todd Mayo pulled up. He had alerted Todd after he'd talked to Isaiah on the phone.

Win arrived a couple of minutes after Todd. Pastor Washington and Todd Mayo had their hands on their hips, looking stern.

When Isaiah and Win got out of the car, Pastor Washington immediately asked, "Isaiah, are you okay? You're not hurt, are you?"

"No. Everything's cool."

Todd pointed his finger in Win's face. "You have a lot of explaining to do, my friend."

"Let's go into my office." Pastor Washington motioned toward the front door. "Isaiah, get a couple of chairs and bring them in."

After the four settled into the office, Washington spoke with a firmness Win hadn't heard in the pastor's voice. "Mr. Bass, what was going on when I called you? You said you were going to work out with Isaiah. I then call and find out you're in some kind of fight. You want to explain?"

"There wasn't a fight. Just yelling and screaming."

"Then Isaiah was lying when he said you'd been hit twice."

"He wasn't lying. That's true, but it wasn't a fight . . ."

"If that's not a fight," Washington said, "then tell me what a fight is."

"It's not like that. Just listen for a few minutes and I'll explain."

"We're all ears."

Win looked at Todd. "I didn't know the young runner I was training was my grandson. I didn't know his mom was Hope."

Todd gasped. "You were training Chip, and you met Hope?"

"After the workout, we went to Chip's house to make a protein drink. While we were there, Grace and Hope walked in. Grace thought I had been lying to her, and she lost it. She slapped me. Then Hope slapped me." Win shook his head. "It almost felt good. I've felt so guilty for what I did, I've thought I needed something done to me. It may sound crazy, but I wanted someone to hit me. I deserved everything they gave me, and much more."

"That explains what happened today," Todd said. He clarified to Washington the situation with Win and Grace.

Todd looked at Win. "When Thomas called me, he said you gave him a letter from your mother saying you were in prison. What's that all about? And before you answer, I want the whole truth. Don't piecemeal it to me like you've been doing. Thomas and I trusted you. No more secrets. Just the truth. It's time to come clean."

Win took a deep breath. "I've been afraid to tell you. I've been embarrassed and ashamed. If I told you everything, I thought you would reject me. I'm sorry I wasn't completely honest, but here's the story.

"I left Baton Rouge after graduation. You remember, Todd. I'd been drinking — real heavy. I was confused. I took the money from the bank account my parents and I had saved for college and headed to California. Hitchhiked. Some hippie types picked me up in Lafayette and I went as far as Houston with them. They were smoking weed. I tried it, and it felt good. It eased the pain. That started me smoking pot.

"I finally made my way to Los Angeles, to Sunset Strip. I stayed in some hippie pads, slept on the streets and in parks. I experimented with LSD but mostly smoked weed. After a couple of weeks in LA, I headed to San Francisco. People said San Francisco was where everything was happening. I hitchhiked, and three guys picked me up. We were smoking grass when the police stopped us. They arrested us, and I spent four years in the slammer. By the time I was released, Mom and Dad had died. I was too ashamed to come home."

Win's eyes seemed haunted with pain. "Had nothing to come to. So, I caught a bus to Seattle and started life over. From there I've told you the rest of the story."

"Sorry, but I don't buy it," Todd said. "When we first met, I felt you weren't telling me something. I wanted to give you the benefit of the doubt. I can't do it anymore. It doesn't sound right that you'd get four years for smoking pot if that was your first offense. Win, look me straight in the eyes and say you've told me everything — that you've not left anything out."

Win looked away and swallowed. "There were other charges."

"What other charges, Win?" Todd asked. "What other charges?"

"Murder."

CHAPTER THIRTEEN

Chip and Hope had been very close in the nearly five years since David Thibodeaux was killed in Iraq. Chip felt a responsibility for his mother. Although he'd gotten into a few fights with other boys shortly after his dad died, he'd turned a corner and kept out of trouble. The main point of tension between them was church. After his father was killed, Chip had strayed from his faith. If God was as good as he'd been taught, why would God allow his dad to be killed at a time he desperately needed him? It didn't make sense.

It was nearly noon when Grace left their home. Chip hugged his mom. "Are you okay?"

"I think so. I didn't want you to learn about your grandfather this way. Your grandmother and I were meeting today, talking about how to tell you. I'm so sorry you had to find out like this."

"Don't worry about me, Mom. I think I'm the only one who is cool with the whole thing. It's you I'm worried about. You never knew your real dad. This has to be tough on you. At least I knew mine."

Hope wept softly. "I never realized there was this big empty place in my heart. I've always said I didn't need to know my real dad because God gave me such a good father. I loved him, and everything was okay. But now . . ."

"Now, you want to know your other dad."

"Yes. No. I don't know. What if he's some kind of creep?"

"What if he's a really nice guy? Before we started our workout, he told Isaiah and me that he wanted to begin our workouts with prayer.

It was the first time I've prayed in a long time."

Hope looked at Chip with a mixture of hope and surprise. "Really?"

"Yeah, it's been a long time since I prayed."

"I'm not talking about that. You mean, he wanted to pray?"

"When he first started talking about his relationship with God, I was a little skeptical, but I'm pretty sure he's for real."

Todd and Thomas were stunned by Win's confession. Isaiah looked upward and whispered, "Oh, dear Jesus."

Todd looked his old friend in the eye. "Win, you killed someone?"

"No, but I was charged with accessory to murder. When we were arrested, I didn't have enough money for a lawyer, and the court appointed one. He was new and looking for the easy way out. I contacted Mom and Dad. You remember, Todd. They were poor. They said they'd sell the house to get an attorney, but that took time. The other guys in the car had robbed a home — and in the process killed a man. Because I was in the car with them after all this happened, the D.A. thought I was a part of the crime, though I told them I'd been at a party at the time of the murder. The guys got a reduced sentence by confessing and giving testimony against me."

Thomas rolled his eyes. "So you're like all the other guys in the neighborhood who've gone to prison. They're all innocent. None of them did anything wrong."

"I didn't say that. I was guilty of possession of narcotics — but not murder. I went to trial, and my lawyer did a lousy job. I had a rock-solid alibi, but he never presented it. He just wanted to get through the process as quickly as possible. I was sentenced to fifteen years.

"While in prison, I studied law. I knew I'd been wrongly convicted and was determined to prove it. I met an attorney who visited a fellow inmate. My friend told him about me, and he took my case. Made an appeal. He located the people at the party I'd attended and won the appeal. A year later, I was found innocent. You can check it all out. It's public record."

"Don't worry," Thomas said. "We'll check everything. But training Isaiah is over. I can't take any chances. There are enough people who can mess him up. We don't need another one. He needs a role model, not a murderer."

Isaiah had to say something. "There's no way Mr. Bass was involved in murder. I watched him when he was slapped. He didn't fight back. He doesn't have a drop of mean blood in his body. Give him a chance."

"Quiet, Isaiah!" Thomas said. "We can handle this."

Todd stood and spoke directly to Win. "Why don't you come to church tomorrow. Let's meet after the last service and talk about where we go from here. But you need to leave Isaiah alone. That's what Pastor Washington wants, and you need to start playing according to the rules. Understand?"

Win hung his head. "Sure."

Todd walked out with a sense of frustration. Win looked like a whipped puppy.

"Pastor, I'm really sorry," Win said. "I won't bother you or Isaiah anymore." He fist bumped with Isaiah. "You've got plenty of potential. Don't let anyone take your dreams away. Listen to Pastor Washington, and stay out of trouble. I'll look forward to hearing in a couple of years that you're the state champion."

As Win drove home, emotional exhaustion overwhelmed him. He wondered if he'd made a mistake by returning to Baton Rouge. Maybe he should sell the house and return to Seattle. First he'd call his friend Calvin. He always had good counsel. Since Win had arrived in Baton Rouge, he'd sent Calvin a couple of emails letting him know what was happening, but he hadn't given a lot of detail.

Win's lakeshore home felt as empty as his heart. Out the window, the old oak stood silent. No breeze. No waving moss. He prayed, 'Father, I need You right now, really bad. I thought You wanted me to come home. I don't know if that was right. I only want to do the right thing. Please, help me. Help me do the right thing. Thank You for letting me meet my family. Thank You for Hope and Chip. Thank You for Grace. Oh, God, please protect them and keep them. I don't know how You could forgive me when I messed up so badly."

Win felt like someone had turned on the faucet of his emotions. "Thank You, Lord. I love You so much," he cried out. "You're the only One who sees something in me. Thank You for Your love, especially when I don't deserve it. Thank You." Win finally sat on the couch and looked around at his nice furniture. *All this stuff. None of it means anything. I'd give it all up in an instant to have a relationship with Chip, Hope, and Grace.*

After an hour, Win decided to call Calvin. "Hey, man, this is your long-lost friend."

"Win, I've been wondering when you'd call. I appreciate your emails and texts, but all of us are anxious to hear the details. Every time we run, we ask each other if anyone's heard from you. The bits and pieces you've given sound like it's really been interesting. Tell me, what's happening?"

"Are you sitting down?" Win told Calvin everything that had taken place. "I've made a royal mess. Everyone had a nice life. Then I drop in, and chaos erupts. I think I've made a mistake by coming home. Maybe I need to return to Seattle."

"Whoa. You can't do that, at least not now. First, you didn't bring the chaos to Baton Rouge. It was already there. No one knew it, but it was there all the time. Your presence is God's way of exposing the chaos that already existed. And second, once the chaos is exposed, you can't just walk out and leave a mess. Remember that Bible study where we talked about God being a God of order?"

"I remember, but I don't see much order to this situation."

"Not now, and that's why you can't leave yet. God didn't send you to Baton Rouge just to show you the mess in your life or in your family's lives. He wants to heal you, Win. And He wants to heal the hurt in your family. Those hurts have been in all of you for a long time. And I believe God is going to heal them completely, but it's not going to be easy."

"That's an understatement. I don't know where to begin."

"When you first shared your desire to return to Baton Rouge, we were skeptical. But the more we prayed with you, the more we felt God wanted to use you. There's such freshness about your faith. We felt God wanted to renew His people in Baton Rouge. Do you remember before you left Seattle, we prayed that God would use you to bring revival to your old friends and neighborhood? Revival can be messy at first. But God has a way to clean up a mess, and His ways are higher than ours. We don't always understand them, but in the end it's all good.

"Win, I don't want you ever to forget what I'm about to say." His voice became more confident. "Brokenness is God's path to renewal and healing. He placed you on the trail of brokenness. God's Spirit has a way of surprising us on that trail. I don't know where it's leading, but I'm sure it's going to bring an amazing amount of healing to all of you."

"I sure hope so," Win said. "I'd hate to think I'm going through all this for nothing."

"Now, what about the two pastors — your friend and the pastor in your old neighborhood? What are their names again?"

"Todd Mayo and Thomas Washington. They've lost any faith in me. I'm going to meet with Todd tomorrow, but I don't think he'll be helpful anymore. He's finished with me. And Pastor Washington doesn't trust me at all. I don't blame him."

"Okay, Todd Mayo and Thomas Washington."

"Calvin, you're not writing down their names, are you? I can handle this myself."

"Wait a minute, Win. You called me because you trusted me. Let me pray about this. I think these guys need to hear from someone who has worked with you for the past thirty-plus years, someone who really knows you. Besides, it sounds like they need God to do a work in their lives. You want to give me their cell numbers, or do I find them on my own?"

"Calvin, they are really good guys. I don't blame them for my mistakes."

"Numbers. Give me numbers," Calvin said.

Win knew Calvin could find the phone numbers without his help.

"Why don't you give them my number," Calvin said, "and ask them to call me? If they don't call, I'll pray about making contact with them."

"Sure, man."

"Let's pray," Calvin said. "God, I pray that You fill Win with such love that all confusion and fear will disappear. Use him as an instrument to bring revival to these men's hearts and also their churches. Give him clear direction at this critical moment."

"Amen. Thanks, Calvin."

"One last thing.

"What's that?"

It could get worse before it gets better."

"I don't see how it could get worse."

"Trust me. It can get much worse."

CHAPTER FOURTEEN

Win arrived early at Indian Heights Community Church. The facilities were impressive. Acres of parking surrounded a large, circular building with a small cross at the center. Parking attendants directed Win to a nearby spot and then the sanctuary. The inside felt almost like a sports complex, with entrances having section numbers and signs pointing to upper and lower levels. Win passed a coffee shop before heading to the upper level.

He found a seat where he could be alone, at the top and far right of the sanctuary. After sitting in his theater-style chair, he looked with amazement at the worship center. Excitement filled the air as the worship team and band prepared. The leader barked out commands, making sure there wasn't an unused second. *Wow. Todd has really done well. This ought to be quite a performance.*

Win closed his eyes, placed his head in his hands, and tried to push the theater atmosphere out of his mind. He wanted to focus on worshiping God, not just meeting after the service with Todd. After sitting in silence for a few minutes, he whispered, "Oh, Father, speak to me today. I desperately need You. I ask You for a miracle."

Someone tapped his shoulder. Chip stood with a huge grin and his arm extended with knuckles. "Mom always says I'm her miracle child, but I don't think I'm the miracle you were looking for."

Win smiled. "What are you doing here?"

"Going to church. What do you think?"

"I didn't think you went to church."

Chip bounced on his toes, gestured as though he were boxing, and laughed. "After seeing Mimi Tyson and Mom Holyfield in action, I decided I'd better obey."

Win's smile grew large. "I don't think it's a good idea for you to sit here. If you're serious about obeying them, you probably want to sit somewhere else."

"Come on, Gramps." Chip's eyes twinkled. "Is that what I call you? Or Mr. Win? Or Speedy?"

"I don't know, but, look, Chip, this isn't a game. I've hurt a lot of people. Your mom and grandmother think I lied. I don't want them to think I'm doing it again."

Chip patted Win's shoulder and took the seat next to him. "Don't worry, Gramps, I'll be your lawyer."

Win rolled his eyes.

"They may not trust you," Chip said, "but they'll trust me. Anyway, they're visiting their lady friends and won't see me until after the service."

"Okay. If you're going to get me thrown in your mom's jail, then I've got some questions for you."

"Fire away."

"Why did you give up on God?"

"You go straight for the jugular." Chip squinted his eyes and looked directly into his grandfather's. "I didn't give up on God. I gave up on church. You see, I . . ."

"Hi, Chip."

Chip and Win snapped their heads to see who'd sneaked up on them. Chip stood and hugged the cute blonde. "Hi, Emma. Good to see you."

"It's great to see you. It's been a long time since you've been here. I was downstairs and looked up and saw you acting like you were boxing. I thought I'd better stop the fight." She smiled. "You want to sit with our youth group? We're going out for pizza afterward."

"I wish I could," Chip said, "but I'm here with my friend." He turned his head toward Win. "This is my new friend, Mr. Bass. He's been training me. This is Emma. We're both seniors at Indian Heights."

"It's a pleasure to meet you, Mr. Bass. Do you come to our church often?"

"No, Emma. First time."

"I hope we'll see you again." Emma smiled at Chip and returned to the lower level.

Chip stared as she walked away.

"I think she likes you, Chip. Go sit with her."

"Good try, Gramps, but you're not getting rid of me that easily."

"So, I'm Gramps now, but Mr. Bass when she's around."

Chip smiled. "Exactly."

"Well, let Gramps give you some advice. She really liked the hug you gave her. She seems like a keeper — real cute, and a nice young lady."

"I don't want to seem rude, Gramps, but I think I'll get my love-life advice from someone with a better track record."

A booming voice came over the sound system. "Let's all stand as we worship."

The energy level skyrocketed as people clapped, sang, and lifted their hands. After a few minutes of praise, Todd welcomed everyone before the band continued. The service flowed flawlessly. The musicians transitioned from one song to another with perfect timing. Dynamic video was used to prepare the audience for Todd's message. Everything was done with excellence. The only part of the service that bothered Win was the offering. Todd took too long and seemed too aggressive in raising funds. But when Todd finished preaching, Win felt inspired and had forgotten the forceful attempt to collect money.

After the service, Win nudged Chip. "This was incredible. I don't understand why you left church. I've not been in many worship services this dynamic. And Todd's message — wow!"

For the first time that day, Chip's face looked serious. "That's the problem. Everything is so perfect. That's not my world. I loved this kind of worship before my dad was killed. When I came to church after that, it seemed phony. Everyone looks so happy, but I don't think they are. That's what I like about you." Chip's face relaxed and he looped his thumbs in his front pockets. "You're messed up." His natural smile emerged again. "But you know it — and aren't ashamed to admit it."

"Thanks for your theology lesson. But I have to get to a meeting with Pastor Todd."

"Uh-oh."

"Uh-oh, what?"

"Mom and Mimi are talking to Pastor Todd right now to see if they can meet with him for a few minutes. That's really why I'm here. I promised I'd talk to Pastor Todd with them."

Win looked upward and took a deep breath. "Why does this keep happening?"

Chip's eyes darted around the room. "Why don't you wait at the back of the sanctuary while I play lawyer?"

"What?"

"I'll tell Mom and Mimi that you're here. I'll explain that you had already set up a meeting with Pastor Todd."

Win grimaced. "I don't think so, Chip."

"Come on." Chip motioned for Win to follow. "Give me a chance."

Grace and Hope waited with Chip for Todd to finish talking and praying with church members. When they finally approached, Todd offered a sad smile and gave both ladies a hug. "I'm sorry this happened. I met with Win after your encounter. He told me everything."

Grace trembled. "Todd, we really need to talk. Do you have time?"

"Sure, but you need to know . . ."

Chip stood behind his mom and grandmother and frantically shook his head.

Todd saw him. "Chip, you want to say something?"

Chip's eyes flittered from Todd to his mom, then his grandmother. "Maybe I can go with Mom and Mimi to your office. I need to tell them about someone I met today. You can finish talking with people, and we'll wait for you there."

"Sounds like a plan. You go ahead, and I'll be right there."

Grace told Hope and Chip she didn't understand why she was so nervous about talking to Todd. "After all, we've been friends since the fifth grade. He's helped me more than any person I know . . ." She looked at Hope. "Except your dad."

Hope squeezed Grace's hand, "It's okay, Mom."

As Chip paced in Todd's office, he grimaced. "I met someone today. I think you ought to know about it."

Hope and Grace waited for the rest of the story.

"Mr. Win is here."

"Surprise, surprise," Hope said.

"He didn't know we were here or that we were meeting with Todd."

"You talked to him?" Grace said.

He hesitated. "I guess you could say that. He has a meeting with Pastor Todd."

Hope stared in silence.

"I can't believe it!" Grace said. "That conniving . . ."

The door opened, and the conniver entered with Todd.

"Todd, what's going on here?"

"Calm down, Grace. Win didn't know you wanted to meet with me. I arranged yesterday to talk to him after the service. This is not his doing. So, let's all take a deep breath, relax, and talk for a few minutes." Todd pointed to the couch and a couple of chairs. Hope sat on one end of the couch and Win on the other. Chip and Grace sat in the fine leather chairs.

"I am going to meet with the three of you separately," Todd said, "but on our way to the office, I told Win there's something he needs to tell all of you."

Win kept his eyes on the wall. "Yesterday when everything happened, I didn't have time to tell you why I didn't return to Baton Rouge." He glanced down. "I'd been arrested for possession of marijuana. I was hitch-hiking to San Francisco when some guys picked me up. They were smoking dope, and they gave me a weed. I smoked with them. Soon after that, the police stopped us and arrested us." Win took a deep breath. "I was in prison when dad and mom died."

Tears formed in Grace's eyes. Hope gasped, and Chip kept his eyes on his grandmother.

Todd frowned at Win. "Tell them everything."

Win looked at Grace with a plea for trust. "The guys who picked me up had killed a man a few hours earlier in a botched robbery. Because I was with them, I was also charged with murder. I was convicted, and four and a half years later, the decision was overturned. I was found not guilty."

Hope jumped off the couch and strode toward the door. Wrapping her arms around herself, she looked at Todd with a plea for protection.

Grace stared at Win, her eyes wide.

Chip's eyes darted around the room, trying to see what everyone was thinking. He finally fixed his gaze on his grandmother.

Win pulled out a paper with Calvin's cell number and handed it to Todd. "He was my supervisor at Dresdtech. They did a complete background check. Calvin has access to most of the court documents that prove my innocence. I'm sure he can give you whatever information you need. And Todd, he said he'd like to talk to you. He asked you to call him this afternoon or evening." Win glanced at Todd, then back at his shoes. "I'll go now. I hope you can help them sort through this. I know I've said it before, but I really mean it. I'm so sorry."

As Win walked out of the room, Chip kept his eyes on his grandmother. At last she knew the truth.

CHAPTER FIFTEEN

Grace called Win's cell, then his home phone. No answer. It was an hour and a half before sundown, and she had a hunch where she might find him. She hurried because the cemetery closed at dark. When she arrived, she saw a lonely figure on a bench under a big oak near Win's parents' grave. "Hey, can I sit with you?" Grace asked gently.

Win gave a small smile and scooted over. "Sure. If you're not afraid."

Grace sat close, but made sure she wasn't touching him. "I used to come here after your mom died. It's strange, but I felt like I could still talk to her."

"I guess I'm not the only crazy person."

With a heavy heart, Grace said, "I'm sorry, Win."

"For what?"

"For what happened to you."

"My stupid decisions caused everything." He stared at the horizon. "I was able to put it all behind me in Seattle. Those guys at Dresdtech treated me great. They believed in me, gave me a chance. I rebuilt my life. When I gave my life to Christ five years ago, I was so pumped. I had meaning. I thought I could face anything."

"And now?"

Win looked with confidence into Grace's eyes. "God's grace and power are just as real as they were then. It's just that all this junk has risen to the surface. I never came home because I didn't want to face my past. But after the Masters World Championships, I knew I had to return. I knew it would be difficult, but I didn't think it would be this hard."

Win looked at the ground. "I almost gave up last night. I called Calvin and told him I was returning to Seattle. He prayed for me, and God gave me strength. I never expected life to get this messy."

Grace grabbed Win's chin and gently turned his face toward hers. "Win, I know you had nothing to do with the murder. I don't have any doubts."

His eyes widened. "Why? Why would you believe me?"

"I'll be completely honest. I called your friend Calvin this afternoon. He emailed me some documents that prove your innocence. I couldn't believe how incompetent your first attorney was. Calvin sent me a copy of statements from fifteen witnesses who were with you at a party in another part of the city before, during, and after the murder. It's unbelievable that your original attorney wouldn't contact them.

She sighed. "But you need to know I believed you before I ever called Calvin. I only made that call for the sake of Hope and Chip. I wanted them to see the evidence. They didn't know the Win I knew."

"Thanks." Win took a deep breath. "It's good to have someone here who believes me."

"I'm sure Chip does, too."

"Why do you think that?"

"When his dad died, Chip was at a very vulnerable age — just entering his teens. He wanted to prove he was a man. He got into fights. He was at my house one day, and I told him about a boy in my school who was my hero. I told him how my hero was the fastest runner in the school. When this boy was in the eighth grade, a tough guy came up to him and wanted to fight." She smiled and looked into Win's eyes.

A smile crept across his face.

"I told him how my hero refused to fight, and the tough guy hit him. My hero walked up to the tough guy, and stood toe to toe with him. Then he turned his other cheek." Grace paused. "Chip asked me what happened. I told him the boy knocked my hero down, and everyone laughed. The tough boy walked away.

"Chip wanted to know how that made him a hero. I told him my hero proved his manhood with his feet, not with his fists. He became the greatest runner our school ever knew. But the tough guy dropped out of school, and I've never heard of him since."

"What did Chip say?"

"He called me the next Saturday and asked if I could take him to the track. He said he was going to be a runner."

Win looked sheepishly at Grace. "Really? That's why he started running?"

"Really. When everything happened yesterday, when I slapped you, Chip knew you were that hero."

Win smiled gently. "I'm just sorry that I quit being your hero."

Grace's voice changed from tender to forceful. "Stop it, Win. Quit feeling sorry for yourself. You told me you were forgiven. If you're forgiven, then act like it."

He lifted his hands in front of him. "You're right. I just don't know if you can understand how difficult it is." Win gazed around the cemetery. "This may sound strange, but this place is beautiful. The old oak trees. I love them. The moss hanging off the trees over there. I've missed that so much. I never realized how much I missed Baton Rouge until I came back.

"Prison almost destroyed me emotionally." Win shook his head. "Being in a small cell with no windows ate away at me. I didn't realize how much of an outdoorsman I was. When I won my appeal, I had a year before my new trial. I researched where I wanted to start a new life. Seattle had big fir trees, beautiful mountains, and great lake views. I loved the mountains and the water, but the fir trees gave me the fresh vision I desperately needed. But it wasn't Baton Rouge." He grinned. "I even like the humidity here. It feels like home.

"The oak trees have the same strength and endurance of the firs," Win said, "but each one has a unique personality. The south-Louisiana storms twist and bend them, but don't destroy them. They become even more beautiful."

Win stood, invigorated. "Come on, let's walk. I want to show you something." He led Grace to a statue of Jesus carrying a lost sheep. "Right now, I'm that sheep. I can't face this by myself. I need Jesus to carry me. After I talked to Calvin last night, I wanted to leave, give up."

"On what?"

"On ever having a family. Baton Rouge is home, the only place I've ever known family. God led me back, and I realize now I have to stay. But I'm too weak. I need Jesus."

"Win, Jesus isn't just the Great Shepherd. He's also the Great Healer. When I talked to Calvin, he asked a question that cut deep. I knew I needed to talk to you."

"What'd he ask?"

"Which was the greater injustice: that the three boys got off lightly or that you went to prison for the murder they committed? I realized how much you've suffered. How I've suffered. Hope and Chip have suffered. Your parents suffered. And none of that takes into account the victim's family, who didn't really receive justice. All because you were tried and convicted unjustly." A tear fell from Grace's eyes. "I wondered what life would have been like if true justice had been served."

Win held Grace's shoulders and looked into her eyes. "I've already asked all the 'what if' questions. We'll never have the answer. It's okay. You said a few minutes ago that I'm forgiven. We can't do anything about the past, but we can make sure that we do the right thing for the future."

Grace looked down and her face flushed. "Let's go back to the car."

"Sure." Win released Grace. "Hey, I'm sorry."

"It's okay." Grace waved her hand in front of her face, trying to fight the tears. Neither said a word as they walked to their cars.

Win opened the door for Grace. "Can we get together again?"

Grace smiled. "I'd like that."

"What about next weekend at my place? You could bring Hope and Chip — that is, if they're open to it. I know a place that makes good jambalaya. I could bring it to my house. It has a great view."

"I'll talk to Hope and Chip and see if it's okay for Chip to continue running with you. I can't promise anything, but I'll see. And next weekend, I'll let you know."

"If he and his mom agree, Chip and I can run together Saturday morning. I'll drop him off, come home, and get everything ready for lunch. When you come, there's something special I want to show you. When I found it, I couldn't believe what I saw."

"Sounds great. I'll get back with you. Where is it located?"

"It's on South Lakeshore Drive."

She looked stunned. "Lakeshore Drive?"

A smile tiptoed across Win's face. "I promise. You won't believe what I found."

CHAPTER SIXTEEN

Each day that week, Chip worked out at Indian Heights before school, in an attempt to avoid Jamie. He arranged with the janitor to open the locker room early so he could shower before classes. After a hard workout Wednesday, he entered the dimly lit locker room. The silence when no one was around always gave him the creeps. He wanted to be cleaned up and gone before Coach Landon arrived.

As he opened his locker, he heard a noise. The locker slammed and someone grabbed him around the neck. He felt something sharp against the left side of his neck.

"Move and you're dead."

Chip's heart pounded. *What's going on?*

"I'm gonna let ya go, and I want ya to turn around real slow. If ya try and run or fight, I'll rip your throat. Understand?"

"Yeah, I understand."

The man's grip loosened, and Chip gasped as he turned. The man he and Jamie had seen getting out of Coach Landon's car at the All Comers' meet stood inches from him, a switchblade pointed at his face.

"I hear you're a snoop, and my boss don't like snoops. He thinks snoops and snitches are trash. You know what we do with trash?"

Chip couldn't speak.

The man pointed at the scar on the side of his face. "You see this. That's nothing compared to what your face will look like if you ever say a word about the conversation between your buddy and your coach." He flashed a caustic smile. "Understand, pretty boy?"

"Yeah, I understand."

"I know your address. I've been following ya. Know your every move, and I know where that pretty little momma of yours works. If you want to see her pretty face again, you won't say nothing to nobody."

Chip took a deep breath and silently prayed, *Oh, God, please help me.*

———◇———

Tuesday afternoon, Todd and Thomas Washington had a conference call with Win's former supervisor, Calvin. After that call, they arranged to meet Win for breakfast early Wednesday morning at CC's coffee shop on Airline Highway.

Win greeted them with a soft voice but with his shoulders back and his chin up. He gave them a firm handshake, letting them know he was no longer wallowing in shame. The last time Win and Todd had met at CC's, Win had left a broken man. This time he arrived with his scars on the mend.

After they ordered a light breakfast and coffee, the men grabbed a table in the corner. Todd spoke first. "We talked to Calvin yesterday. He's quite a guy. Really sharp, and has a lot of respect for you. After speaking with him, we wanted to talk to you as soon as possible."

"Do you believe what he told you about me?"

Thomas looked at Todd. "I'd like to answer that." He turned back to Win. "We believe him. I'm really sorry for doubting you. To be honest, I'm pretty embarrassed. I gave Calvin my lecture how we don't need a bunch of white folk coming down here who don't understand our culture and situation. I gave him an ear full about our community and our people. I told him he needed to learn a little more about our people and African-American culture. That was a big mistake."

Win chuckled. "I feel your pain."

"No one told me he was black. I felt terrible when he told me his brother was killed in gang violence in Chicago's South Side. Calvin is the kind of guy our young people need to meet: climbing his way out of the ghetto, overcoming the odds, getting an education, a great job. Anyway, he laid out the evidence that proves your innocence. Emailed us scanned documents. I'm truly sorry you suffered the way you did."

"So you believe me?"

"We believe you," Todd said. "But you also admitted you did time for using drugs. I think I understand what happened because I know you, Win. But Thomas doesn't."

"I guess that means I can't work with Isaiah."

"That's not what it means," Thomas said. "I have an obligation to Isaiah's mom to make sure her son is in safe hands. She trusts me, and so does the community. I don't take that lightly." He leaned forward, elbows on the table. "Here's what I propose. There's a man from our church who just retired from the Army — Special Ops. He's adjusting to civilian life. He hopes to land a job in the next couple of months. I'd like him to work out with you and Isaiah while he's in this interim."

"A babysitter?"

"Call it what you want. But those are my conditions. Also, I'm still concerned about someone finding out that you rescued LaKeisha. That could cause you and anyone with you big problems. My Special Ops friend will provide an extra level of protection if something did happen."

"Okay. Maybe we can start Saturday. I'm hoping Chip will run with us."

———✕✕———

A voice bellowed from one end of the locker room. "Put that knife down, Boone."

Coach Landon strode toward them. "Now!" he shouted. "Did you hear me? Put it down!"

Boone slowly lowered the knife.

The vein on Landon's neck pulsed. "You stupid . . ." Coach Landon grabbed the knife. "I told you never, never to come to these school grounds. You come near one of my boys again, you'll regret it for the rest of your life. Understand?"

Boone sneered. "Yeah, but Dutch isn't gonna like this."

Coach Landon's eyes narrowed. "I told Dutch what happened because I wanted to keep him in the loop. And I'll tell Dutch how stupid you are. I'll handle this. If you ever . . ." Coach's ears, neck, and face flushed red. "If you ever put a foot on these school grounds again, you can tell Dutch that our deal is over. Now get out of here."

The man walked halfway out of the locker room, then turned and pointed at Landon. "You still owe us. Just remember, we can repossess that fine car of yours. And I don't think you want to order Dutch to do anything."

Chip stood speechless.

Coach Landon turned toward Chip, his hands on his hips. "Let's go into my office. We need to talk."

Chip's legs felt like rubber. His body calmed as he collapsed into the chair in front of Coach Landon's desk.

Coach Landon stared at Chip. "Look at me." Coach squinted and spoke in a soft tone. "I'm sorry you went through that, son. This has never happened before."

"How did that guy know who I am and that I heard you and Jamie talking?"

"Jamie told me about seeing you, and I panicked. I called Boone's boss in Lake Charles. Asked him what to do, and he said not to worry. I had no idea he would have that creep threaten you."

Landon rubbed his chin and took a deep breath. "Chip, these guys are bad. They control the flow of steroids in Lake Charles and most of south Louisiana. You don't mess with them. Whatever you do, you can't tell anyone about what happened today, or about Jamie. Understand?"

Chip rolled his eyes. "Yeah."

"You may not like it, but don't tell anyone. These guys will hurt you — or anyone else who stands in their way."

Chip shook his head. "Why? Why are you doing this, Coach?"

Landon looked at the trophies on his shelves and grabbed one for a state championship. "At first, it was about this. After a few championships, I discovered I could make good money. Do you know how much a high-school coach makes — and how much time he puts into his work?"

Chip stared at Coach Landon.

"Not much. I make up my shortfall selling steroids. It's a business. The supplements help guys like Jamie develop muscle, get stronger and faster. And I'm able to live a decent lifestyle, rewarded for my hard work."

"Yeah. Rewarded with the knife of Boone, the Scarface."

Coach glanced down. "This year has been difficult for everyone. The economy. There's not much money floating around. Scarface, as you call him, works with some guys out of Lake Charles, and they're really uptight. They've placed a lot of pressure on me. It's all about money, Chip. At first, I thought it was about winning, but it's not. That was the hook in my heart."

Chip shook his head.

"There's a question I need answered. Rumor has it you're training with the guy who beat you at the All Comers' meet. That true?"

"So what? You're drugging Jamie and working with him until track season starts. What do you expect me to do?"

"Watch your mouth. I don't have a problem with you training with him. I just want to know who he is and what kind of training he's doing with you."

"He's some rich old man who used to live in Baton Rouge and has moved back. He's a good runner for an old guy. That's all."

"What's his name?"

"Why do you want to know? You're going to send your goons after him? He didn't make his money selling drugs."

"Stop it!" Landon shouted. "Get this straight. These guys will hurt you and anybody with you." Coach Landon pointed at Chip. "You need to cooperate, or we're all going to have problems."

"His name is Win Bass."

Coach Landon shook his head. "You're kidding."

"No. That a problem?"

"He's a legend in Louisiana track. The guy still holds the state record in the quarter mile." Coach Landon's voice softened. "Wow. I've always wanted to meet him. I can't believe you're training with the guy."

Landon stood and looked into Chip's eyes. "Okay, keep working with him until track season starts in a few weeks. Tell him he can call me if he needs to know anything about what we'll be doing when the season begins. And Chip, don't tell him anything about what happened today or anything about Jamie. It's better for you — and for him."

CHAPTER SEVENTEEN

A few months earlier, the U.S. economy had taken a huge hit. The bubble in the nation's housing market had burst, and money dried up. Because Baton Rouge's home prices had appreciated slowly, the city escaped much of the direct fallout. But people who had invested heavily in the stocks of large homebuilders saw their portfolios plummet. Todd Mayo was one of those.

Win had been able to buy his home on South Lakeshore Drive through a short sale. Paying in cash, he'd gotten the home for little more than half its value.

Before Todd left CC's coffee shop, he reminded Win that he needed to meet him to discuss a business decision he'd made. But Todd wanted to meet more discreetly — not at CC's and definitely not at the church. They decided to meet the next day at Win's place.

When Todd arrived, he asked how Win was doing and if he'd set up a running schedule with Isaiah and Chip.

"Grace talked to Hope, and she was willing to allow Chip to work out with me. I think Grace may have done some arm-twisting. I also called Pastor Thomas and Chip. We've set a time. It was odd, though. Chip didn't want to work out at Indian Heights. He wanted to train at Istrouma. That works great for Isaiah. We begin Saturday morning at the old Istrouma cinder track."

Win poured them both a cup of Community dark roast. "Before we talk about your business decision, there's something really weird I've needed to ask you about since we met the first time. But so much else has happened.

Todd leaned toward Win. "All right. Shoot."

"After the All Comers' meet, I had a strange encounter with a guy in the parking lot. He said he was the father of one of the boys I beat. At the time, I didn't know which one he meant. Now I do. He was talking about Chip's friend."

"Jamie."

"Yeah."

Todd shook his head, "Oh, boy. What happened?"

The guy was extremely angry because I beat his son. He threatened me."

"I'm not surprised. The guy is a bully, but also a coward."

"Why would he do that? Is he crazy?"

"He's an egomaniac. In Eric's world, he's the center of the universe. Jamie's mom left him because of abuse. The guy made lots of money building homes, but he has a reputation for cutting corners. I think his reputation finally caught up with him.

Todd sipped his coffee. "I've watched several of the meets at Indian Heights, and I've never seen him at any of Jamie's. My guess is that he heard about Jamie doing so well last year at state. He's probably trying to affirm his greatness through Jamie's success."

"Didn't Chip beat Jamie in state?"

"Still, both made it to the finals, and both were juniors. Jamie will probably get a scholarship this year. But I don't think this is about Jamie. It's about Eric. Rumor has it he's bankrupt. He's made a lot of shady deals during this housing bubble, and it's burst. Now that he's no longer successful, he's probably trying to find his worth in Jamie's success."

"Well, thank you, Dr. Mayo, for that evaluation of human personality. Now how can I help you with your business decision?"

Todd clasped his hands tightly and cleared his throat. "Win, I'm in trouble. Big trouble, and I need your help."

Win looked intently at Todd. "Sure. What can I do?"

"After you told me about your investment, I wondered if you might be an answer to prayer. When I came here and saw your house, I felt I should talk to you. I don't think the timing of our meeting after forty years is an accident."

"I agree."

"Win, I'm upside-down on my mortgage. I'm going to lose it if I don't come up with a big chunk of change. If I lose my house, I lose my testimony, and no one will believe anything I say."

"Whoa. How did you get upside-down on your house, and why would a financial problem make you an untrustworthy pastor?"

"It's complex. Elaine and I wanted a house that gave testimony of God's goodness and shows His desire to bless His people. I've taught our people for the past ten years that God's desire is to prosper us in every way. I wanted them to see what God does when we trust Him. I probably became overly excited and had more house built than I could afford."

"Wait a minute. How did you get a loan for something you couldn't afford?"

"You know how easy it's been to get money the past few years. I wanted a nice house. So I found a company that would work with me. Then some problems arose in the church, and a few of the big contributors pulled out. We lost about twenty percent of our congregation. Until then I'd been anticipating a raise, but everyone has taken a cut. I used my home equity to borrow money to keep doing some of the things I've always done. Now the money supply has shut down. I'll lose everything unless I come up with a lot of money."

Win let out the breath he'd been holding. "How much?"

"One-hundred grand."

Win looked at the ceiling. "When do you need the money?"

"I have two months. If I don't come up with it by then, I lose the house. If I lose the house, I lose my credibility and my church." Todd stood and paced. "Man, I can't believe this. I've tried to obey God. Elaine is confused. She doesn't understand what's happened. I don't understand why God hasn't provided."

Todd stopped in front of Win and put one hand on his shoulder. "I need your help. If it's not an accident that you're here at this moment, maybe God wants to use you as His provision." With a pained look, Todd popped the question. "Can you lend me a hundred thousand?"

CHAPTER EIGHTEEN

Win struggled with Todd's request. He could easily cash in more stock and pull his old buddy out of the hole he'd dug. But red flags popped up in every part of his heart. He decided to take a long walk to clear his mind.

Win's home on South Lakeshore provided great access to places to walk, pray, and process his new life. Hundreds of joggers, many of them LSU students, used the street as a walking and jogging trail. The course went four miles around the lake and the edge of the campus. On the days he didn't do speed work, Win enjoyed walking a lap around the lake.

Before he stepped out the door, his cell phone rang. He was surprised but happy to hear Hope's voice. She fumbled for words, telling Win of her concern for Chip. Before he ran with Chip the next morning, she wanted to talk.

"Why don't you put on some jogging shorts and walking shoes, and let's walk around the lake? I find that I think more clearly when I walk."

"I'm not into exercise, but okay. I really need to talk before you meet tomorrow with Chip. I'll be there in forty-five minutes."

The thought of finally having time alone with his daughter put a lump in Win's throat. He paced the family room and wondered what he should say. *Should I apologize first? Is she still afraid of me? Do I ask her about growing up? What about her husband?* With every round of thoughts, he paced faster. His senses were on overload. The colors seemed more distinct, the scent of the flowers more soothing. He danced in circles, giving imaginary high-fives and thrusting his fist in the air as though he just won the 400 meters.

After ten minutes, reality settled in. *She's not coming here to develop a relationship with me. She has a concern about Chip.* Win began to wonder about her urgent matter. "God, give me wisdom. Help me to be a father that reflects You."

Win met Hope in the driveway. A broad smile crossed his face. "Welcome."

Hope shyly glanced downward and with a gentle smile greeted her father. "Hi."

Win spoke rapidly. "Do you want to come in? Do you need anything? Water? Do you want to go ahead and walk?"

She turned and glanced at the lake. "This is beautiful."

"It's a special place. I think your mom will like it."

"I'm sure she will. Who wouldn't?" Hope meandered around the front yard as joggers passed. "I've not exercised much. I don't know how far I can go. I know I can't go fast."

"No problem. With the mild weather, this is a great day to begin. When I started five years ago, I was only able to walk one-and-a-half miles. I slowly added to my mileage each week. It didn't take long before I was jogging three miles. Then the sky was the limit."

Hope sighed. "I wish I could lose some weight. I've tried every diet imaginable. Nothing works."

"I know a diet you've probably never tried. I lost 60 pounds on it."

Hope raised her eyebrow and smiled. "All right, I give up. What's the diet?"

"The driveway diet."

"You're right. Never heard of that one. Tell me about it."

"You walk to and from a designated driveway you know won't tire you too much. Each day, you walk one driveway farther. Walk at least five days per week. If you don't change your eating patterns, you'll lose a couple pounds in a month. If you make minor changes to your eating, you can lose six pounds in two months. You develop walking as a lifestyle, and before long, you're down to your desired weight."

"Are you serious?"

"If you want to try it, I'll help you. I'll walk with you a couple of times each week to keep you accountable."

The gentle smile reappeared on Hope's face. "You're a sly old man. I'll have to think about it."

"Okay. How far do you want to go?"

"Let's start with your mile and a-half. See if I can do that."

As they walked, Win said, "What's up with Chip?"

"I don't know. He came home from school Wednesday and went straight to his room. Had a sullen look, real quiet. Not like him at all. I tried to talk to him, but he wouldn't open up. He's never been like this."

"Do you think it has anything to do with me? He may need time to think through everything that's happened."

"He finally talked a little this morning. He said he didn't want to work out at Indian Heights. Didn't want to run with Jamie, only you. He wanted to see if you could contact Isaiah and run at Istrouma after school every day."

A group of joggers passed them and one bumped Hope. "Maybe we ought to move to the other side of the street. The weather is so nice that there's a ton of people out today." Win looked at Hope. "I understand his hesitation with Jamie. There's been some tension between them since the All Comers' meet. Coach Landon is working privately with Jamie. But I don't understand why he would want to train at Istrouma. Maybe he doesn't want Jamie to see what kind of training he's doing."

"I don't know. He's usually outgoing. He's always teasing me. That's gone. The blank look in his eyes scares me."

"What do you want me to do? I'll help any way I can."

"Just try to find out what's going on. Run with him. He really likes you. See if you can find out anything."

Win stopped walking. "Hope, are you saying you trust me?"

"No. I'm saying I'm very concerned about my son, and I'll do anything to help him."

"Have you told your mom you're consulting with me?"

"I figured if you're my father, I don't need permission."

Win looked at the ground and cleared his throat. "I've never known what it's like to be a dad. Most guys have a six- or seven-pound precious little baby placed in their arms, and they're thrilled. When I learned I had a forty-three-year-old daughter, I was overjoyed and overwhelmed. I don't know how to be a dad. Don't know where to begin. I want to be a good one, but I have to start with the learning curve at the university level." Win looked directly in Hope's eyes. "I love you, Hope. For years, I've watched dads with their children and wondered what it felt like. Now I know."

Hope's eyes moistened, and she looked away. "Thanks. I guess we've made it to today's last driveway. Let's head back."

CHAPTER NINETEEN

Saturday, Win woke an hour before his alarm went off, filled with excitement. As he brewed coffee, the aroma seemed twice as strong, the sun brighter, and the clanging of pans like a set of cymbals. After a small breakfast, he spent time reading the Bible and in prayer, though he had difficulty concentrating.

Win arrived at Istrouma fifteen minutes before everyone. Isaiah had arranged with his coach to have the gate to the football field and track opened early, but when Win arrived, it was still locked. He took the opportunity to stretch in the parking lot on Winbourne Avenue, looking out at the homes of high-school friends.

Mild temperatures and plenty of sunshine made it another great day for training. The facilities manager arrived about the same time as Isaiah and his Special Forces friend. Isaiah smiled at Win. "This is Steve Joiner, the man Pastor Washington mentioned."

Steve, an athletic man in his mid-forties, stood erect, almost at attention. He extended his hand. "Great to meet you, sir."

Win wasn't sure whether to shake hands or salute. "You, too."

Isaiah asked about Chip. Though Win was a little concerned, he expected him to show any minute. The three discussed the day's workout as they made their way to the track. As they jogged, Win said they would begin with 100-yard strides and continue with a ladder drill, progressing from 100 to 200, then 300 and finally 400 meters, and continue by going back down the ladder.

"Sir," Steve said. "I'd like to throw a conditioning exercise in the mix."

Win wasn't excited about the input. He thought Steve's reason for being there was to babysit Isaiah. If he tried to second-guess the workout schedule, it would be counterproductive. "I don't know. This will be a pretty intense workout. I don't think we'll need any more conditioning."

"I understand, sir. A great 400-meter runner must first be a great athlete. We can start with something small. It'll make Isaiah a better athlete and a better 400-meter runner."

Win continued glancing at the parking lot every few seconds, hoping to see Chip. "What do you have in mind?"

"After we finish our strides, sir, I'd like us to do something I've done for years. We start at the goal line and run ten yards. We drop and do ten push-ups. Get up quickly and run to the twenty. Then ten jumping jacks. Take off and run to the thirty, drop and do ten crunches. Repeat that until we make it to the goal line. Rest thirty seconds and repeat the same until we're back at the first goal line."

Win again checked the parking lot. Finally, Chip arrived. "Whatever. I don't think it'll hurt," he said as Chip made his way to the track.

After introductions, the four men stretched and ran six 100-meter strides, each faster than the previous. Steve smiled and shouted, "All right, men. Conditioning time. This is all-out. Whoever is the last person to get back to the goal line has to run an extra mile after the workout."

With a heavy sigh, Win lifted his hand. "I only agreed to the conditioning exercise."

"I'm sorry, sir, but there must be accountability. Without it, we can't progress. I want Isaiah and Chip to be the best they can be."

"Yeah, but remember, I'm the coach."

"Yes, sir. I understand. This will make these boys better, and you'll be a proud coach. I know that's what you want."

Win bit lower lip. "Okay." He turned toward Steve. "But from now on, you discuss any workout issues alone with me before we start."

"Yes, sir. Will do."

"And no more 'sir'. Just Win. Okay?"

"Yes, sir. I mean, sure, Win."

Isaiah stayed close, enjoying the exchange, but Chip remained aloof. When Win glanced at Chip, he saw a distant look.

Steve reminded everyone of the elements of the drill and the extra mile the final finisher had to run. Steve's challenge produced a determined look in all their eyes as they stared down the field. He yelled, "Go!" and everyone took off like horses at the Kentucky Derby.

Win and Steve kept the lead until the forty-yard line, with Chip close and Isaiah only a yard behind. Win was determined Steve wouldn't show him up, especially in front of his trainees. By the time they arrived at midfield, the lack of Win's upper-body conditioning began to show. As he strained with the pushups, Steve and Chip passed him, and Isaiah caught him. When they finished, Steve was first, Chip second, Isaiah third, and Win last. Everyone high-fived and fist bumped, then turned and repeated the process. Same results.

"I guess I'm not in as good a shape as I thought," Win told the guys.

"No, problem, sir. I don't know any men your age who could have hung in with us."

Win smiled and pointed as though he was about to rebuke Steve.

"I mean, no problem, coach."

Everyone laughed.

They completed the workout, and Win told Chip to wait for him while he ran his mile. Steve spoke up. "Wait a minute, guys. We're a team. If one person is weak, the entire team is weak. We help each other. I'm going to run one of Coach Win's laps for him."

"I don't think so," Win said. "I lost. I run."

"No, Mr. Win." Isaiah said. "I'm going to run one of your laps, too."

Chip finally smiled. "Me, too."

"Okay," Steve said. "Let's all run one lap together. We're a team. One of us wins, we all win. One of us loses, we all lose." The four men ran one final lap around the track.

CHAPTER TWENTY

Grace tried on several outfits before choosing a conservative light blue blouse with her new designer jeans. She planned to arrive at Win's an hour before Hope and Chip. As she drove, she felt like a teenager on her first date. She kept thinking, *Why am I so nervous? We're just going to have lunch together.*

Another thought haunted her: Win's surprise. She had an idea what it was, but wouldn't let her mind go there. As she turned off Stanford Avenue onto South Lakeshore, her suspicions were confirmed. It had been a long time since she'd been on South Lakeshore. It was nothing like she remembered from forty-four years earlier. It was just as beautiful, but the fields were packed with large homes.

As she turned into Win's driveway, he stepped outside. "It's great to see you. Welcome."

Grace's face turned red.

Win read her thoughts. "Don't worry. We can talk about it inside. Let me help you with these goodies. You've brought enough for an army."

"We can't eat only jambalaya. I brought some salad and gumbo, and Chip and Hope love my banana pudding. It's their favorite dessert."

As they carried the food into the kitchen, Grace gaped at Win's home. "This is really nice."

"It's a blessing. But I don't need all the space."

"I can't believe you bought this home — and right here. Why?"

"This might be hard to believe. When I decided to move back to Baton Rouge, I contacted a Realtor and told her I wanted a home near LSU and on water. My home in Seattle sat on Lake Washington. The Realtor found this place, about to go into foreclosure. She showed me photos. When I came here, I loved what I saw, and I knew I couldn't beat the price. I sold some stock and bought it for about sixty cents on the dollar. It was a great deal, but before I came here with the Realtor, I had no idea . . ." Win cleared his throat, and his voice trembled. "I had no idea it was across from the old oak."

Grace looked away as her face turned red.

"Come with me. There's something I want to show you."

Grace hesitantly agreed. It was the moment she'd tried to escape for four decades. "Okay."

As they walked toward the old oak, Win saw the pain in Grace's face and wondered if he made the right decision to show her the message. "Are you okay?"

"I'll be okay. I've known for a long time I needed to return. I thought if I put it out of my mind, then I could live without having to deal with the truth."

"What do you mean, the truth?"

"I don't want to talk about it now. Just show me your surprise."

Win took Grace to the back of the tree. She looked at the heart carved into the old oak with "Win + Grace" in the center. "It's still there, after all these years. Can you believe it?"

A tear dropped from Grace's eyes. "Yes. I can believe it."

"Maybe this was a bad idea. I'm sorry."

"Don't be." Grace looked at Win. "When you told me you lived on South Lakeshore Drive, I knew I had to face the truth. It's haunted me for years."

Win tilted his head. "What do you mean?"

Grace looked into his eyes. "Win, I need some time alone."

Win tapped his finger against his lips. "Whatever you need. Just know I didn't want to hurt you in any way."

Grace smiled and patted his shoulder. "Don't worry. I'll be all right."

Win returned alone to his house. He paced the living room, occasionally glancing across the street to see if Grace was okay.

⸻

Grace leaned against the oak and slid to the ground. Looking across the lake, she had the most honest conversation with God she could remember. "I'm sorry it's taken so long to talk with You about this. You've been waiting for years, but I've been afraid. I wanted to talk to Rick when he was alive, but I couldn't. I don't know why I've been afraid to talk to You. I know You love me." A tear fell.

Grace walked to a special spot about fifteen feet from the oak, fell to her knees, and sobbed. After ten minutes, she felt a firm but tender hand on her shoulder. "You okay?"

"I'm all right," she whimpered.

Win helped Grace to her feet. "I'm sorry. I didn't know if I should come out. I was worried about you."

"Thanks. We need to talk."

"Sure, inside or outside?"

"We need to talk right here, on this spot. Do you remember? This is where we parked on prom night. The place where Hope was conceived."

He smiled gently. "Yes. I know."

"After you left Baton Rouge, I came here at least once a week until she was born. I talked to God on this spot. Every time I had the same prayer: 'Oh, God, please bring Win home.' As long as I came here, I had hope you would return. When you didn't come back, I decided to name our child Hope. As long as I had her, I had hope."

Win squeezed Grace's hand. "I don't know what to say. I . . ."

"Shh. Don't say anything. Just listen. When Rick and I married, I buried some issues, things so deep I couldn't talk about them to anyone. When Elaine told me about her relationship with Christ, I tried to talk to her. I did, about some things. My bitterness, my hurt. She told me about Christ's forgiveness and the well of grace He offered. I trusted Him, and it changed my life. I've grown so much in my faith, but I keep coming against this barrier. It's like a huge wall, so high I can't get over it. I've known what it is for years, but haven't been honest enough to admit or deal with it."

Win grabbed both of Grace's hands. "What? Deal with what?"

"You've always been the bad guy, and I've been the victim. You abandoned me. You left me a single mother. You didn't return to your parents' funerals. You, you, you. It's been easy for me to blame you, but that night, on this spot . . ." Grace looked at the ground as her eyes again moistened. "You didn't force me, Win. We made love because I wanted you. I loved you.

"No one ever talked about that," Grace said. "Everyone just talked about how terrible you were to run off and leave me. I know you have your issues. But I was wrong. I violated God's standard." She looked directly at Win. "If I would have said no, would you have continued?"

Win squirmed. "I don't know. I don't think so. No, I would have stopped. But, you can't go there."

"I have to go there. No one else will. I failed God. I've never openly admitted that. You were an easy scapegoat. As the years passed, everyone has always thought, *poor Grace*. When I came this morning, I knew God wanted to bring this to an end, to remove the wall that's kept me from having intimate fellowship with Him."

As Win and Grace looked at one another, tears filled their eyes. Win gently said, "Let's pray together. We both did wrong. Let's ask God to cleanse us. He gave us Hope, even though we failed Him. Think what He might give us when we're honest about our failures."

Win and Grace held hands and poured out their hearts to God. As they finished praying, a voice shouted, "Mom, what's going on?"

CHAPTER TWENTY-ONE

Win hosted Grace, Hope, and Chip with energy he hadn't felt in years. He was thrilled to have lunch with his high school sweetheart, daughter, and grandson.

Hope didn't share the excitement. She spent most of her time with arms folded and smiles forced. Chip maintained his reserved demeanor, but occasionally displayed a glimpse of his old self. As he helped Win in the kitchen, he smiled. "Well, Romeo, I guess I may need that love-life advice after all. You're getting better at this thing, Gramps."

"Wait a minute. Your grandmother and I were praying about some things, that's all. Putting the past to rest."

"You'd better explain that to Mom. I don't think she's too happy about you holding Mimi's hands."

"You said you would be my attorney. Are you still working for me? I may need a defense lawyer."

A smile crept up Chip's face. "Maybe."

"Maybe?" Win laughed.

"Yeah. What's the pay?"

"I don't know if you'll make a good lawyer, but you'll definitely make a great businessman." Win chuckled. "Wait here. I'll get your paycheck." He returned with two shoeboxes. "I told you and Isaiah I'd get you some nice running shoes. The other day while you were warming up I checked out your sizes. I went yesterday to Varsity Sports and bought both of you a pair of trainers and a pair of racing flats."

Chip high-fived Win and thanked him with a huge smile. "These are awesome. Can I try them on now?"

"Sure. Go for it."

As Chip tried on the shoes, he laughed. "What about Drill Sergeant Steve, *sir*? Did his workout keep him from payday, *sir*?"

"Hey, you sound like the old Chip."

"I didn't know I aged so quickly. Who is the old Chip?"

"The funny, full-of-life one. Earlier, I thought I'd lost that Chip. Seemed like something was bothering you."

"Don't worry, Gramps. It's my love life. You know what that does to a man, right?" His shoes laced, he jogged around the kitchen, then back to the family room to show Grace and Hope.

Win grinned and stood in the entry of the family room, watching Chip show his mom and grandmother the shoes. Hope's expression changed. A genuine smile appeared.

Sensing it was a good time, Win asked Hope, "I see you're wearing your walking shoes. Want to go for our driveway-diet walk?"

Hope looked thoughtful. "Yes, I'd like that."

As they headed out the door, Chip warned, "Gramps. Watch out, sir. Her left hook is mean."

Win chuckled. "Don't worry. I know about her left hook."

Once they were out of earshot, Hope looked at him accusingly. "What's going on between you and Mom?"

"Forgiveness. That's all."

"Not what it looked like to me. Be honest. Are you trying to make a move on Mom?"

"Hope, your mom and I are trying to deal with the past. It's really difficult. That's all there is to it." He laughed softly. "But remember, we are adults."

"You know, don't you, that you forfeited your right to be my dad?"

"I see. You think I'm trying to replace the man who loved and raised you. Everyone has told me Rick was a great guy — that he really cared for you and your mom. Even if I wanted to, I could never replace him. Hope, that's not what's going on."

"Then what were you and Mom doing before we arrived?"

Win smiled. "Are you worried?"

"No, but . . ."

"But you think I'm trying to win your mom's heart. That's not what was going on. I'll admit I still care deeply for her, but I also know that I lost the right to have a relationship with her when I took off for California. I don't deserve to come anywhere close to the entrance of her heart. I know I've hurt her, you, and a lot of other people. I'm trying to make it right with God and with you. That's all."

"I wish I could believe you."

"Then why are you here? Why are we walking together right now?"

As they arrived at the parking lot on Stanford where many joggers began their workouts, Hope's face tightened. She stopped and looked directly into Win's eyes. "It's Chip. I don't understand why, but for some reason he really connects with you. I know you're good for him. Maybe it's that he needs an older man in his life. I just know he's going through something right now that I don't understand. And you seem to be helping."

"Chip is a good kid. Has a great head on his shoulders. I think you're right. He's going through something, but I know he'll come through it fine." Win smiled and patted her on the arm. "We'd better head back or Chip will think you knocked me out."

When Win and Hope returned, Chip told him Isaiah had called.

"What'd he want?"

Chip looked at the ground.

"Well?"

Chip sighed. "He said the Istrouma track would be closed Tuesday afternoon. Some kind of school event. He wanted to know if we could work out at Indian Heights."

"No problem for me. Do you think it will be open?"

"It'll be open, but . . ."

"But what?"

"Coach Landon and Jamie will be there. I don't know if I want to work out when they're around."

"Chip, you're going to have to work out with them in a few weeks when track season begins. Might as well start now."

His eyes widened with alarm. "I know, but . . ."

"Are you okay?" Hope asked.

"No. I'm not feeling well. Can we go now?"

CHAPTER TWENTY-TWO

Todd sat under the "a taste of Louisiana hospitality" sign at CC's, waiting for Win. His father, like most north Baton Rouge dads in the '50s and '60s, was a plant worker who'd never gone to college. He'd come to Baton Rouge from a poor southwest Louisiana farm after World War II. He'd worked hard and taught his boys that if they kept a good work ethic, they could accomplish anything they wanted.

Todd had been the first in his family to attend college, and his dad had been extremely proud when he'd received a track scholarship. He'd had high hopes. Because Todd was a gifted speaker, he'd dreamed Todd would become a wealthy attorney. When Todd decided to go to seminary, his dad's dreams had been shattered. Although a good man, he wasn't particularly religious. To him, becoming a preacher wasn't the right step. Soon after Todd began seminary, his dad died.

Losing his dad left a huge hole in his heart. Though Todd's life had been transformed by his personal faith in Christ, he kept a hidden desire to fulfill his dad's dream. He knew his calling to ministry was honorable, but the secret drive toward material success sometimes took him down a different path.

Win arrived and took a seat across from him. Todd smiled. "Looks like we're on different sides of the table today."

"It does," Win said, "but we're at the same table. That's what's important."

Todd smiled and drummed his fingers. "I was just thinking about Dad. Our dads were two of a kind. They loved sports, and they loved us. I really miss Dad." Todd told Win about his dad's death and his dreams for Todd's success. He explained how he'd responded when Todd had taken a different direction. "He took it really hard."

"Why? You're respected in the community. Have a huge church. You're a good man with a great family. I don't understand."

"He never saw any of that. I've been thinking about our talk. I've wondered what drove me to go so deeply in debt. I think it's been this desire to please Dad, even though he's gone."

Win gave a weak smile. "I understand."

Todd took a deep breath. "But I still have a problem. One hundred grand. And I need it soon. I wish understanding would make it go away, but it doesn't. Can you help me?"

"I can help you, Todd, but not with $100,000. That's a quick fix to a problem far deeper than money. Until you deal with the underlying problem, you'll always be chasing your dad's dreams. It seems like you lost that original passion for Christ and replaced it with a desire for material things. To be honest, when I went to church, I was impressed with the service, with you, with your message — but the strong pitch for money made me uncomfortable."

"What are you saying? You can't help me, or you won't help me?"

"I'm just saying that giving you money would rob you of dealing with the real issue."

Todd's face turned red. He spoke quietly but forcefully. "I'm in a desperate situation. And you're telling me to deal with the real issue. So, tell me, what's the real issue?"

"I'm not a pastor, and I certainly don't understand everything in the Bible. But I know what God has been doing in my life through all of this. He's brought me to a place of desperation — and it's been good. I've grown more than any time in my life. My love for Jesus has deepened. God may be bringing you to that same place. He'll show you what to do, and you'll come out of this with a greater love for Jesus than you've ever known."

"I can't believe you're saying this. I thought if anyone would understand, it would be you." Todd slammed his fist on the table and pointed at Win. "I've never seen such spiritual arrogance."

Win's eyes widened. "What?"

"I helped you when you needed it. I put you in contact with

Grace. And this is what I get. A know-it-all attitude. This holy man who doesn't have time to help his brother in trouble." He smiled sarcastically. "That's really like Jesus."

Win slumped. "That's not fair, and you know it. I'm trying to help you. It's just not the way you want."

Todd stood to leave. "You have an unusual way of showing it. I'd hate to see what you do to your enemies." He smirked. "Don't worry. I'll find someone who'll help."

Win arrived early at Indian Heights High School. Classes had just ended. Steve, Isaiah, and Chip had not arrived. He kept replaying his discussion with Todd. Had he made the right decision? Before the others arrived, he took a half-mile therapeutic jog. Chip was the first to show up. He seemed distant and kept looking toward the gym.

Steve and Isaiah arrived, and they began their workout. Steve's conditioning drills became even more difficult. In the middle of the drills, Coach Landon and Jamie came on the field. After the drills, Chip introduced them to his running partners.

Landon gave Win a big smile. "I've wanted to meet you for years. You're a legend in Louisiana high school track and field. The older guys still talk about your mile relay team and your 400-meter record. It's an honor to meet you."

"Thanks, Coach. It's great to meet you. I've already met Jamie. He's a great runner. Looks like he's been working hard since our All Comers' meet."

Landon nodded. "He's got great potential."

"I hope you don't mind me working out with Chip until track season begins."

"I think it's great. Jamie tells me there's a rumor that you're his grandfather."

"Yes, he's my grandson."

"No wonder he's such a good runner. It'll be helpful to train with you."

"Let me know if there are drills you want me to help Chip with in the next couple of weeks."

Win, Chip, Isaiah, and Steve returned to their workouts. Win asked Chip, "What's happened to Jamie?"

"What do you mean?"

"He's developed a lot of muscle tone, and quickly. I don't remember him being that muscular."

"I think Coach has him working hard in the weight room."

Steve jumped into the discussion. "That means we need to do more. I have some drills that will blow the opposition out of the water."

Win looked away and rubbed the back of his head. "I don't know. I'm concerned about Jamie." He turned back to Chip. "I don't remember him having pimples."

"Yeah," Isaiah said. "He has a ton of zits."

Win smiled. "Okay, guys. Enough talking. Let's finish our workout. I was last again today in Steve's conditioning drills. I'll run the mile."

Steve glanced at Isaiah and Chip. "We'll all run with you."

———✕✕———

Steve's input into the group developed a cohesion that made them feel like a team. Though they ran for two different schools and for different reasons, a sense of unity emerged. While they were slowly jogging during their cool-down, Steve turned to Chip. "I was in the 103rd Airborne in Iraq in 2004. I met a guy named Thibodeaux. With that kind of a name, I figured he came from Louisiana but never asked him." He looked at Chip. "I wonder if you might be kin."

"Maybe. My dad was in Iraq."

"What's his name?"

"Mike. Mike Thibodeaux."

"This is amazing. You're Mike Thibodeaux's kid."

"You were in Iraq with my dad?" Chip asked. "You knew him?"

"Oh, man. I can't believe this." The two stopped jogging, and a huge smile crossed Steve's face. "Yes. I knew him. He came into the country, and his team replaced ours about a month before I was transferred out of Iraq . . ." Steve stopped abruptly, and his expression changed. "I'm sorry. I heard about what happened."

"You actually knew my dad in Iraq. I, I . . ." Chip shook his head. "What was he like over there? Did he ever say anything about my mom or me?"

Steve put his hand on Chip's shoulder. "Your dad was a man's man. A great soldier. I remember one night we sat around talking about family. He talked about his sweetheart and his boy. He loved you guys. You were his pride and joy."

Chip looked at the ground. "I can't believe you knew my dad."

"I owe my life to him. His squadron replaced mine. I should have been killed by that bomb." He placed his hand on Chip's shoulder. "I owe you and your mom. If you ever need anything, or your mom ever needs anything — and I mean anything — you let me know." Steve glanced over Chip's shoulder, and his face tightened. "Win, I think we'd better go. Trouble may be brewing."

"What do you mean?" Win asked.

"Maybe it's my paranoia from Spec Ops training, but there's a guy who's been watching us the entire workout. He's standing just behind the bleachers, sort of out of sight. I don't have a good feeling about him."

Everyone turned and looked. "Don't worry," Chip said. "That's just Jamie's dad."

Win's stomach churned.

CHAPTER TWENTY-THREE

As Win and the guys walked toward the gate, Coach Landon yelled for Chip to come back, saying he wanted to talk with him. Chip looked at Isaiah. "Want to go with me?"

"He's your coach. I don't think he wants me around."

"He may not, but I do. Maybe we're running for different schools, but like Steve says, we're on the same team. Come on."

Win waved Chip and Isaiah off. "You guys go ahead and meet with Coach Landon. Steve and I will wait in the parking lot."

A pensive look crossed Win's face. "Steve, we may have a big problem. This guy was angry with me for beating Jamie in the All Comers' meet. He told me he didn't want to see me run against Jamie and Chip."

"What's the problem? You weren't running against them. You were training Chip. No big deal."

"The problem is . . ." Win took a deep breath. "When he told me that, he was ready to fight. I think he had a gun in his truck."

"Oh." Steve squared his shoulders. "We might have a problem. But don't worry. If he tries anything, I'll have him on the ground before he knows what hit him."

"Let me handle this. We don't need to make a scene."

"Yes, sir."

Jamie's dad strode toward the exit as Win and Steve approached it. Eric Braun arrived at the gate first and stood in the middle, blocking Win and Steve.

With his eyes straight ahead, Win calmly said to Steve, "Stay cool.

I'll talk to him."

Eric stood with his hands on his hips and feet spread. "I told you I didn't want to see you anywhere near these boys when they're running."

"I've not been working with your son. I'm training Chip and a friend, Isaiah."

Eric smirked. "Jamie tells me Chip is your illegitimate grandson."

Win stared into Eric's eyes and silently counted to five. "If you'll excuse us, we're headed to our car."

"No." Eric raised his voice. "I don't excuse you. I excused you the first time, you stupid . . ." He grabbed Win's throat with his right hand.

In a flash, Steve hit Eric's arm, freeing Win from his grip. Before Eric could respond, Steve had his arm behind his back, pulling it toward his shoulder.

"Mister," Steve said, "do you know how many ways I can kill a man with my hands?"

No response — only a whimper of agony.

Steve raised his voice and pulled the twisted arm closer to Eric's shoulder. "Well, do you?"

"No."

"Let me give you a hint. It's a lot fewer than the ways I can break his arm."

"Ahhh. Please, stop."

Steve released his arm. "If you ever lay a hand on my friend again, you'll never use that arm."

As Eric cradled his arm, Win tried to gather his composure. He wasn't sure what to do or say, but he remembered the gun in Eric's truck. "We're going to our car now," Win said. "I'm forgetting this ever happened. I want you to walk over to the bleachers and stay there. Don't come to the parking lot until Chip and Isaiah are with us and we've left. Go ahead. Leave."

Holding his arm, Eric walked toward the bleachers.

———◇◇———

Chip introduced Isaiah to Coach Landon and Jamie. "He runs for Istrouma. We've been working out together."

"I thought I had seen you before. You run the 400 meters?"

"Yes, sir. I'm a junior. It's great training with Chip."

Landon smiled. "You guys looked good out there." He turned to

Chip. "Everything okay?"

Chip looked at the ground and back at Coach Landon. "It's been cool. No problems."

"We start the season in a couple of weeks. From what I saw you doing today, you'll be ready. Don't you think so, Jamie?"

Jamie had been pretending to not listen. He kept his head turned toward the locker room until Coach Landon addressed him. "Yep. They looked great."

"You guys are going to be working together in a couple of weeks. I want all your differences put aside by then. Understand?"

Both boys smirked and said, "Sure."

Chip and Isaiah started walking toward the gate. Isaiah turned to Chip. "What's going on with Jamie's dad? He looks like he's hurt."

"I don't know. I hope there wasn't a problem."

When they got to the parking lot, Chip asked what had happened.

Steve glanced toward the bleachers. "Jamie's dad tried to choke your grandfather."

"What?"

"It didn't last long. I broke his hold immediately. He won't forget what happened for a few days."

"Why'd he choke you?"

"He's still upset that I beat you and Jamie at the All Comers' meet. After the meet, he told me he didn't ever want to see me running with you and Jamie."

Chip's eyes went wide. "And he choked you because of that?"

Isaiah chuckled. "Pastor Washington ain't gonna believe this."

Steve pointed to Isaiah. "There's no reason for us to tell Pastor Washington."

Win wasn't so sure. "I don't want Pastor Washington to think I'm hiding anything. Maybe we ought to explain what happened."

Steve shook his head. "I don't know. There's already suspicion about you. Even if I tell him the whole story, it'll just bring up more questions. I think we ought to forget what happened. I don't think we'll ever hear from that guy again."

CHAPTER TWENTY-FOUR

Grace had struggled with her feelings from the moment she'd heard Win had returned to Baton Rouge. As days and weeks passed, those feelings grew more complicated. Anger and bitterness turned to attraction and longing — attraction to the man who had devastated her life and a longing for a relationship that had died forty years ago.

She normally sorted through life in two very different ways. After Rick died, she'd begun attending a women's prayer group. An interdenominational and inter-racial group of ladies prayed weekly for renewal in the city's churches. The group had been praying for ten years, asking God to pour out His Spirit in the churches in Baton Rouge. Jenny Brown had started the group and still led it.

Jenny's smile and kind spirit made all the ladies feel at ease. Grace connected easily with Jenny the first time she attended. They'd become prayer partners and close friends.

When Todd had called Grace and told her Win was in town, she had immediately called Jenny.

"I have a strange feeling about this," Jenny said. "It's not just about you. There's something much bigger."

As the weeks passed, Jenny continually reminded Grace, "Remember the big picture. God is up to something bigger than you or I understand." Her wisdom and encouragement helped Grace keep her emotions balanced.

Friday morning was sunny and mild, a great day for outlet mall shopping — the second way Grace sorted through issues. When she needed time to think, she often drove to the outlet mall in Gonzales, a small town just off Interstate 10 headed toward New Orleans. Today, she desperately needed a shopping trip.

As Grace made her way onto I-10, her thoughts drifted to her senior year of high school and her relationship with Win. The silence in the car resurrected old memories. She turned on the radio and hit the scan button. *I'm not going to let the past haunt me.* The radio found an oldies station, and a huge smile crossed her face. She couldn't believe the song being played: "Chapel of Love" by the Dixie Cups.

In 1965, their senior year, it was Grace and Win's favorite, and they asked the band to sing it at the prom. Her mind wandered back to that night. Life had seemed simple and love so real. Soon, they expected, they would also go to a chapel and get married.

She and Win danced all night. He twirled her and pulled her into himself, singing with the band, "Chapel of Love." Her heart pounded.

Win smiled and sang as he twirled her again. He bent his body forward, rotated his shoulders, and slid backward. With his index finger, he motioned for her to follow. Her face beaming, Grace moved smoothly and softly across the dance floor to the beat of the music. Win sang with the band about loving until the end of time.

Grace covered her mouth and pushed the off button. *Stop it. You can't do this.* Thoughts of Rick hit her like a tidal wave, sweeping her into a sea of guilt. *I'm sorry, Rick. You were and are the love of my life. No one will ever replace you.* A tear trickled down her face.

Grace took a deep breath. *No. Rick wanted me to have the freedom to love again.* One of the last things Rick had done was to tell Grace she shouldn't feel guilty if she found someone else. Grace had assured Rick no one could replace him. He was the love of her life.

She glanced in the mirror, then at the road ahead. "It seems strange to try to talk to you, Rick, but here goes. I don't know if you can hear me, but I need help. I'm confused. I love you, and you'll always be in my heart. But I have these feelings. I didn't want them. I didn't go looking for them. I don't know where they came from."

Grace heard only the sound of the engine. She switched on the radio again.

Their song had ended.

———————— ✕ ————————

By the time Grace reached the mall, her emotions were in overdrive. She parked in front of an athletic shoe store, took a deep breath, and stepped inside.

"I'm looking for a good, comfortable pair of walking shoes for my daughter," she told the salesman.

"Do you know her size?"

"She and I wear the same size. If they fit me, they'll fit her."

After trying on several pairs, she told the salesman she'd take a pink and white pair of Nikes and also a purple and white pair.

"Two pairs?"

"Yes. My daughter is walking with her father. I thought maybe I could get a pair and walk with her."

He smiled. "Make it a family affair. That's nice."

Grace blushed. "Well, it's not exactly . . ." She realized it was too complicated to explain. "Kind of." She smiled.

She spent the rest of the morning browsing, walking, and thinking. As she went from shop to shop, the fog seemed to lift.

Once Grace had visited enough shops to clear her mind, she drove to a nearby coffee shop. The place was fairly empty, and she grabbed a table near the front. Three men sat at a table in the back. One looked like Todd. She glanced again. It was Todd.

She left her purse on her chair and walked to the back. The three seemed in deep discussion. Todd was signing some papers. The two men had their backs to her, but they didn't look like anyone with whom Todd would be doing business. One, dressed completely in black, had slick black hair with a short ponytail. The other wore a muscle T-shirt. His head was completely shaved, and a tattoo covered his entire head, resembling some kind of bird.

She decided to walk away, but at that moment Todd looked up. He gripped the table. "Grace?"

Grace blushed. "I'm sorry. I didn't mean to disturb you. I saw you and didn't know . . ."

The two men turned and stared at Grace. The one with slick hair wore a black silk suit and had a black shirt with a large gold necklace. "Who's your girlfriend? Introduce us."

Todd's eyes darted around the room as though he were looking for an escape. "Sure. This is Grace Johnson, a longtime friend of our family."

The man with the slick hair extended his hand. "I'm Joey."

When Grace extended her hand, he grabbed it, slowly brought it to his lips, and kissed it. "It's always a pleasure to meet a lovely lady."

Grace stepped back. She felt as though she were looking into the eyes of a snake.

The other man smiled and winked. "Everybody calls me Bald Eagle. Nice to meet you, ma'am. Want to join us?"

"No, thanks. I was just stopping for a cup of coffee. I need to head home." She turned to leave.

"Wait," Todd said. "I'll walk you to your car. Excuse me, gentlemen. I'll be right back."

Once she and Todd were out the door, she asked, "Who are those guys? They give me the creeps."

"Just some guys I'm doing business with. They're from New Orleans. Forget what just happened. It's no big deal."

"What do you mean, no big deal? A forty-year-old man kisses a sixty-year-old woman as though he wants to sleep with her, and a guy with an eagle tattoo on his head gives me this sensuous wink. And you say, 'It's no big deal!'"

"Calm down. Don't overdramatize this. You have to deal with all kinds of people when you do business. I promise, this is no big deal."

"When he kissed my hand, I felt pure evil. I thought I was looking into the eyes of a water moccasin about to sink its fangs into my hand." Grace wrapped her arms around herself. "Uggh. I feel like I need a bath."

With pleading eyes, Todd shook his head. "If you don't mind, don't tell Win about this."

Grace's eyes opened wide. "Why?"

"He might misinterpret it. People can sometimes be judgmental without knowing all the facts."

She shook her head. "Todd, I can't promise you that. I'm still working through my feelings about Win. I don't know what I will tell him — and what I won't tell him."

"I understand. Just try to keep this between you and me."

"I need to go."

Once Grace was on I-10, the emotions of the day took their toll. Tears rolled down her face. She returned to Baton Rouge more confused than when she'd left. *Rick, where are you when I need you?*

As her emotions settled, she began to accept what she already knew was true. Rick, with his listening ear, was gone. She had to walk a new way.

She pulled off the interstate at the Bluebonnet exit, pulled into a gas station, and called Win. "I really need to talk. Can we have lunch?"

CHAPTER TWENTY-FIVE

Win sensed the urgency in Grace's voice and agreed to meet at Ralph and Kacoo's restaurant. As he walked across the parking lot, he recalled his first luncheon with her. *Things have really changed since we met.*

He found Grace seated, staring at the table, her body trembling. He gently touched her shoulder. "Are you all right?"

"Yes. No." She paused and looked into his eyes. "I'm not sure."

He pulled Grace to her feet and wrapped his arms around her. She didn't resist. Grace whimpered as Win held her and told her, "It's okay."

When the hostess approached, he requested a table in a quiet corner. Win had never seen Grace hurting like this. After ordering two iced teas, he reached across the table to grasp her hand. "What's going on?"

Grace couldn't speak for several seconds. She slowly removed her hand from Win's gentle grip and looked at him with downcast eyes. "I'm confused. Scared."

Win's heart ached to see her in such pain. He wanted to fix the hurt, but a voice deep within said, *Be quiet. Listen.* He sat in silence.

"I love Rick. I can't stop loving him, and I don't want to stop loving him."

Win bit his lip.

"But I'm having some feelings. I don't understand them."

Win tilted his head and squinted. Everything in him wanted to ask, but the inner voice kept saying, *No. Not yet.*

"I keep thinking about what we had, and what might have been. I know I can't live in the past, but when I'm with you, it feels good. And I don't want it to feel good. But it does. When it feels good, I feel like . . ." A tear dropped onto the table.

Win took a napkin and wiped her tears. The waitress came to take their orders. Neither was hungry, but they ordered salads. Grace struggled. She looked down. Her eyes darted around the room and came back to Win. Her face flushed, and she turned away.

"What? What's wrong?"

"I care about you, Win Bass, but sometimes it feels like betrayal. Like I'm unfaithful . . ." She paused. ". . . to Rick."

"What?" Win felt as if he'd been hit in the stomach.

"I know that's not true. I'm confused. I spent forty years with Rick. We were soulmates. I know things are different now."

"I'm so sorry. I don't want to cause you more pain."

"I don't want you to back off," Grace said. "I care about you. I was afraid to talk to you about this because I thought I might lose you again. It's just so hard."

"Grace, you don't ever have to fear talking to me. I don't want to replace Rick. You had something special with him. I'm glad he was there for you all these years."

Grace reached across the table and grabbed Win's hand.

Win glanced at their hands and back at her eyes. "I never stopped caring about you. There's always been this empty place in my heart. I've known for forty years that only one person could ever fill that emptiness. I've felt so guilty. I didn't think I deserved the chance to pursue a relationship. But it seems we keep being brought together."

"Deep down, I know I'm not betraying Rick. But I don't know what to do."

"We're both different from who we were in high school. We can't develop a relationship with the person we knew forty years ago." Win paused. "I want a relationship. But I don't want to do anything to cause you more pain. I've caused enough of that."

The waitress brought their salads. Grace stirred hers with her fork. It was an easy way to escape Win's eyes when she told him, "I'd like to continue seeing you."

"Me, too." Win stared at Grace as she focused on her salad. He sensed something was wrong. "That's not all, is it? Something else is bothering you."

There was a long pause. "I went shopping today. Wanted to get out of town and think. I went to the outlet mall in Gonzales, and I ran into Todd." Grace paused again.

"What about Todd? What happened?"

"I'm not sure. He was with two guys. Definitely not deacons at the church. They creeped me out."

"What do you mean?"

"Todd was signing some papers. He told me he had some business dealings with them. One of them kissed my hand. Chills ran up my spine." Revulsion spread across her face. "I've never felt such evil. The other guy flirtatiously winked at me. Called himself 'Bald Eagle.' His head was shaved and covered with a tattoo of an eagle. Todd could tell how uncomfortable I was, and he walked me to the car and asked me to not tell you about the meeting."

Win twisted in his chair. "He didn't say what the meeting was about?"

"No. I felt so dirty after the guy kissed my hand. He scared me, really bad."

Win shook his head. "I had a talk with Todd a couple of days ago. He has some financial problems. But I didn't think he would . . . I don't know what to think."

"These guys weren't like anyone I've ever met. They really shook me up, and I don't understand why Todd didn't want me talking to you. Do you think he's involved in something . . . something . . .?"

"Illegal?"

She shook her head. "I don't know. Maybe I'm overreacting."

"Let's not jump to any conclusions. After my experience in California, I know how easily situations can be misinterpreted, but I have an idea. The guy in prison, who put me in touch with the lawyer, became a private investigator after he was released. We've kept in touch. He's really good at what he does. Let me see if he can find anything about these two guys. With a name and look like 'Bald Eagle,' he should be easy to identify if the guy has a record."

Grace took a deep breath and wiped her tears. "Okay." She laughed and excused herself. "I'd better clean up the mess I've made with my mascara."

Win fidgeted with the napkin as he thought about what had happened since his arrival in Baton Rouge. After settling in Seattle, he'd developed a routine life. When he'd placed his faith in Christ, his heart and his world had changed. Running had led him down a path he'd never imagined. The World Masters Track and Field Championships. Returning to Baton Rouge. The discovery of the family he never suspected. Falling back in love with his high-school sweetheart. A guy threatening him. *Whew! When will this let up?*

He thought about the passage from Proverbs he had memorized with Calvin: "Trust in the LORD with all your heart, and lean not on your own understanding; in all your ways acknowledge Him, and He will direct your paths." He placed his head in his hands and silently prayed. *God, I need You. I don't have any idea what's going on. Please, direct me. Show me what to do.*

Grace's voice and soft touch brought him back to earth. "A penny for your thoughts."

Win smiled and shook his head. "Just thinking about life, about us. Hey, we haven't yet had an official date. Would you go with me to church this Sunday?"

Grace looked down and back to Win and smiled. "I'd love to."

"Maybe lunch after church? I'll see if I can have some information on these guys by then."

"Sounds great. I'd really like that."

Win waved to the waitress for the check. She also brought a note from a customer. *Interesting. Maybe a quick answer to my prayer?* He unfolded the paper.

Your girlfriend is real pretty. Hope she stays that way.

Seeing Win's expression, Grace asked, "Is something wrong?"

Win scanned the restaurant for anyone he recognized. No one. "Look around. Do you see either of those two guys who were with Todd?"

Grace's eyes darted around the room. "No."

"Let's get out of here." He stopped as he passed the waitress. "Is the person who gave you the note still here?"

"No, sir. He left about ten minutes ago."

"What did he look like?"

"I'm sorry, but I can't tell you."

"Why not?"

She unfolded a $100 bill. "He gave me this and told me not to say anything about what he looked like."

"Would two bills just like that change your mind?"

"I don't want to get in the middle of something."

"Just tell me this. Was there one person or two?"

"I'm sorry, sir."

"Did the person have a tattoo all over his head?"

"I'm sorry. I have a customer. Please, excuse me."

Grace grabbed Win's arm as they left the restaurant. "What's going on?"

"Someone was watching us while we ate. With what happened to you earlier, I'm concerned. Do you think you ought to stay alone tonight?"

Grace's eyes flashed. "Win!"

"No." Win shook his head. I was thinking that maybe you ought to stay with Hope and Chip tonight. With everything that's happened, I'm worried."

CHAPTER TWENTY-SIX

Win drove behind Grace to her home and made sure no one had followed. She insisted on staying at her house and promised she would call if anything unusual happened.

He gave her a peck on the forehead. "Be careful." He smiled and headed to South Lakeshore Drive.

Win called later that night to check on Grace. He did the same thing each morning and evening until he saw her again. Worried about Grace, he had a difficult time sleeping. But it didn't affect his mood once he awoke on Sunday morning.

As he hopped out of his Lexus in Grace's driveway, he grabbed the dozen red roses. When she came to the door, he said, "I think it was Valentine's Day the last time I gave you some of these." He smiled. "That's Valentine's Day in 1965."

She laughed and told Win to make himself comfortable while she finished getting ready. Win walked around the family room and saw a photo he assumed was Rick. Bald, much older than Grace, and a little overweight, Rick didn't look at all like he'd imagined. He picked up another photo of Rick, Grace, Hope, and Chip. They looked like the perfect family. *It should have been me in that picture.*

The family room carried the feel of Grace's personality: warm, elegant, and orderly. Win took his seat on the fine leather couch, glancing at the perfectly placed knickknacks and photos. He breathed deeply, trying to calm his nerves.

He glanced back at the photo of Rick, and saw something a little out of place: an old Coca-Cola bottle about two-thirds full of water.

Win tilted his head and squinted. *That's different. I wonder what . . . why?* He walked over and examined the bottle.

Grace came in as he held the bottle near his eyes. "I see you found my special gift."

Win raised his eyebrows. "You collect Coca-Cola memorabilia?"

"No. That was the last birthday present Rick gave me."

Win didn't know what to say.

Grace saw Win's perplexity and smiled. "Rick was a giver. That was his love language. He expressed his love by giving things. It was his greatest joy. I had to be careful before my birthday. If he heard me say I liked something, he immediately bought it for me. I didn't even need to have a birthday, and he'd buy it. He just loved to give. I often teased him about it. He was diagnosed with cancer a couple of months before my birthday. He figured it would be the last one that he would experience with me, and he wanted to get something special."

Win's eyes narrowed. "So he bought you an old Coca-Cola bottle?"

A big grin appeared on Grace's face. "Let me show you something." She took the bottle and lifted it so Win could read the bottom. Embossed was the location of the bottling company: Baton Rouge. Below that, read *1947*.

"He bought you a bottle with the city and year of your birth embossed on it." *Hmm. A really big giver.*

Grace saw his skepticism. "Why do you think the bottle is two-thirds full?"

"I give. Tell me."

Grace picked up a card that lay behind Rick's photo. "Here. Read it."

Win's face turned red. "I don't know. Are you sure?"

"Go ahead and read it."

My dearest Grace,

I'm a blessed man to have had you in my life all these years. God has truly been good to me. You have been and always will be the love of my life. This year will probably be the last time I give you a birthday present. I thought a long time about what I wanted to give you. I wanted something that after I'm gone would remind you how valuable you are. I ordered this old Coca-Cola bottle that I found on the Internet.

I've filled it half-full of water because I want you to know that no matter what happens in life, no matter how difficult things become — when you lose me or whatever happens after I'm gone — God never forgets you. He knows your heart and your hurts. He's stored every tear you have ever cried or ever will cry in His bottle. I'm reminded of a passage in the Bible where the Psalmist had experienced heartaches, and he said to God in Psalm 56:8, "You take account of my wandering; put my tears in Your bottle." So never forget that God is keeping track of every one of your tears. He knows your pain. He cares. He always will. And so do I.

Love you, Rick

"Wow. That's beautiful. Rick must have been a great guy."

"He was."

"I do have a question. He said he filled it halfway, but it's two-thirds full. Why?"

Grace chuckled. "I clean it every week and refill the bottle. If I've been hurt and I've cried, I add just a little more water."

"I guess you've added a lot since I returned to Baton Rouge."

A smile crept onto Grace's face, and she paused a few seconds. "It definitely has more water than a few weeks ago."

"We'd better head out or we'll be late for church." As Win opened the door for Grace, his nervousness returned. He was concerned not only about his first formal date with Grace, but also what he'd learned about the men who'd been with Todd. He needed to talk to Grace about it, but that wouldn't be easy. He also needed to talk to her about the actions of Jamie's dad. Then there was the note he'd received at the restaurant. He feared his presence in Baton Rouge had placed Grace in danger.

Win lowered the convertible top, and Grace rubbed the fine leather interior. "I don't think I've ever been in a car like this."

"I'm gonna sell it."

Grace turned her head. "What?"

"Life changes, and people's desires change. I don't need it."

"So just like that." She snapped her fingers. "You're going to sell it."

"Yep."

"Why?"

"I've been doing a lot of thinking." Win chuckled and glanced toward Grace. "I've done more thinking since I arrived in Baton

Rouge than I've done in the past ten years."

"What are these deep thoughts that make you want to get rid of such a nice car?"

"The kids in Pastor Washington's after-school program. Pastor Washington told me about the growing problem of human trafficking. I want to help him develop a way to educate the community to the problem. I don't know how, but maybe I can provide computers and training for his after-school program. He could teach the kids how to safely use the Internet. I've been thinking about this since the night before we met, the night God touched me so deeply. It's hard to explain, but fast cars and big houses don't appeal to me like they used to."

"Does that mean you'll get rid of your house, too?"

"Let's talk about that at lunch . . . But I do think I can sell this car and buy a less conspicuous car, a nice one, and have enough profit to put an entire network of computers in Pastor Washington's church to help with their after-school tutoring program. It won't hurt me to downsize."

"Has he asked you to do this?"

"He has no idea I'm thinking about it."

"Shouldn't you talk to him about it first?"

"Do you have a problem with me doing this?"

"It's just . . ." She stroked her chin. "Different. I'm not used to someone wanting to sell their nice car so kids can have a computer center. But that's great, especially the part about educating the kids of the dangers on the Internet." Grace whispered to herself. "Really great." She tilted her head upward. "I hope."

At Indian Heights Community Church, they found seats near the front.

Hope didn't know Grace was coming with Win. When she saw them, her face flushed. She pulled her mother to the side. "Mom, what's going on?"

Grace smiled. "I have a date."

Hope rolled her eyes.

Chip walked up. "Just wanted to say hello to everyone."

Win extended his arm to give Chip knuckles. "Great to see you. The reason I missed yesterday's workout was that I was tied up with some research. How'd it go?"

"Great, but we missed you — and the extra mile you always have to run."

"Very funny. Hey, it's good to see you at church this morning."

"Don't worry, Gramps. We're two of a kind. Same motivation."

"What do you mean?"

Chip winked at Win. "Excuse me. I gotta go. You remember Emma. She's waiting for me. We're going for pizza after church."

Win laughed and pointed at Chip as he walked off. "You're wrong about my motivation. You know that."

The countdown began on the big screen with one minute until the start of worship. Everything during the service ran smoothly. Precision timing. Great music. Wonderful presentation of biblical truth by Todd. And a hard sell for contributions. After the service concluded, Win told Grace he was going to try to set up a meeting with Todd.

Win waited patiently for Todd to finish talking to some of the members before approaching him. "Grace told me about her encounter with you Friday. We need to talk."

"I really don't have anything to say. I've already talked to you, and you weren't interested in helping. Besides, I'm really busy this week."

"I'm not talking about your conversation with me. I know who the guys are that were with you when you saw Grace. Todd, this is . . ."

Todd abruptly turned. "Oh, Jim, I need to visit with you for a few minutes." He walked away and began a conversation with one of the deacons.

Grace had watched the incident and gently took his arm. "Let's go to lunch."

———⬥⬦⬥———

Win invited Hope to join them, but she politely declined. They went to Parrains, one of Grace's favorites. They found a booth that gave them privacy to talk. After ordering, Win sighed. "I talked to my PI friend."

"Was he able to identify those men?"

He paused. "The guy who calls himself 'Bald Eagle' is an associate with the New Orleans mob."

Grace shook her head. "I didn't know the mafia still existed in New Orleans."

"Some people think they died out, but my friend tells me that some guys connected to the New York crime bosses moved to New Orleans. They're involved in loan sharking and real estate development. And extremely dangerous. One of the top guys spent time in prison on kidnapping charges."

All the blood drained from Grace's face. "Your friend thinks the guys with Todd are connected to them?"

"A guy named 'Bald Eagle' is an associate. He's not a part of the family, but he does a lot of the dirty work for them. And there's a soldier named Joey who fits the description of the guy with the slick black hair."

"A soldier?"

"That's a member of the family. He gives orders to the associates. He normally wouldn't meet with a loan customer. But with Todd's fame, he probably thought it would be good to meet him."

Win took a deep breath. "That's all speculation. We don't have proof anything illegal is going on." Win tapped his fingers on the table. "Still, I'm really concerned. And with the note I got at the restaurant, I'm very worried about you."

Grace placed her hand on her forehead and looked at the table. "I can't believe this is happening."

"There's one more thing I need to talk to you about."

Grace glanced up with a quizzical look.

"When I ran in the All Comers' meet against Chip and Jamie a few weeks ago, I had an encounter with Jamie's dad."

"Oh, no."

"That's what Todd said when I told him. Eric Braun threatened me."

"What?"

"I saw him again last week when we were working out at Indian Heights. He tried to choke me."

"Choke you? "This has to be a bad dream. Tell me this isn't happening."

"I'm sorry, but it is. Isaiah's Special Ops friend Steve had Eric's arm twisted behind his back before I could even react. It's just so strange that Eric's reacting this way. Do you know anything about the guy — why he would act so violently?"

Grace sighed. "All I know is what Hope told me. He and Jamie's mom were divorced about the time Chip's dad was killed in Iraq. He grew up in New Orleans in a poor neighborhood. He met Jamie's mom at LSU. They seemed to have a good marriage until he started commuting to work in New Orleans. Hope said he became involved with some really bad people. Started drinking heavily and doing drugs. He made lots of money and started his own construction and real estate development company here in Baton Rouge. That's when the violence began."

Grace shook her head. "He physically abused Jamie's mom. They divorced. That's about all I know. Except that Jamie's mom won't attend any school events if she thinks he's going to be there. She's really afraid of him."

Win nodded. "I don't know what to do if he comes around when I'm with Chip. Steve was a great protector. I don't think he'll try anything when Steve is there, but he's not our bodyguard."

Grace's voice trembled. "Win, what do we do about all of this?"

"I wish I knew. Sometimes I wonder if I made the right decision to move back. In some ways, it seems divine destiny brought me home. When the housing market collapsed last fall, I thought, *This is the perfect time to buy a house back in Baton Rouge.*

"But after all that's happened, it's really shaken me. On the other hand, I would never have known about Hope and Chip." Win looked at Grace and smiled. "And we wouldn't be together here. Now I'm the one who's confused."

Grace looked down. "I have a prayer partner — Jenny. I'd like to ask her to pray about all this."

"I don't know, Grace. We don't know for certain that Todd is involved in something wrong. I don't want to start rumors. That wouldn't be fair. It could wreck his ministry."

Grace leaned forward, crossing her arms on the table. "If he's doing business with the mob, his ministry needs to be wrecked."

"We're not sure that he's doing business with them."

"I won't tell her who it was that was meeting with these guys, but I'll say I'm concerned. We need someone praying for us. This is way over our heads."

CHAPTER TWENTY-SEVEN

Win breathed deeply and smiled as he walked outside his home on Tuesday, March 10. Life had seemed to settle after Grace spoke with her prayer partner, Jenny, about the situation. They prayed together, and Jenny gave wise counsel. Chip and Isaiah completed their training with Win. Steve's conditioning exercises helped both boys to get ready for track season. Win would no longer be running with them, and he had no more encounters with Jamie's dad. Hope warmed to Win, at least a little. She dropped ten pounds and two dress sizes. She and her mom walked together regularly. Win and Grace decided that prayer was the best course in dealing with Todd. It seemed to work, as they saw no more signs of suspicious characters.

The mild breeze, the sun's reflection off the lake and the blossoming flowers refreshed not only Win's body, but also his spirit. *This is great.* He'd made a habit of drinking his morning coffee out by the old oak. He sat under the heart he'd carved on the tree four decades earlier. He looked out at the lake, read his Bible, prayed, and listened to podcasts Calvin had recommended. *Life can't get any better. Thank You, Lord.*

Calvin had recommended that Win listen to a series of messages about spiritual revival in America. They had been delivered at the Billy Graham Training Center, *The Cove.* Win was intrigued by the speakers. He found it fascinating to learn how revivals had helped form the nation. Different speakers emphasized the place of prayer in those revivals.

As a retired businessman, Win's curiosity was piqued by one speaker who said, "The last great awakening in America began in the fall of 1857, when the banking system collapsed in New York City. Three weeks prior to the economic crash, a man started a prayer meeting in the financial district of New York City. The prayer meeting grew from a handful of men to thousands of people, gathering in every major city around the nation." The next phrase captured Win's imagination. "This move of God's Spirit is considered by many historians as the last Great Awakening of evangelical Christianity in America."

Win walked back to the house, pondering what he'd heard. He wondered what it might take for America to experience another great revival. He thought about the television preachers he'd seen begging for money — and wondered how Todd had gotten so caught up in his financial problems. From what he could tell, Todd had a genuine love for God. Yet he seemed to risk his walk with God for the pleasure of possessions. *Will it take another financial crisis to bring a spiritual revival?*

As he started to open the door of his 5,000-squarefoot home, he stepped back and snickered. *Who am I to judge anyone? Maybe I'm the one who needs to reevaluate things.*

Inside, he flipped through the television channels to catch up on the news. He saw the ticker at the bottom of the screen and switched to a business channel. Financial analysts announced, "The Dow-Jones industrial average hits a twelve-year low. The S & P 500 hits its lowest point since September 12, 1996." He clicked the off button. *That's interesting. Is God trying to say something?*

The doorbell rang. Grace stood there, smiling. "What are you doing here?" Win said. "Come on in."

"I hadn't heard from you in a few days. You weren't at church yesterday." She glanced around the room and smiled again. "Wanted to make sure you hadn't left town."

Win laughed. "That's a low blow. I visited Pastor Washington's church. I really enjoyed it. I wanted to see Steve and Isaiah. Since we won't be working out together, I didn't know when I'd see them again."

"You haven't called, and I wondered if our talk the other day scared you away."

"So that's what this is about. No, I figured you needed some space to work through everything."

"I had another talk with Jenny — not just about those mafia guys, but also about us. I told her about my feelings of betraying Rick. She really helped."

"What'd she say?"

"Lots. It was good to have someone to be really honest with. Once I talked it out, I knew the truth. I'm not betraying Rick. He would want me to get on with my life. No one will ever replace him. But, I think I'm ready to . . ." Grace looked down with a smile.

Win lifted his eyebrows. "Ready to?"

She looked into his eyes. "This may seem a little aggressive, but I'd like to ask you out on a date."

"Really? And where might this date take us?"

"I thought I'd bring you somewhere you'd really like to go."

"Okay. I give. Tell me where that might be."

"Chip has a track meet in a couple of weeks. I thought we might go to it."

He grinned. "I accept your invitation. But that's a long way away. What about lunch today?"

"Little early for lunch, don't you think?"

"Let's make it breakfast. I haven't eaten yet. Besides, I've been thinking about some things I'd like to bounce off you."

"Things?"

"Like selling this house. I told you we'd talk about that, but we never got around to it."

"Sell this place? Why?"

"It's nice, but what does a single guy need with 5,000 square feet?"

Grace looked around. "Hmm."

"If I could sell it for close to its market value, I could buy another nice place — something smaller —and have enough profit to build a training center for Pastor Washington and his kids."

"Well." Grace sighed. "Your vision seems to be growing daily, from selling your car to selling your house."

"That's right." Win smiled. "I'm feeling real good about this."

"I still have the same question: Have you talked to Pastor Washington?"

"No. I want to make sure it's what I should do before I talk to him." Win grabbed his keys and started to leave. Grace stood motionless, staring at him with reverence. Her face flushed.

Win stopped directly in front of her and looked into her eyes. Grace stared at Win, then closed her eyes. Win bent his face toward hers. When his lips were only an inch from hers, Grace's phone rang. Win jumped back.

It was Hope's ringtone. She laughed. "I guess our daughter is checking on us."

Win smiled. "We'd better be out of the house before you call her back. Let's go."

CHAPTER TWENTY-EIGHT

Over the next couple of weeks, Grace and Win's relationship continued to grow. She insisted that she pick up Win for the track meet. On Friday afternoon, they arrived early at Indian Heights High School. Hope came a little later and sat with them.

Five schools were participating in the meet. Win hoped Istrouma would be one of them, but it wasn't. He knew that if Chip and Isaiah were running together, it would calm both boys' nerves. This race would be different for Chip. He and Jamie had always run with each other. This time, they were on the same team but running against each other.

As Win explained the phases and strategy of the race to Grace and Hope, Eric Braun started up the bleachers.

"Oh, no. Look," Grace whispered.

Eric took a big puff from his cigar and grinned. He walked straight to Win, his eyes on him the entire time. Win tensed.

"Hello, Mr. Bass. See you're here with your girlfriend." He turned toward Grace and Hope and smiled. "Hi, ladies. Should be a great race today. My boy tells me he's ready." He looked at Win, blew a circle of smoke in his face, and laughed. "These cigars are the best money can buy. Davidoff, Swiss — Millennium Series. Cost twenty-six dollars a pop." He chuckled and blew another circle of smoke. "Now, if you'll excuse me."

Win waved off the smoke, thinking, *I'll never forget that smell.* As Braun walked away, he called out, "Eric."

With a scowl, Eric looked back. "You want something?"

"No. Just thought you would want to know."

"Know what?"

Win glanced at Eric's pants. "Your fly." He smiled. "You forgot."

Eric's face turned red. He placed his cigar in his mouth and turned away, zipping his pants.

"Eric."

Braun turned again toward Win. His faced burned with rage.

Win took his index finger and flipped it against his cheek as though something was on Eric's face. Eric wiped his face, turned abruptly, and walked away.

Grace and Hope covered their mouths to keep from laughing. Grace poked Win's side. "I didn't see anything on his face."

He smiled. "Me, either."

———◇———

As Chip stretched, his stomach churned. It wasn't just the normal race jitters. This was completely different. He'd never had the state's best 400-meter runner watching in the stands. He'd never had a grandfather come to his meet. He regretted his dad had never been able to see him race, and he'd never dreamed his grandfather would see him.

Coach Landon told Chip and Jamie to run some strides to prepare for the race. Soon the first call came for the 400 meters. Chip's nerves rose about two notches. When they'd run in previous years, Jamie had always been at least one second behind Chip. Though Chip was running the best times of his life, Jamie's improvements were remarkable. Chip felt he could beat the competition from the other schools, but he lacked the same confidence about Jamie.

The only time my grandfather has seen me race was when he and Jamie beat me. Now he may see Jamie do it again. The loudspeaker boomed, "Final call for the 400 meters." Chip and Jamie made their way to the starting line.

Chip was given lane four and Jamie, lane two. "Runners, take your marks." Chip stretched as he placed his feet in the starting blocks. *Focus. Forget everything else and everyone. Just focus.*

"Runners, get set." Two seconds seemed like an eternity. One last thought. *Focus.* He stared at the track. Boom.

Eight runners were off with a fast start. Chip and Jamie took an early lead. Chip was ahead of Jamie, but not by much. Both boys had a natural and relaxed stride down the straightaway. Chip kept a few strides ahead of Jamie, but he knew those would be made up in the final curve.

By the end of the curve. Jamie caught up. Chip felt his presence. When they came out of the curve and on to the final 100 meters, they were dead even. The closest runner was ten meters behind.

Win jumped to his feet, shouting, "Stay focused! Stay focused! You've got it!"

Grace and Hope screamed, "Go! Go, Chip!"

Eric Braun shouted, "You've got it! Take him! Take him, now! Go!"

The tension grew with every stride down the final straightaway.

By the time Chip and Jamie were at the fifty-yard line, Chip's legs felt like a ton of bricks. Lactic acid took its toll. Chip pumped his arms and maintained his form. Jamie did the same. They were almost a mirror image. Stride for stride, they stayed with each other.

At the thirty-yard line, it appeared they would both break the school record. Both boys had fire in their eyes. The only thing Chip saw was the finish line. He knew the same was true with Jamie. He could feel it.

Ten yards from the finish line, they were still even. Chip stretched his chest toward the finish. Jamie did the same. They crossed the line in a tie.

For Chip, everything became slow-motion. The cheers from the crowd seemed muffled. He bent over in pain, then looked up. He saw his mother, grandmother, and grandfather applauding. Hope blew a kiss. Win and Grace smiled.

He saw Jamie bending and struggling to breathe. Chip walked over to congratulate him. As he placed his hand on his shoulder, Jamie grabbed his chest. Then collapsed.

Fear flooded Chip's heart. Jamie lay on the track, his eyes open. He didn't seem to breathe. His hands and face turned blue. People started screaming.

Chip shouted, "Coach! Coach!"

Eric Braun flew out of the stands, vaulted the fence, and pushed Chip away. He grabbed Jamie's head and shouted, "Someone call 911! Call 911!"

CHAPTER TWENTY-NINE

Pandemonium broke out at the Indian Heights track. A crowd of athletes gathered around Jamie as he lay on the ground. Coach Landon yelled for them to move back.

Chip looked at Jamie, lying lifeless in his dad's arms. He tilted his head backward, grabbed his face with both hands, and fell to his knees, crying, "No. No."

Hope and Grace ran onto the track. Hope grabbed Chip and pulled him into her arms. "It's okay. It's okay. He'll be okay."

With an anguished voice, Win told Eric, "He needs CPR."

Eric's face contorted with agony. "Help!" he cried.

Win dropped to the ground and placed one hand on top of the other and pressed hard and fast on the center of Jamie's chest. Jamie still didn't breathe. After about 30 presses, Win tilted Jamie's head back and lifted his chin. He pinched his nostrils and gave two mouth-to-mouth breaths. He repeated the process and continued until emergency medical techs arrived. They showed up within five minutes, placed Jamie on a stretcher and whisked him away. Eric hopped in the ambulance with Jamie.

Win walked over to Chip, Hope, and Grace.

Tears streamed down Chip's face. "Will he be okay?"

"I don't know," Win said softly. He helped Chip stand and hugged him.

───────◇◇◇───────

Coach Landon approached Chip and his family. "You okay, son?"

Chip looked at the track. "Yeah."

"Excuse us folks," Landon said gently, "but I'd like to talk to Chip alone for a few minutes. Do you mind?"

"Come on, Chip. Let's walk over here." He placed his arm around Chip's shoulder while they walked toward the goal post. Chip kept his eyes focused on the ground.

Landon spoke softly. "I know this is hard. But it's not your fault. It didn't happen because of your race with Jamie. These things just happen. We don't always understand why." Chip continued to stare at the ground.

Coach Landon bent down so he could look directly into Chip's eyes. His voice became firm. "Chip, you can *not* tell anyone about the conversation I had with Jamie." He paused. "I'm sorry this happened. Hope to God it never happens again. But the guy in the locker room with the knife, he's very dangerous. He won't hesitate to visit you and your mother late at night. He and his friends are dangerous."

Chip continued staring at the turf.

Landon grabbed Chip's arm. "Look, Chip. You *can't* tell anyone about the conversation we had. Do you understand?"

Chip pulled away from Landon, glared at him, and spat on the ground. He turned and strode away.

"Don't forget," Landon said. "These guys will hurt you."

———◇◇◇———

When Chip returned to his family, Win suggested they pray for Jamie. Win, Chip, Hope, and Grace gathered in a circle, holding hands and crying to God for Jamie's life. Win prayed, "Oh, God, I ask that you spare Jamie. Touch him. Be with the doctors. Comfort his mom and dad right now. Help them to know Your peace. We ask for a miracle. In Jesus' name. Amen."

Grace and Hope quietly wept, while Chip stared at the ground.

Win put his hand on Chip's shoulder. "Why don't you get your clothes from the locker room, and let's head home. "

Win felt a need to talk to Grace about his observations of Jamie a few weeks earlier. He suggested that he and Grace pick up something for dinner and meet at Hope's house in an hour.

Once Win and Grace were in her car, he rubbed his face and groaned. "Oh, Grace, I have a really bad feeling about this."

"What do you mean?"

"We were working out a few weeks ago, and I saw Jamie for the first time since the All Comers' meet. I was shocked."

"Why?"

"He had put on a lot of weight — all muscle — in just a few weeks. That tells me steroids were involved."

"Couldn't the muscle gain have come from Coach Landon's workouts with him?"

"Possibly, but it seemed too much too soon. Also, I didn't remember him with such bad acne."

"I didn't, either, but what does that have to do with steroids?"

"Some people have that reaction to steroids."

"You think steroids could have caused this?"

"It's not something that normally happens, but it's possible. The heart can enlarge, and with extreme exertion, a person can have a heart attack."

Grace looked at Win as though she wondered how he knew so much about steroids.

Win read her. "When I ran in the World Masters Track and Field Championships, they tested people randomly for steroid use. A few tested positive. Several of us had a long discussion about it one night. That was a real eye-opener. I just hope it's not what happened to Jamie."

"How would he have gotten steroids?"

"Don't draw any conclusions yet. Let's wait and see what the doctors say."

"Do you think he'll be okay?"

"I really don't know."

"Just when I thought things had settled down, this happens." Grace tried to gather her composure. "Where are we going to pick up dinner?"

"I heard about a little place on Coursey called Dempsey's. It's supposed to be a hole-in the-wall place, but it has great seafood and shrimp po' boys. Let's check it out."

Dempsey's was packed. As they completed their take-out order for po' boys, Win's phone rang.

"Steve, what's going on?"

"I saw a news flash on television. Is Chip okay?"

"He's okay. A little shook up about Jamie."

"So it was Jamie."

"What's the news saying?"

"They're not giving much information. Just that a key member of Indian Heights track team collapsed at the meet and that he's been hospitalized. They said they'll have a full report on the six o'clock news. What happened out there?"

Win explained what had taken place, then asked, "Steve, remember when we saw Jamie at the track a few weeks ago. Do you think he could have been using steroids?"

"That's exactly what I was thinking. Do you think Chip might know something?"

"I don't know."

"If I were you, I'd talk to Chip before the news report comes out."

CHAPTER THIRTY

As Win and Grace headed back to Hope's home, Win told her about his conversation with Steve. "I'm afraid," he said.

"Of what?"

"That this isn't going to have a good ending."

"What do you mean?"

"I don't know. All I know is that my stomach is knotted. We need to get home before the news comes on. We need to be with Chip, whatever the report."

Grace's hands on the steering wheel trembled. Neither spoke for the rest of the drive.

When Grace and Win entered Hope's house, they asked about Chip.

"He's in his room. He went in and slammed the door. I'm worried about him."

Win asked, "Do you think he'd talk to me?"

"You can try."

Win tapped lightly on Chip's door, then slowly opened it and peeked side. "You okay?"

Chip just sat at his desk. His facial muscles twitched. His eyes were downcast with a deep look of sadness.

"There's going to be a news report on WAFB about Jamie in a few minutes. Thought you might want to watch it."

"Sure."

"Chip, you do know this wasn't your fault?"

"That's what Coach said."

"He's right. You want to talk about it?"

"No."

"Okay. But if Jamie was on some kind of steroids, the doctors will know. And I'm sure the authorities will ask if you knew whether Jamie was taking anything."

The blood drained from Chip's face. "Why would they want to talk to me?"

"Chip, I'm your grandfather, and I'm your friend. If you need to talk to anyone about this, you can talk to me."

Chip gazed downward. "I don't need to talk to anyone. I just don't know why they would ask me anything. I don't keep track of Jamie and what he's doing."

"You were his running partner. But let's not go there yet. It's about time for the six o'clock news. Let's see what they say."

Chip and Hope sat on the couch together as they waited for the broadcast. Grace sat in a nearby chair. Too nervous to sit, Win stood behind Grace.

"Welcome to WAFB's Six O'clock News. A tragedy struck the Indian Heights High School track team today. Four-hundred-meter runner Jamie Braun collapsed after breaking the high school record. He was pronounced dead upon arrival at the Baton Rouge General Hospital."

"No!" Chip shouted. "Please, God, no!" He slid to the floor, weeping. Hope placed her arms around him and cried. Grace embraced both of them.

Win stared at the ceiling, tears running down his face. "Oh, God, we desperately need you."

The reporter's next words stunned them. "A source inside the hospital says steroid use is suspected as a possible cause of the heart failure."

Sobs turned silent. Grace stood, grabbed Win's hand, and lifted it to her face. Hope looked at Chip, who had a glassy stare.

When the report ended, Hope placed her hand on the back of Chip's head and softly pulled it to her shoulder. "I'm so sorry."

After a few seconds, Chip pulled away and looked at Win. His face turned pale and he ran into the bathroom. Dry heaves.

Hope and Grace looked at Win. He walked into the bathroom, took a deep breath, and quietly rubbed Chip's back. Once Chip was able to stand, he told Win, "I need to lie down."

"Come on." Win helped him to his bedroom.

When Win returned to the living area, Hope asked, "Will he be all right?"

"I'm concerned about the emotional and psychological impact this is going to leave."

Grace rubbed her upper arms as though comforting herself. Then she walked to Win and gently grabbed his arm. "Do you think Chip knows anything about Jamie using steroids?"

"I hope not. But one thing's for sure. The authorities will ask him. He and Jamie were too close for them not to question him."

Hope collapsed on the couch. "Oh, God, why is this happening?"

Win sat next to her and tried to put his arm around her. She stared at the coffee table. "No. Don't. Please."

"I'm sorry. Just wanted to help."

"I think we all," Grace said, "need to pray for God's guidance and peace."

After each of them prayed, Win's phone rang. He didn't recognize the number. He almost didn't answer, but with everything happening, he checked it out. "Hello, Win Bass here."

Win looked down and frowned. "Sure, I'll do what I can," he said with no emotion. "But I don't know anything. If I can help, I'll do whatever. It'll be about an hour before I can get there."

Both Grace and Hope had a questioning stare. Chip came into the room. Grace tilted her head and squinted. "What's that all about?"

"It was the police. For some reason, they want to talk to me. They asked if I would come downtown."

Chip slammed his hand against the wall. "That's stupid. You don't know anything about Jamie."

"It seems like Jamie's dad . . . ." Win's lips trembled. "He thinks I know something. He told them they needed to talk to me." Pain crawled over Win's face. "Grace, can you drive me to my house to pick up my car?"

"Mom, before you go, I need to talk to you." Hope hesitated and looked at Win. "Alone, if you don't mind."

"Sure." Win looked at Grace. "I'll wait for you at the car."

CHAPTER THIRTY-ONE

"Mom, I don't trust him."

Grace's eyebrows shot up. "Why?"

"What do we really know about him? He's only been around for three months. He comes to town with a Lexus sports car and buys a big house on South Lakeshore Drive. Pays cash. He woos you. Helps me lose weight."

Hope's voice grew louder with each observation. "He trains Chip. He's Superman. Nobody is that good. What do we really know about him? Maybe he's dealing drugs. Maybe the police know something we don't."

"Mom, stop it!" Chip shouted. "He didn't do this to Jamie."

Hope's face looked incurably sad, and her voice softened. She grabbed Chip's arms. "Oh, sweetheart. I know you've had a great time with him, but I'm frightened for you." She glanced at Grace. "For all of us."

Chip's eyes filled with desperation. "Mom, you're not thinking rationally. I'm certain he had nothing to do with Jamie's death. He's being falsely accused — again. Can't you see that?"

"I'm not accusing him. We just don't know him. And I'm worried about you — both of you."

"Hope, it's going to be fine." Grace softly rubbed Hope's arm. "I talked to Win's former boss. Everything Win's told us is true."

Hope shook her head. "And how do you know that this supposed boss is legitimate?"

"Mom, I can't believe you're saying this."

"How do you know? How does either one of you know he's not lying to us?"

Chip slapped his chest. "I know, Mom. I know."

———⊰⊱———

As Grace drove Win to get his car, he said, "Grace, I'm afraid."

She glanced at him. "Why?"

"I haven't had this feeling since 1965. When I was arrested. All of the same elements are here. A person is dead. Drugs are involved. And someone's pointing the finger at me." Win banged his fist on the console. "I can't believe this."

"It's going to be okay," she said. "Do you want me to go with you to the police station?"

"No. I have to face this. But, it's my worst nightmare."

"Is there anything I can do?"

"Do you know a good attorney?"

"Not a criminal lawyer. But I know enough people to find someone."

"Someone really good?"

"I think I can."

"Please get to work on that after you drop me off. I don't want to be in the position I found myself in 1965."

When they pulled into the driveway on South Lakeshore, Grace looked at Win with a tender smile. "Before you go, there's two things I want to do."

"What's that?"

"First, I want to pray for you."

"Please do."

Grace grabbed Win's hand and closed her eyes. "Oh, God, I ask You to be with Win. Give him peace, a supernatural peace. Give him strength and courage, strength he doesn't have and courage he's never known. Help him to answer all the questions. I ask for wisdom. You promised You would give us a liberal amount of wisdom if we ask. So, we're asking for Your wisdom. Fill him with Your Holy Spirit. And bring him home safely. In Jesus' name. Amen."

"Amen." Win opened moist eyes and smiled. "Thank you. I really appreciate that. I believe God will answer you. What's the second thing you want to do?"

"This." Grace leaned toward Win and gently kissed him on the cheek. "I want you to know I trust you. Will you do me a favor? Call me when you arrive at the station, before you go in, and then when you're out. If things go too long, I'll have the attorney call the station."

Win gazed deeply into Grace's eyes. "Thank you."

CHAPTER THIRTY-TWO

Win sat in the parking lot at the Mayflower Street police station for several minutes before going in. *Why do they think I have information?* He breathed deeply. *Stay focused. Remember, you're here on a volunteer basis. Don't forget your rights. Just be honest. Be wise.* His mouth felt dry. *Stay calm.*

Win's mind went back to the night he was arrested in California. He remembered the pressure he'd felt and how quickly he'd become confused. He prayed again. "God, I desperately need You. Please, help me."

He phoned Grace. His voice trembled. "I'm here. Headed inside. Thanks for your trust — and your prayers."

"I'm still praying and will continue to pray. Don't forget, God is with you."

"Thanks."

He sighed and slowly walked into the police station. Memories flooded his mind. Many things were different from forty-four years earlier, but the feelings of fear hadn't changed. Win reported to the front desk, and soon Detective Bobby Bourgeois greeted him. "Thanks for coming in. We appreciate it."

Win smiled softly and followed the detective to a small room with a table and a couple of chairs. The scene was all too familiar. "Have a seat. I'll get my partner."

Win knew the drill. They left him alone for about ten minutes. Empty walls. Simple table and chairs. He recalled some of the California inmates calling it "the box." That room had hosted petty thieves, rapists, and murderers. It was a place where lies, truths, and half-truths played games and often looked like identical triplets. *I remember this. Sitting here, waiting for them to begin their questioning. Their mind games. I hope there aren't any tonight.*

Win bowed his head and silently prayed, *Oh, God, I need You. It seems I'm always telling You that. It's been true every time, but it's really true now. I'm scared. I don't know what to expect. Show me how to respond. Help me to help these officers discover what happened to Jamie. I pray for justice for Jamie.*

The door was flung open, and Detective Bourgeois introduced his partner, Johnny Ramirez. As Detective Bourgeois sat, he made small talk, then said, "I understand you were at the track at Indian Heights and saw what happened today?"

"Yes, sir."

"I don't know if you're aware that Jamie Braun passed shortly afterward."

"I heard it on the news. I'm so sorry for him and his family."

"Traces of steroids were found in his blood, and we've been given the assignment to find out what happened. We thought you might be able to help."

"I'm so sorry," Win said. "This is awful. Whatever I can do, I will."

"You're right. It is terrible. This is a tragedy for the city and for the Braun family. Mr. Braun told us you attempted to give CPR."

"I did. If there's anything I can do to help, I want to do it. That's why I came."

"Great. That's what we were hoping."

Detective Ramirez matter-of-factly asked, "Had you met Jamie Braun previously?"

"I met him a couple of times, but didn't know at first who he was. The first time I saw him was several weeks ago at a track meet at Catholic High. I saw him again when we were working out at Indian Heights High a few weeks ago. Until today, that's the only contact I've had."

Bourgeois again took control of the conversation. "Eric Braun seems to think there was more contact than that. Why do you think he would think something like that?"

"I don't have any idea. For some reason, he seems like a bitter man. I beat his son when we ran the 400 meters in the All Comers' meet. He was angry. Maybe that anger drives him to place blame on me. I don't know."

"So you're a runner."

"Yes, sir."

"I assume, then, that you know something about performance-enhancing drugs."

"I know a little about them, but not much more than the average person."

"How'd you learn about them?"

Win rapidly tapped the table with his finger. "Some guys were talking about them at the World Masters Track and Field Championships in 2007. But that has absolutely nothing to do with Jamie Braun."

Ramirez came back into the conversation. "You nervous, Mr. Bass?"

"Of course I'm nervous. It's not every day that someone is asked to come into an interrogation room like this."

"You ever been in an interrogation room?"

The outer edges of Win's lips turned downward. "I have a feeling you already know the answer."

"Why don't you tell us about it?"

Win looked at the ceiling and sighed. "I was arrested in California forty-four years ago for using marijuana. I was a mixed-up kid, just out of high school. Never used it since. And we both know that has nothing to do with Jamie Braun. So could we go to any questions about him? That's why I came. I want to help."

Bourgeois continued the questions with a more gentle tone. "Look, we just want to get to the bottom of this. Mr. Braun feels you had something to do with it. So we have to eliminate you as a possible suspect. That's all. Where do you live, Mr. Bass?"

"South Lakeshore Drive."

"Nice area. Have a good view of LSU?"

"Yes."

"On the lake. Must have cost a lot of money."

"It's nice."

"How long you been living there?"

"A few months."

"What kind of work do you do?"

"I'm retired."

"Must've done well to retire on South Lakeshore."

"I worked hard for four decades."

"Did you ever meet privately with Jamie Braun?"

Win's eyes narrowed with disgust. "No." He raised his voice. "I've already told you. I only met him at the All Comers' meet and on another day when I was working out at Indian Heights High."

Ramirez moved from the far corner and stood directly in front of Win. "You're lying. We have a witness who saw you alone with Jamie Braun. Why don't you go ahead and tell us about it?"

Win's jaw dropped. "What? I can't believe you're saying that." Win stood, squared his shoulders, and pointed his finger at Detective Ramirez. "No, you're lying. I came here in good faith that you guys needed my help, not that you were going to accuse me. I thought you wanted honest answers. Well . . . truth is a two-way street. There's one thing all three of us know that's true. And that is . . ." He pointed at Ramirez. "You're lying. No one has ever seen me alone with Jamie, because it never happened. Gentlemen, this interview is over. If you want to talk to me further, you'll do it with my attorney's approval. Unless you're planning to arrest me, I'm leaving. Call me if you want my attorney's number."

Win stormed out of the station. He clenched the steering wheel and cried out, "Oh, God. I can't believe this is happening." His chest tightened, and his muscles became rigid. Then he took a deep breath and calmness slowly filled his heart. He knew Grace was praying. He dialed her number.

"Grace, I'm out of the interview."

"How did it go? I've been praying since you went into the station."

"Not well. Did you find a lawyer? I'm going to need one."

"I found one, a very good one. But we'd better talk before either one of us makes contact with him."

CHAPTER THIRTY-THREE

When Win got home, he walked to the old oak and slid to the ground against its trunk. He gazed at the stars and prayed. "God, I know You're there. I just don't understand why this is happening."

For more than two hours, he sat in silence. The night skies spoke with great clarity, the order and vastness of the universe overwhelming Win. *God is greater than I can imagine. His ways are so much higher than I can fathom.* As he pondered God's greatness, the heaviness from the day's events lifted. When he stepped inside, Grace called. Her voice felt like healing oil.

"Before I go to bed, I wanted to make sure you're okay."

"I'll be okay. This is all so crazy. Jamie dying today, the police thinking I had something to do with it . . ."

"Why do they think that?"

"Eric Braun is very angry, and he's trying to place the blame on me. But let's talk about all that over breakfast tomorrow. You up to it?"

"Just tell me when and where."

———✧———

Win picked up Grace Saturday morning, and they found a little restaurant on the southeast side. Win told Grace what happened at the police station. "You said you found an attorney."

Grace pursed her lips. "Yes, but . . ."

Win raised an eyebrow. "But?"

"But he's a deacon at the church. Good friends with Todd."

Win covered his face with his hands while Grace continued.

"I've seen him at church and knew he was a deacon. I didn't know he was a defense lawyer. I called Jenny last night, and she told me about him. She said he's one of the best criminal attorneys in the state. I figured I'd better talk to you before contacting him."

Win rubbed the bridge of his nose. "Why does everything have to be so complicated?" He gazed toward the ceiling, then back at Grace. "Okay. Let's contact him. Maybe we can ask him tomorrow at church if we can set up an appointment."

Win and Grace met briefly with Ray Landry at church. He knew Grace, and Todd had told him about Win after their first meeting at CC's. After Win told him how urgent it was to speak with him, Ray told him to come to his office before it opened the next morning.

As Win entered Mr. Landry's office on Jefferson Highway, he thought, *I wish I'd known him forty-four years ago*. The plush suite spoke volumes about Landry's success as a trial attorney.

"Take a seat. It's great to meet you. Todd told me several weeks ago that he'd once again met his best friend from high school. He was really excited."

Win looked toward the floor. "Yeah."

When Win didn't say any more, he asked, "Something wrong?"

Still looking at the floor, Win took a deep breath.

"Look, everything you say in here is private," Landry said. "The first meeting is free, but we'll call it a consultation. If we go further, you can formally hire me. But this discussion will have complete attorney/client privilege. So you're safe to talk."

Win looked up. "Thanks. This is really difficult." He explained what had happened at the track with Jamie, and he also detailed the history of his California arrest. After an hour of talking, Ray Landry asked Win if he wanted to hire him formally. If so, they needed to fill out some paperwork.

"I do, but there's something else you need to know."

He raised an eyebrow. "Go ahead."

"Grace was at the outlet mall in Gonzales the other day, and she ran into Todd. He was with two guys. They looked . . ." Win glanced around the room. "They looked different."

"What do you mean?"

"One had a shaved head with an eagle tattoo that covered his head. These guys acted strangely toward Grace and frightened her. Todd told her not to talk to me about them. But I had the guy with the eagle tattoo checked out by a PI friend. The tattoo guy is connected to the New Orleans mafia."

Landry looked shocked. "Are you sure?"

Win rubbed his eyes. "I'm sure."

"You don't think this has anything to do with the track meet and the kid who died?"

"I don't know. It's strange that both of these incidents happened around the same time. I don't know what to think. But with your relationship with Todd, I needed to tell you if you're going to enter into an attorney/client relationship with me."

Landry began pacing.

"I'd like to hire you," Win said. "But I don't know where all of this is leading. You may not want to represent me."

Landry stopped pacing and turned to Win. "Let's do this. I'll work as your attorney. I don't think the steroids have anything to do with Todd. If that becomes an issue and I feel I need to recuse myself, I'll do it. If that happens, I'll make sure you have the best representation you can find in Baton Rouge. Will that work?"

"It's good for me. But what about your relationship with Todd now that I've told you this? Have I complicated things?"

"I'm a defense attorney. A person is innocent until proven guilty. I know Todd. I don't know these guys, but I'm sure Todd had a good reason to meet with them. I won't say anything to Todd. I don't know what this is about, but it's not my business. I trust him completely. Let's leave it there."

CHAPTER THIRTY-FOUR

At 3:45 that afternoon, Win prepared in his front yard for his four-mile walk around the lake. It always helped stimulate his thinking, and he had a lot to process. Though he wasn't running, he still stretched. He'd discovered the importance of flexibility in older age when he'd begun running again. Injuries seemed to happen much more frequently. Stretching kept him healthy. As he stretched his calves and hamstrings, Chip pulled up.

"Why aren't you at track practice?"

"Coach Landon cancelled practice. Said he'd let us know when or if we would start up again. So I thought I'd come over."

"You want to walk with me, or would you like to go inside and visit?"

"Let's walk."

As they headed around the lake, Chip shared his feelings. "Coach Landon isn't sure if we will continue to compete this season."

"How do you feel about that?"

"I don't know. I have all sorts of feelings."

"Like what?"

"Guilt. Anger. Frustration. Disappointment. And probably a hundred other feelings I can't name."

"Why do you feel guilt?"

Chip looked toward the sky. "That's a tough one. Jamie and I were best friends for so many years. When he beat me in the All Comers' meet, Coach decided to train him and didn't want me to be a part of it. Jamie and I had a big argument. Our relationship ended. I just wish I could go back and change everything."

God, give me wisdom to know what to say and when to say it. For the next half mile, neither spoke.

When they got near the fraternity houses at LSU, Chip opened up again. "Jamie and I talked about running for LSU. He'll never have that opportunity."

"Chip, I don't want to pry. If I'm out of order, just tell me."

"Okay."

"There's something that's bothered me. You mentioned it a few minutes ago. Why didn't Coach want you to be a part of the training he was doing with Jamie?"

Chip's face flushed and he turned his head away. "I don't know. You'll have to ask Coach. He's the one who has that answer."

"Is there something you're not telling me?"

Chip shook his head. "Absolutely nothing. Look, maybe it was a mistake to come here."

"I'm sorry. Maybe I shouldn't have asked." A small smile crept on Win's face. "Besides, you're stuck with me another couple of miles. We're not halfway around the lake yet."

Chip chuckled. "You're right." He kept his eyes directly ahead of him as they passed a church facility called *The Chapel.* "One of the reasons I came today is to see if you would train me. I don't want to quit. I've gained so much conditioning and speed, and I won't have another chance for a scholarship to LSU. If I don't train, I'll lose my conditioning. Coach isn't working with us. I don't know how long that will last, but I need to keep working out. I don't want to lose anything before district and state. Will you train me?"

Win bit his lip. "I want to, and maybe we can figure out a way to do it. But Grace told me your mom is pretty upset. She's afraid. She thinks I may have had something to do with Jamie taking steroids. She loves you and doesn't want anything to happen to you."

"But you didn't have anything to do with it. That's all that matters."

"Your mom is my little girl. I love her, and I don't want to do anything to hurt her."

"So you won't help me?"

"I didn't say that. There might be a way I can help. Are you willing to run with Steve during the week and Isaiah on the weekend?"

"Yeah."

"Let's do this. I'll develop a training schedule for the next two weeks. I'll go over it with Steve. I'll be the coach, and Steve the trainer. Steve can give me a progress report every day. I'll adjust the workouts accordingly. Maybe you and Isaiah can train together on Saturdays. I won't have to be there. That way, your mom won't be upset with you or me. You'll stay in shape, maybe even better shape than working with Coach Landon. Think that might work?"

Chip flashed a triumphant grin. "That'll work."

When they got back to Win's house, Chip asked, "You coming to the funeral tomorrow?"

"I don't know. I don't want my presence to incite Jamie's dad. But I'd like to pay my respects. What about you?"

"I'll be there. They're letting school out at 1:30 so people can be there by 2:00. I think the church will be packed. I'm going to be a pallbearer. They asked me to say something, but I didn't think I could. Carrying his casket will be hard enough."

"I'll come late and sit in the back. I'll sneak out before the final prayer."

"Okay. Call me and let me know what Steve says."

Win called Steve about the idea of training Chip.

"That's a great idea. But where?"

"I don't know. If the track season has been suspended at Indian Heights, the track should be free. Check with Chip. I'll call tomorrow morning and give you the workout schedule for this week. I think you should start right away. Jamie's funeral is tomorrow. Maybe work out Wednesday through Friday after school, and then you can also train on Saturday morning. If you have any questions, I'll have my cell with me, and you can call."

"You think Coach Landon will have any problem with Isaiah working out with Chip on Saturday?"

"I don't know, but what he doesn't know won't hurt."

"You think it'll be safe to train, considering what happened to Jamie and the explosive nature of his dad?"

"Hey, you're the man. I'm confident Chip will be safe with you."

CHAPTER THIRTY-FIVE

A slow drizzle came down all day Tuesday. Despite the weather, Indian Heights Community Church was packed with students, family members, and friends of Jamie Braun.

Jamie's family sat on the front row, with Jamie's dad on the far left, his brother and sister between his dad and mom, and his mom with her boyfriend on the far right. The pallbearers — all the 1,600-meter relay team and some of the 400-meter relay team —sat behind the family. Coach Landon sat at the far left of the row. The rest of the track team sat behind the pallbearers.

Chip's mind wandered as he stared at the back of Jamie's mother's head. *Jamie wanted both his parents to come to one of his events. They never did until now. I don't think this is what he had in mind.* Chip's foot bounced nervously as people walked by the open casket to show their respect. Hope walked by with tears streaming. Mimi held her arm. They glanced at his body and quickly turned their heads.

Chip fought back tears. *That's my best friend in that box. I'll never see him again. I can't believe this is happening.* As the line dwindled, Chip turned to see if Win had arrived. He walked in and took a seat on the back row of the lower level.

The service began with Pastor Todd making a statement about the purpose of the gathering. After his opening remarks, he read a Scripture passage and led in prayer. Pastor Todd spoke to the family directly. "No one can fully understand the pain you are feeling right now. We hurt with you. We hurt for you, and we're praying for you." After speaking for five minutes, he said, "I'm going to ask Jamie's track coach, Coach Landon, to come now. He'd like to share a few words about Jamie."

It was the first time Chip had seen Coach wear a coat and tie. Landon slowly made his way up the stairs and unfolded his notes on the cross-shaped pulpit. "This may be the most difficult thing I've ever done. It's not natural. A high school coach doesn't normally speak at one of his athletes' funeral. But I wanted to be here, because I cared about Jamie."

Chip's foot stopped bouncing. *Give me a break. I can't believe you're saying that.*

"Jamie Braun was a great runner. His life was an inspiration to all of us. He worked hard. He wanted to prove he was the best runner at Indian Heights, and he did. The last thing he did was to break the school record."

Chip's jaw dropped as he leaned forward. *We* broke the record. Remember. *We* did it. Chip looked at the floor. *I can't believe I'm thinking that. On this day, I worry about who gets the credit. He was my best friend. Can't I let him have his glory just one day?*

Coach Landon spoke for another several minutes. As he said, "thank you" and began to walk off the platform, Pastor Todd approached the microphone and said, "Coach, could you wait for a few minutes? I'm going to ask Eric Braun, Jamie's dad, to join us. Mr. Braun, please. We have a small presentation we'd like to make."

Coach Landon and Eric Braun stood on either side of Pastor Todd. "Coach Landon, something historic took place last Friday. A school record was set by Jamie Braun." He looked at Eric. "Mr. Braun, your son achieved something no other athlete at Indian Heights High School has ever done. He ran 400 meters faster than any athlete at Indian Heights. Jamie isn't here to receive the recognition. We wanted to present this plaque to you."

Eric Braun read aloud the inscription. "In memory of Indian Heights High School's greatest 400-meter runner."

The auditorium erupted in applause. Chip looked around. He managed a smile, stood with everyone, and clapped. *What about me? I did it, too.* He looked down again. *Why am I thinking that? This is Jamie's funeral.*

When Todd asked Coach Landon to stay on the platform and Eric Braun to join him, Win's stomach churned. As the three stood side by side, Win broke into a sweat, and his body trembled. *Something's wrong with this. Very wrong.* As he watched the three men on the platform, he became deeply grieved.

Though the lights illumined the pulpit area, a dark shadow appeared behind them. The darkness stood in contrast to the light on the pulpit. Win felt he was going to vomit. He stood and staggered out of the auditorium. Once in the lobby, his trembling ceased and his temperature returned to normal. *God, what's going on in there?*

An usher saw Win and asked, "Sir, are you okay?"

He assured him with a nod. "I'm okay."

Win left the church and headed to CC's coffee shop. He sat silently in the corner, thinking about the memorial service. *Why did I react like that?* Strange. Really strange.

As Win thought about the episode, he realized it was the pulpit and the seeming darkness behind the cross. Something felt wrong about Coach Landon and Eric Braun standing behind the cross with Todd in the middle. Win had never seen that kind of darkness on the platform. It spooked him. His feelings seemed as bizarre as the situation.

After a half hour, Grace called. "Where are you?"

"CC's on Airline. Having coffee. Want a cup?"

"I'll be right over. I saw you in the back, but when the service ended, you had disappeared."

"I'll explain when you get here."

When Grace arrived, Win told her what he felt.

"It seemed a little odd to see Coach Landon and Eric Braun in church and on the stage," she said, "but I didn't sense what you felt."

"Maybe I'm too mystical." He chuckled. "How many people do you know who are called to repentance by an old oak tree?"

Grace smiled. "That's true. But remember, you're not the only one who was called to repent by that old tree."

It felt good to talk to Grace. She knew when to listen and when to speak. Her counsel seemed to flow straight from heaven. Win took Grace's hand. "You know, I'm falling in . . ."

Grace slipped her hand out of Win's and placed her fingers on his lips. "Not yet. I need more time."

Win's afternoon went from bizarre to sublime. Weird feelings at the funeral turned to wonderful conversation with the only woman he'd ever loved.

After Grace left CC's, Win called Chip.

"How are you doing, Chip?"

"Okay. I'm headed home. Have you talked to Steve?"

"Everything is set for tomorrow at Indian Heights. He'll meet you after school Wednesday through Friday, and also early Saturday morning."

"Great."

"How did the graveside service go?"

"Okay. I'm having some crazy thoughts, though."

"Maybe we can talk about them sometime."

"I'd like that."

"Chip."

"What?"

"Nothing."

"No. What? What were you going to say?"

Win took a deep breath. "I don't know. With all that's happened, be careful."

There was silence on the other end of the phone.

"Chip, you still there?"

"I'm here. I'll be careful."

CHAPTER THIRTY-SIX

Wednesday through Friday afternoons, Chip and Steve worked out together. Everything went well. Chip enjoyed these workouts more than the ones he'd done with the track team. By Friday, Coach Landon hadn't said when or if they would restart practice.

Just before Chip arrived at Indian Heights on Saturday morning, Steve called him. "We're here at the parking lot. How long before you arrive?"

"I'm just down the street at the light. As soon as it changes, it'll only be a minute."

"Great. Then I'm leaving Isaiah. I picked him up from a breakfast meeting at the church. He needs to change into his workout gear. Do they leave the restrooms open on weekends?"

"I doubt it, but there's a cubbyhole where you enter the men's restroom. He can change there, and no one will see him."

"Okay. I'm dropping him off and heading to the gas station down the street. I'm on empty. I want to make sure I don't run out of gas when we leave. I'll be back at the track in ten minutes. Go ahead and warm up. I'll be right there."

"The light just changed. I'm almost there. I see Isaiah getting out of the car."

"I see you, too. I'll be back in less than ten minutes."

Chip waved as he passed Steve.

Isaiah found his cubbyhole and changed while Chip stretched on the football field near the parking lot. He faced away from the lot while he loosened his hamstrings. He heard a car door shut and assumed Steve had returned without getting gas. He heard footsteps. As he turned, two strange men stood fifty feet from him and stared. One had a shaved head with a bald eagle tattoo.

Chip's heart raced. His eyes darted toward the restrooms and back at the men. *Should I run? Should I scream?* He knew he could outrun them. He planted his right foot.

The man with the eagle tattoo pulled a pistol from the back of his pants. "Don't try it. You run, and you're dead."

A wave of terror welled in Chip's belly. "What do you want?"

"Just shut up," the man with the gun said. "Don't move, and you won't get hurt."

The second man pulled out zip cuffs and handcuffed him. "Now, we're going to walk to our car, and you're going to walk with us with your mouth shut. Understand?"

"Yeah." Chip's eyes darted to see if there was any hope for someone to stop the men. *Are they going to kill me? Oh, God, help me.* As the men walked Chip to the parking lot, he glanced toward the restrooms and saw Isaiah hunched under the bleachers. He was watching everything.

As they exited the track, the man with the tattoo pulled out his cell phone. "Boss, we have him. We'll be in Leesville in about three hours."

Leesville. Where's that? What will they do with me there?

"Okay. We'll call when we get there." The men pushed Chip into the back of a black SUV and sped away.

Win had stored a special ring on his cell phone for calls from Steve. He was surprised that he called at the beginning of their workout. He hoped no one had strained or twisted anything. "Hey, Steve. Everything okay?"

"Win, Chip's been kidnapped. You need to get over here now."

Win's body trembled. "What? Calm down. What are you talking about?"

"Someone kidnapped Chip. I left the boys for ten minutes to get gas. When I came back, Isaiah was shaking. He said two men with a gun grabbed Chip and shoved him into a SUV and took off."

Before Steve finished his sentence, Win was already in his car. "I'll be there in a few minutes. Have you called the police?"

"That was the first thing I did. They're on the way."

"Me, too." Win sped out of his driveway, down Lakeshore, and up Stanford. He was on Interstate 10 within a couple minutes.

"Oh, God. Please, protect Chip. Don't let anything happen to him." Tears streamed down his face. It took very little time to get to Airline Highway and then to Indian Heights High School. Once he passed the red light before the school, he saw the police car in the lot and an officer talking to Steve and Isaiah. Speeding into the lot, he slammed on his brakes, stopping just before the police car. He hopped out and ran up to Steve, Isaiah, and the policeman. Another officer was talking on the radio. He put down the radio and pulled his pistol.

Win yelled, "Have you heard anything?"

"Calm down, sir," the policeman said. "Who are you?"

"I'm the boy's grandfather!" He grabbed Steve's shoulders. "What happened? What . . ." Win's head dropped on Steve's shoulder, and he wept.

"I'm so sorry, Win." Steve spoke with absolute determination. "We're going to find him. We'll get him back. I promise you and I promise his father, Mike Thibodeaux, that I'll get his son back."

CHAPTER THIRTY-SEVEN

The police officer interviewed Isaiah. "Can you describe the two men?"

"They were both white. One was completely bald, with a tattoo of some kind of bird covering his head."

When Win heard Isaiah's statement, he gasped and covered his face with his hands. *No. It can't be.*

The officer saw Win's reaction. "Sir, do you know this person?"

"I don't, but Chip's grandmother ran into a man a few days ago who fits that description. She told me about the encounter."

"What's her name? Do you have an address and phone number?"

Before he could respond, Win's cell phone rang. He turned his back to the officer. "Grace, I was just talking about you."

"Really? I was having my time alone with the Lord, and as I prayed, I had this overwhelming sense I should call you. What's going on?"

Win took a deep breath. "Chip has been . . ." He found it almost impossible to say.

With alarm, Grace asked, "Been what?"

"Grace, he's been kidnapped." There was no response. "Grace, you there?"

"Kidnapped? When?" She sobbed between words. "Where? Does Hope know?"

"Hope doesn't know yet. I'm at the Indian Heights track. The police are here. I think you'd better get to Hope's house right away. I don't know if you need to come here — or what needs to happen next. There's something I need to find out. I'm headed to Todd's house."

"Todd's? Why?"

Win paused and looked down. "One of the guys who grabbed Chip was bald with a tattoo of a bird on his head."

"Oh, no," Grace cried. "No!"

"Grace, let me pray with you, then I'm headed to Todd's." Win walked toward the officer with Steve and Isaiah, pointed to his phone, and lifted his finger to let them know he would only be a minute. "God, I pray for Chip, wherever he is right now. I ask You to protect him and bring him back safely. I ask for a supernatural amount of grace for all of us. I pray for Hope. I ask that you give Grace wisdom. Guide her as she talks to Hope. Oh, God, I pray for a miracle."

Win told the officers the call was from Chip's grandmother. "She's headed to the home of our daughter to tell her what's happened. They'll be here shortly."

"Good. We have some detectives on their way here. They're a part of the investigation into the Braun kid's death. They'll want to talk to them both."

I'd better get out of here before they arrive or I'll never get to Todd's house. "Okay. I'll tell them." Win grabbed his car keys. "I'm going to check something. I'll make sure they get here quickly."

Steve walked Win to his car while the officer continued to interview Isaiah.

"What's up, man?" he asked softly.

"Those detectives on their way — they think I had something to do with selling steroids to Jamie. I need to talk to Todd Mayo right away. He may have some information about this. But I'll never get to him once the detectives arrive. If I'm not back by the time they've finished talking to Isaiah and you, then call me."

"Will do." Steve gave Win a firm handshake and a pat on the shoulder. "Be careful."

"Steve, pray." Win's voice broke again. "Please ask Pastor Washington to pray."

"I'm not only going to pray, but I'm going to put feet to my prayers. Chip's dad died in my place. I'm going to find who did this. Trust me, I'll find them — and I'll find Chip."

Hope was busy with Saturday activities when the doorbell rang. "Mom, What are you doing . . .?" She grabbed her mother. "What's wrong, Mom?"

Grace did her best to keep from crying.

"Mom, come in." She guided Grace to a chair. "What's happened?"

It seemed like an eternity before Grace could speak. "Chip's been kidnapped."

"Oh, God! No!" Tears ran down her face as she grabbed her mom's shoulders. "What are you talking about?"

"Win just called me. The police are at the school."

Hope stood and spoke rapidly. "We have to get there right now. There's got to be some kind of mistake." She searched for her purse. "Come on, let's go."

Grace and Hope made it to Indian Heights High in less than ten minutes. Detectives Bourgeois and Ramirez were there, talking to Steve and Isaiah.

Hope ran to a police officer. "Have you found my son? This has to be a big mistake. Please, tell me it's a mistake."

"Calm down, ma'am. Are you Chip Thibodeaux's mother?"

"Yes. Please tell me this isn't true. Maybe this is some kind of a hoax."

"I'm sorry, ma'am, but this young man saw two men with a gun force your son into a vehicle." He nodded toward Isaiah. "Do you know him?"

"Yes, but not very well. He runs with Chip sometimes."

"He was changing into his workout gear near the men's restroom when two men came up to Chip. He heard shouting, and he peeked around the building. The two men had a gun pointed at your son, then cuffed him. He heard them say they were headed to Leesville. Do you know anyone in Leesville?"

"Leesville? No. I've never been there."

"We're wondering if he might have heard 'Leeville.' Detective Bourgeois is talking to him about that."

"I don't know anything about Leeville, either."

Grace spoke up. "Chip's grandfather said a man with his head covered with a tattoo of a bird was one of those who took Chip."

"Yes, ma'am. And he said you met a man who fits that description a few days ago."

"Yes, that's correct."

"What?" Hope said. "When did that happen?"

Grace told the officer about the incident at the outlet mall.

The officer interrupted Detective Bourgeois. "I think you need to hear this." He brought both detectives to Grace and Hope and introduced them.

Detective Bourgeois looked at Hope. "I'm so sorry, ma'am. We're going to do our best to find your son as quickly as possible. Having an eyewitness gives us some hope."

The officer pointed to Grace. "She had an encounter a few days ago with a man with a bald head that was covered with a tattoo of some sort of bird."

"Really? Where and when did this happen?"

Grace again gave details about her experience at the outlet mall. "I went to the coffee shop and saw a close friend who happens to be my pastor. He was talking to two men. I approached him to say hello. There was something strange about the two men. I don't know how to explain it, but they seemed evil. The way they looked at me. One was bald with an eagle that covered his head."

"Did they tell you their names?"

"One said his name was Joey. The other called himself 'Bald Eagle.'"

Detective Bourgeois raised his brow and looked at Detective Ramirez.

"What?" Hope said. "You know them?"

"We're familiar with the tattoo guy," Detective Bourgeois said. "Do you know if these guys were friends of your pastor?"

"I don't think so," Grace said. "I told Chip's grandfather about the incident, and he had a PI check these guys. Both were tied to the mob. But it never crossed our minds that they would do anything to Chip."

Hope burst into tears, and Grace held her tightly until the crying slowed.

The detectives continued their questions. "Is Chip's grandfather your husband?"

"No." She sighed. "It's a long story. But Hope is our daughter."

"What's his name?"

"Win Bass."

Bourgeois looked at Ramirez, who had a sarcastic smile. "You know where he is right now?"

"I'm not sure, but I think he went to see my pastor, Todd Mayo." Grace gave him Todd's address.

The police officer broke in. "Win Bass. That's the same guy who was here just a few minutes ago."

Steve heard the conversation and walked over. "I called Mr. Bass and told him what had happened. That's why he came."

"We need to talk to you about that — and about your relationship with Mr. Bass." Bourgeois turned to Ramirez. "We need to get some people over to Mayo's house immediately. Make sure there's plenty of backup. Tell them we'll be there as soon as we can."

CHAPTER THIRTY-EIGHT

Win's heart was racing. He pulled up to Todd's home and sprinted to the door. He punched the doorbell a half dozen times, then banged on the door.

Elaine looked startled as she opened the door. "Win, what's wrong?"

"Where's Todd?"

Elaine gaped at Win.

He raised his voice. "I said, 'Where's Todd?'"

Elaine tried to gain her composure. "What do you want with him?"

Win pushed the door open and walked in. "Where's Todd?" he shouted.

Todd rushed into the entry area. "Win, what's going on?"

Win lunged, grabbing Todd by the shirt. "Where is he? Why are you doing this?"

Elaine screamed, "Stop! Stop!"

Todd pushed Win back. "What are you doing? Have you gone crazy?"

Win pointed at Todd. "You know what I'm talking about. You told Grace not to tell me about the two men you met."

Todd glanced at Elaine, who looked confused. "Calm down, and let's go outside and talk about this."

"Outside? You don't want Elaine to hear. Well, she's about to know everything. The police will be here any minute. But I thought you might first want to tell me where Chip is."

"What are you talking about?"

Elaine watched with horror. "Todd, what's going on? What two men?"

"Don't tell me you don't know anything. Chip was just kidnapped by two men. One had a shaved head covered by a tattoo of a large bird — exactly like the guy with Todd when Grace saw him at the outlet mall."

Todd covered his face with his hands and staggered to the couch. "Oh, God."

Elaine ran to Todd. "What? What's he talking about?"

Tears filled Todd's eyes. "I can't believe this."

Win's voice became more forceful. "Look at me!" He gritted his teeth. "Believe what, Todd? Tell me right now. Believe what?"

"I don't know anything about Chip being kidnapped. Please trust me on this." He turned toward Elaine. "I ran out of options to get money to pay our house note. When the foreclosure proceedings began, I panicked. I found a group in New Orleans that offered a loan at an incredibly high interest rate. I talked to them on the phone, then met them at the outlet mall. When I met them I knew I was in deep trouble, but I never expected anything like this."

Todd looked at Win. "I'm so sorry."

Win's phone rang. It was Steve. "Hey, I'm with Todd."

"You'd better get out of there, quick. Several squad cars are on their way. I don't think you need to be there when they arrive. These detectives have finished talking to Isaiah, and now they're talking to Grace and Hope. They're headed to Pastor Mayo's as soon as they're finished. Go to our church. I'll meet you there."

Win pointed at Todd. "I'll be back, and I want answers."

<hr>

When Win got to Mount Calvary Missionary Baptist Church, Pastor Washington was waiting. "Come inside. Let's talk. Steve and Isaiah are on their way. They'll be here any minute."

Pastor Washington placed his hand on Win's shoulder. "Sit down. You all right? Steve told me Chip was kidnapped and that Isaiah saw everything. Have you heard anything else?"

"I just left Todd's house. He says he doesn't know anything about the abduction. I have my doubts."

"Whoa. You think Pastor Mayo had something to do with this?"

"I don't know, but he met recently with some guys with ties to the New Orleans mob. One of those guys took part in the kidnapping."

"Let's not be hasty. There must be a good explanation for the meeting, and that doesn't necessarily mean he had anything to do with the abduction. What did he say when you went to his house?"

"He claims he contacted them to obtain a loan, and that was his only contact. He says . . ."

Steve and Isaiah burst through the door. Isaiah walked to a corner of the room and stood with a glassy stare. Steve placed his palm on Win's shoulder and looked him in the eye. "We're going to find him. I promise."

Win looked at the floor.

Pastor Washington asked, "What are the police saying?" He glanced at Isaiah and nodded. "Is he okay?"

"I don't know. He's pretty shaken. And confused."

"Confused?" Pastor Washington said. "About what?"

"The police think the kidnappers are associated with the New Orleans mob."

Pastor Washington looked perplexed. "Why?"

Steve placed his hands on his hips. "One was bald with a tattoo of a bird on his head. It fit the description of a guy with ties to the mob."

Pastor Washington stumbled backward. "Oh, no."

Win stepped toward Washington. "What? Oh, no, what?"

"LaKeisha said one of the men that grabbed her was bald with a tattoo of a bird on his head."

Win fell to his knees.

Steve cleared his throat. "Isaiah told the police he heard the abductors say they were going to Leesville. The detectives thought he must have heard *Leeville*. They said Leeville is south of New Orleans on the Gulf Coast. Told us the mob has always used the coast as a haven for drug trafficking. They said they were sure the mob had a place somewhere in Leeville.

"They said Leesville didn't make any sense. It's near the Texas border. Lots of military there. Not the kind of place mob guys would hide." Steve shook his head. "When they discussed that, Isaiah became confused. Then he said he didn't know if he heard Leeville or Leesville. The more he tried to answer their questions, the more confused he became. I think he's in shock."

"How strongly do the police feel they went to Leeville?"

"Pastor, they were adamant about Leeville."

"Give me a few minutes." Pastor Washington walked to Isaiah and placed his arm around his shoulders. "You okay?"

Isaiah stared at the ground and nodded.

"Let's go into my office and visit for a few minutes."

Win and Steve discussed options while Pastor Washington talked to Isaiah.

After a half-hour, Pastor Washington returned. "Isaiah heard Leesville, not Leeville."

Win jumped to his feet. "Are you sure?"

"One hundred percent positive."

"Should we let the police know?"

"I don't know, Win," Steve said. "They were adamant these guys wouldn't have gone there. They're certain Isaiah heard Leeville." Steve took a deep breath. "I have an idea. Pastor, why don't you call Detective Bourgeois about your talk with Isaiah?" He handed him the detective's business card. "Meanwhile, Win and I will go to his house and discuss the situation. We'll see if we can come up with some ideas that might help find him."

Win shook his head. "Pastor, I really need to talk to LaKeisha. She may know something that's helpful."

"I don't think they'll let you in to see her, especially if they get wind of what's going on," Washington said. "Let me call out there and tell them you need to talk to her. I'll pave the way for you to talk to her by phone."

Steve grabbed Win's arm. "He's right. We'll call her from your house."

Pastor Washington handed Win the phone number of the home for girls who'd been trafficked. "Wait at least fifteen minutes before you call."

CHAPTER THIRTY-NINE

Once they were outside, Steve told Win, "I don't think we ought to go to your house. If the police are looking for you, that's the first place they'll check. Let's go to my place. It's not far."

"Why'd you tell Pastor Washington we were headed to my house?"

"He's very honest. When the police ask if he knows where we are, he'll tell the truth. I decided he didn't need to know where we're going. My house is on Brady Street, just a block from Istrouma High."

"I grew up a block from there, on Dalton Street."

"Follow me. If I lose you, it's just west of 38th."

The small, wood-framed house reminded Win of where he'd grown up. It sat on concrete bricks, no foundation — and had a detached, one-car garage. Steve had the garage door open. "Pull in here. The police will be looking for your car. It's hard to miss. It'll be safe here. If we need to go somewhere, we'll take my truck."

Steve went to the back bedroom and told his bedridden mother a friend was visiting. He started his computer in the small living area and pulled up Google maps. The two began looking at the locations of Leeville and Leesville and discussing where Chip may have been taken.

Win called the girls' home and finally reached LaKeisha. After reminding her of their encounter, he explained what had happened with Chip. "Is there anything you can tell me that might be helpful?"

"I don't know much more than Pastor Washington told you. One of the kidnappers who took me was like the guy you described with the tattoo. And I can tell you this. They took me to Leesville, and that's where the people from Houston met them. They took me from Leesville to Houston."

———◇◇———

Three hours after the kidnapping, Chip sat zip-cuffed in the rear seat of the SUV. The two kidnappers had talked little during the trip to Leesville. The smell of whiskey and stale cigar smoke made Chip sick to his stomach.

They pulled into a Wendy's, and the bald tattoo guy snipped Chip's zip cuffs. "I'm gonna be real nice to ya. Takin' these off, and we're going inside. You'll go into the john with my partner. If you look at anyone suspiciously, you're dead. Talk to anyone, you're dead. You try to run, you're dead." He placed his gun in his pocket and raised his brow. "Understand?"

"Yeah."

Chip glanced around the parking area to see if there was any possibility of running. *No way. I'd better wait. Maybe they'll let me go once they understand I won't talk to anyone about what I saw with Coach. Oh, God, please send someone to help me.*

A few minutes later, the three walked out of Wendy's and crossed the parking lot. *This may be my only chance. I can outrun them.* He bolted and ran toward the street. A car turning into the parking lot grazed Chip, sending him onto the pavement. An elderly driver jumped out of the car. "I'm sorry. Are you . . ."

Bald Eagle grabbed Chip and pulled him away. "Sorry. He's drunk. Don't worry. He's cool." He pushed Chip into the SUV. "You crazy, man!" He punched Chip in the eye. "If you try it again, we'll kill you!"

Chip's face was cut from Bald Eagle's punch, and he had a few bruises from hitting the pavement, but nothing broken. Just banged up.

Bald Eagle zip-cuffed Chip's hands. He raised a bag with hamburger and fries. "This was for you, but not now." Bald Eagle turned to his partner. "Turn left. Then north on Highway 171."

"Don't we always meet the dudes from Houston here in Leesville?"

"Not this time. We're headed to a little town — Hornbeck."

Halfway to Hornbeck, Bald Eagle turned to Chip. "It looks like we'll be seeing a lot of each other the next few days. Hope you don't try anything else stupid. You need somethin', you ask Bald Eagle. Me and Bruno here got everything."

Chip produced a fake smile. *I think you ought to be called Stupid and Stupider.* A sickening thought crossed his mind. *Why did he tell me their names? They know I can identify them. They'll never let me get out of here alive.*

Bald Eagle made a phone call. "Boss, we're in Hornbeck. Where to from here?" He jotted a few notes, smiled, and looked at Bruno. "We're headed into the boondocks."

"I thought this was the boondocks."

"You ain't seen nothin' yet. We still got a few minutes of boondocks driving."

"Is Frankie there?"

"He's got everything set up. We're about to be big-time boy scouts."

<hr />

"Steve, why do you think Pastor Washington is so sure Isaiah heard Leesville?"

"Isaiah never had a daddy. Pastor's like a father to him. When Isaiah was small and would throw a fit, only Pastor Washington could settle him. They have a special bond. That's why he didn't want to take any chances with you. He loves that kid, and Isaiah knows it. I'm sure he was able to calm Isaiah. If anyone knows what Isaiah actually heard, it's Pastor Washington."

"Why would they would take Chip to Leesville when the mob works out of New Orleans?"

"That's a big question." Steve looked up and rubbed his chin. "That PI friend of yours — he said these guys are for sure with the mafia?"

"He said that Bald Eagle guy is an associate with the mafia."

Steve smiled. "Maybe that's it."

"What?"

"Associates aren't necessarily a part of the mob family. They do a lot of the dirty work for the mob, but they also work independently. Maybe they're not working for the mafia. Maybe they're working for someone else."

"Someone not from New Orleans."

"Think about it. Who might have a motive to kidnap Chip?"

Win placed his head in his hands. "Maybe the person who fed

Jamie the steroids. When I talked to Chip about Jamie and steroid use, he would clam up. Maybe he knew too much."

"That's a big possibility. But there's another. Maybe money is the motive."

"Hope doesn't have a lot of money."

"Win, are you blind?"

"What?"

"Chip's grandfather comes to town. He's a multimillionaire. And a few months later, Chip is kidnapped. Don't you think there's a possible connection?"

"I'd never forgive myself if something happened to Chip because of me. What scares me most is what LaKeisha said about them bringing her to Leesville." Win turned pale and started blowing out large breaths.

"What's wrong, Win?"

"I rescued a girl in Houston who had been trafficked. She had been kidnapped in Baton Rouge. You don't think it might be . . ."

"Stop. We have to think rationally. We need to figure a way to find and rescue Chip. Now, think. Who do you know that has one of those motives?"

"Todd definitely has the financial motive. He's desperate for money to stay out of foreclosure."

"You really think he'd do something like this?"

"I didn't think so. But he recently met with the bald-headed guy."

"What about the other motive? Do you think Chip knew who was feeding steroids to Jamie?"

"Yes. I do."

"Have any idea who?"

"Not really. Possibly Coach Landon."

"Why Coach?"

"He didn't want Chip and Jamie working out together. That seemed strange. But how does this get us closer to finding Chip?"

Steve sighed. "You're right. It doesn't."

"What do we do?"

"I think we ought to head to Leesville."

"Even if they're in Leesville, how do we find them? I wouldn't know where to start."

"If they're actually on the coast in Leeville, the police will be searching there. But they're not checking west in Leesville. I trust

Pastor Washington's instincts with Isaiah, and if they went to Leesville, I know the area. I know people in the town."

Win tilted his head. "You know Leesville? How?"

Steve chuckled. "Almost everyone who has served in the Army is familiar with Leesville. I did my basic training at Fort Polk, just outside the town. I was involved in a church there and still know some of the locals. I also have a good friend who just retired from the military and lives there."

"So what are you thinking?"

"The area is heavily forested. Lots of places to hide, and no one will ever know you're there. I've got equipment, but we need to get you some."

"Like what?"

"Guns, ammo, vest, camouflage gear, and some boots — to start with."

Win took a deep breath. "You don't understand. I've never shot anything in my life. Never owned a gun. I wouldn't know where to begin."

"I hope you're a quick learner."

Win paced the room. "How will we find them?"

"You believe in prayer, don't you?"

Win pursed his lips. "Of course I believe in prayer."

"We'd better start praying now. And we need to get some equipment and head to Leesville as soon as possible. From what I know about these kinds of things, the sooner we locate Chip, the better his chances of survival."

Win looked down. "And I guess the opposite is true, also." He sighed. "You're right. We need to act right away."

CHAPTER FORTY

As they turned off Highway 171, Chip's heart pounded. The village of Hornbeck sat deep in western Louisiana's pine forests. Near Toledo Bend Reservoir, it reflected why Louisiana's license tags read, *Sportsman's Paradise*. He remembered hearing that at one time, it had been a hiding place for notorious outlaws.

During World War II, Fort Polk and the surrounding area became the launching point of what was known as the Louisiana Maneuvers. The deep pine forests in Western Louisiana furnished ample places to practice battles, perform tactical missions, and provide hideouts for the "enemy." Much had changed since then, but outlaws still loved the hideouts the forests provided.

As Bruno drove them toward Toledo Bend Reservoir, Chip looked closely, trying to see how to escape if he had the chance. The sight of the forests frightened him. The further they drove, the thicker the forest, and everything looked the same: multitudes of pines reaching to the heavens. Because he'd grown up in the city, he knew almost nothing about surviving in the woods. *I need to remember everything. I need to know how to get out of here.*

The SUV came to a junction, and Bruno asked, "Which way?"

Bald Eagle glanced at his notes. "Right."

Not long after passing a church, they saw a sign for "Beckom Cemetery" pointing toward a road heading into the forest. The SUV slowed, and Chip wondered, *Are they going to bury me there?* He felt like someone grabbed his throat and squeezed.

Bald Eagle glanced at his notes. "Stay on this road. We're headed the right direction."

Chip's senses settled as they passed the cemetery. A few minutes later, they turned right at a sign that read Rattan Road. Within another couple of minutes, they came upon the Pleasant Hill Baptist Church on the left. Rattan Road veered to the left.

They were deep in the forests, with very few houses in sight. Chip's heart pounded. *If there's a church out here, people must live in these woods. Maybe someone will see us.*

They came to another junction, and Bald Eagle checked his notes. "Man, this is spooky out here."

"This is the boondocks."

"Okay. Turn on Prospect Road." As they turned, they passed an abandoned house. A few hundred yards later, they came to an old dirt road.

Chip's heart raced, and he prayed. He'd never prayed this much. *I have to remember these roads. Please, God, don't let me forget.*

Bald Eagle told Bruno to go slow. "We're close." They traveled a quarter-mile down the dirt road and passed a tiny church that looked like it hadn't been used in a long time. They passed a small green house tucked in the woods on the left.

Chip strained to see the small structure. No one seemed to be home. *I wonder who lives there. God, if anyone lives there, help them find me.*

"Turn here."

"There ain't nothin' there."

"On the grass, stupid. See the tracks." It appeared some logging trucks had created a trail into the heart of the forest.

Chip fought back tears. He didn't want Stupid and Stupider to see his fear. Within a hundred yards, he noticed dogs barking. After two hundred yards, Bald Eagle gave the order: "Stop here or we'll get stuck. We're far enough into the woods that nobody will see the SUV. Let's walk."

Bald Eagle and Bruno grabbed Chip's arms, making sure he didn't try to run. The farther they walked, the louder the barking. Chip's eyes darted left and right. Nothing but pine trees and thick brush. As they came to a clearing, they saw the dogs: two pit bulls, each on a leash, jumping and snapping. Chip stopped and tried to step back.

Bald Eagle looked at Chip and laughed. "What's the matter, pretty boy? Scared?"

A voice came from the left. "Don't try to pass those bulls. Go back about twenty yards, walk fifty feet into the woods, and come toward my voice. You'll see the camp once you're in the woods."

Once off the trail, they got a clear view of the camp. Three pup tents had been erected in the middle of a fifty-foot clearing. An old log lay in front of the tents with a fire in front of it. Behind and to the right of the tents was the strangest thing Chip had ever seen. It looked like a small jail cell. *What is that? What are they going to do?*

Bald Eagle, Bruno, and Frankie greeted one another. "So this is our paycheck." Frankie chuckled. "Welcome to the Hilton." The three men laughed.

Frankie looked at Chip. "Don't get the wrong idea. Those tents aren't for you." He pointed to the jail-like structure. "This is your special place."

Chip's eyes grew wide. "What is it?"

"It's the Hilton in the woods. Exotic, man. Exotic."

Chip stared at the structure. A six-foot cube, its iron bars had rusted from the weather. A door on one side measured about five feet high and two feet wide.

As the men pushed Chip toward the door, he swallowed hard and stumbled. Bald Eagle grabbed him before he fell.

Chip grabbed the bars, holding on and breathing heavily. "Please. Don't put me in there. I'm begging you. Please, don't put me in there."

"What's the problem?" Frankie said. "It was full of weeds and brush when I got here. But look at it — all clean and everything. I put a tarp over the top to protect you from the rain. Even got you a sleeping bag."

Frankie softly slapped Chip on the cheek. "Come on, pretty boy. Be thankful. I'm even going to take off these cuffs. Your hands can be free in there. Now isn't that nice? Besides, this one is bigger than most of these cages. They're normally used to trap wild hogs. But we knew you ain't wild. So we got you a nice big'un."

Frankie shoved Chip into the cage and cut the cuffs. "Now, you're safe in here." He smiled. "But if you give us any problems, those dogs are real hungry." He put a lock on the door and turned to the others. "Want a beer?"

CHAPTER FORTY-ONE

Steve grabbed his gear from his bedroom, and the two headed to a sporting goods store. "I have a semiautomatic rifle and plenty of magazines. I have everything I'll need. But we need to get you geared up."

Win kept rubbing his face on the way to the store in Denham Springs. "Will they let me buy a gun? I was arrested in California and convicted of possession of marijuana."

"If we need to, we'll buy the stuff in my name. For sure, that won't be a problem." Steve glanced at Win. "You having second thoughts?"

"I'm having second, third, and fourth thoughts. This makes me sick. I can't imagine shooting another human being."

"The bad guys don't mind shooting you or Chip."

"I know." Win shook his head. "If I'm in a situation where I have to shoot someone, I don't see how I could pull the trigger."

"So if we get in a situation where someone has to die — Chip or the bad guys — you're okay with Chip being killed."

Win stared at Steve. "That's not what I meant."

"Look, I didn't choose this situation. You didn't choose it. But we have to make a decision right now. Are you in or out? Are we going after Chip — or are we going to let these guys do whatever they're going to do to him?"

Win thought for several seconds. "I'm in."

As Steve and Win entered the sporting goods store, Steve said, "Let me do the talking."

Hope wanted to go to Todd Mayo's home right away. But Grace convinced her to wait until mid-afternoon to make sure the police had completed their interviews.

Just before they left, Hope's phone rang.

Grace whispered, "Who is it?"

Hope mouthed, "Eric Braun." She said, "Eric, would you mind if I put you on speaker phone? I'm so rattled, I'm not thinking straight. Mom is here. I want her to hear any insight you might have."

"Sure." Eric's voice boomed over the speaker. "I don't really have any insight. I just wanted you to know the police contacted me and told me about the abduction. I wanted you to know how sorry I am for you."

"Thank you, Eric," Grace said. "We appreciate that."

"Look, I don't know if this has anything to do with Jamie's death. I'd appreciate it if you could keep me in the loop. Let me know anything the police find out. I just want to know who did this to Jamie. I know you understand."

"Sure, Eric. We're headed to an appointment now. If we learn something we can share with you, Hope or I will let you know."

"I appreciate it."

As they drove to Todd's house, Grace asked, "Did you find Eric's call strange? Calling so soon after all this happened."

"Maybe. But that's the least of my worries right now."

Hope and Grace saw a stranger's car in Todd and Elaine's driveway. Grace looked at Hope. "You think we should go in?"

"There's nothing that's going to keep me out. I need answers. Right now."

Elaine looked washed-out when she answered the door. "Oh, Hope. I'm so sorry. Please, come in."

Ray Landry, Win's defense attorney, sat in the kitchen with Todd. Both stood and Todd tried to hug Hope, but she drew back. Elaine pulled out a chair and motioned to Hope. "Please, have a seat."

Fire blazed from Hope's eyes as she stared at Todd, and an awkward silence filled the room. Finally, Grace spoke. "When I saw you at the mall, you were with two men. One has been identified as the person who kidnapped Chip. We need to know what you were doing with those men — and what you know about Chip's abduction."

Ray Landry raised his hand to signal Stop. "I don't think this is the place or time . . ."

"No, Ray. They deserve answers."

"I don't think it's wise. As your friend, I understand. But as your attorney, we need to discuss this in different circumstances."

Todd's chin dipped to his chest, then he looked directly at Ray. "I understand your concern, but I have to answer any questions they have. If it puts me in a bad legal position, so be it. They need answers. I may not have them, but I've decided transparency will be my way of life — from now on. And if anyone deserves transparency from me, it's Hope and Grace."

"I don't agree, but I'll go along."

Todd turned to Hope. "Please believe this. I don't know anything about the kidnapping." His voice cracked. "But I'm so sorry I ever met those guys from New Orleans. There's no excuse for what I've done."

He looked down and cleared his throat. "I hope my actions haven't put Chip in danger. We were going through foreclosure on our home. I asked Win to help, and he turned me down. I blew up. Became really angry." He looked back at Hope. "I made a stupid decision. I found an extremely high interest rate from a group out of New Orleans and contacted them. I was meeting with them when your mom ran into me. I was scared. Afraid the church would find out. Afraid of these guys."

Hope sneered. "So, you're telling us you'd never seen them before or after that meeting."

"That's right. I promise, Hope. I had no idea this would happen."

Grace leaned forward. "Why? Why did you get involved with thugs like this? That's what I don't understand."

"That's all Elaine and I have talked about since the police left. I think it began ten years ago. Somehow, I became infatuated with money." He shook his head. "I lost sight of Jesus. I became more interested in building a ministry than God's kingdom. Numbers, budgets, and influence . . ." Todd's eyes watered. "They became more important than loving God and people." He paused. "The change was slow and subtle, but it consumed me."

Todd looked at Elaine with eyes that pled for mercy. "A friend once told me that heresy was truth out of balance. He said if you paint a picture of a person and all the features are perfect, except you make the ears bigger than the rest of the face, you've created a monster." He pursed his lips. "I created a terrible monster. I lost sight of the true picture of Jesus." Todd wept. "I'm so sorry." He looked at Hope. "I deserve this monster. But not you. Not Chip. I don't understand how it happened."

———⧓———

Steve told the sales clerk he was looking for an AR-15. What the clerk placed on the counter looked half machine gun and half rifle. The handle formed a V with the stock. The magazine, which held thirty rounds, was directly in front of the trigger. The gun had a Picatinny Rail forearm from which the barrel extended.

Win's body stiffened. *I can't do this.*

As Steve examined the gun, the sales clerk spoke briefly with another customer. Steve turned to Win. "This is a cool piece of equipment. Much like what I used in the military." He handed it to Win. "Check it out."

As Win reached for the handle, his hand trembled.

"What's wrong?"

"I don't think I can do this. I can't shoot someone."

"If you can't hold the rifle, you'll definitely never shoot it. I guess I can't count on you."

"I didn't say that."

"Then what are you saying?"

"Nothing. Buy it. I'll get over my nervousness."

Steve set it on the counter. When the clerk returned, he told him that he wanted the rifle and a half-dozen clips and some boxes of ammo.

The clerk asked him to fill out paperwork. "It'll take about 45 minutes, and it's yours."

"Okay, my friend and I need to buy some clothing."

Steve picked up a pair of Mossy Oak camouflage boots. "These will help you feel the terrain. Try 'em on."

"Why will I need to feel the terrain?"

"We'll talk about that when we get on location, but noise is an issue when you're in the woods. As you move slowly through the trees, you'll want to feel any twig you're about to step on. But we have a bigger problem than that. I have to know for certain you're going to do this. Tell me now if there's any possibility you'll back out."

Goosebumps popped up on Win's arms. "I'm in. It's just so difficult." As they exited the store, Win thought, *What am I getting into?*

⸺⸺⸺◇◇⸺⸺⸺

Todd tried to answer all of Hope and Grace's questions. As they got up to leave, he said, "I'd understand if you never go to Indian Heights Church again. But I have a request. I'd like you to be present tomorrow morning."

Grace waited a moment. "Why?"

"I'm going to resign. What I've done has hurt the cause of Christ. I've failed God. I've failed the church. I've disqualified myself from leadership. But that's not why I want you there. I want to call our church to pray and fast for Chip's safety and deliverance. I'd like to ask the people to gather around you two and pray."

Hope's voice quivered. "We want prayer, but I need to think about whether I can handle going to Indian Heights."

"Grace, have you talked to Win? I need to ask his forgiveness."

"I haven't talked to him since he called and told me about the abduction."

"If you hear from him, please tell him to call me. It's important."

CHAPTER FORTY-TWO

Steve had kept calm in the store, despite Win's wavering attitude. But as they hopped in the truck, he exploded. "Your grandson is out there somewhere — held captive by some thugs. No telling what they'll do to him. And you can't decide what you're going to do."

Steve shook his head. "I'm ready to do this by myself. If you're going to be a part, I have to know you're with me all the way. If you don't care enough about your grandson to go after the bad guys, I'll do it alone. His dad took my place in Iraq. If it weren't for him, it would've been me killed in that desert. If you're going to continue going back and forth, then I've had it. Make up your mind."

"That's not fair, and you know it. I told you I would. I'm just struggling. I'm in one hundred percent. But I've never been a soldier. We're talking about killing another human being."

"If that other human being is going to kill your own flesh and blood, how could you hesitate?"

Win's face turned red. "Don't tell me I don't love my grandson just because I find it difficult to kill someone. I lived in a prison for three years with guys that killing was second nature to them. I vowed I'd never become like that."

"Okay, you want out. Then, you're out."

"I love Chip more than you can ever imagine." Win's voice became firm. "I'm going to find and rescue him. But I'm having a hard time with shooting someone."

"I'm headed back. I'm dropping you off, and you can get in your fancy car, go to your comfortable home, and relax. Meanwhile, I'm going to find your grandson. His life is more important to me than kicking back in a big brick mansion."

"Steve, that's enough! We're turning on each other. Before we leave this parking lot, let's calm down. Turn off the motor, and let's pray."

Win bowed his head. Steve stared at him, but as Win began praying, Steve lowered his head and closed his eyes. "God, we need You. I need You. Please, calm our hearts. Give us strength and wisdom. Show us what to do. I pray in Jesus' name. Amen."

"Amen."

Win turned to Steve. "I have to go to Leesville. I can't do anything else. I love Chip too much."

"I'm sorry I yelled. Sorry I said what I said."

"I'm sorry, too."

Neither spoke as they drove across the Atchafalaya Basin. Before they came to Lafayette, Steve tried to engage Win. "You seem to be in deep thought. You have any more ideas?"

"It all seems weird."

"I know. Who would kidnap him — and why?"

"It's not just Chip. I returned to Baton Rouge as a result of rescuing LaKeisha from a kidnapping. Now my grandson is kidnapped."

"You think LaKeisha's kidnapping might have something to do with Chip?"

"I don't know. It just seems strange."

Steve stopped in Lafayette to fill the gas tank. As he was pumping, Grace called. For the first time since they'd left Baton Rouge, Win smiled. "I was just thinking about you. I really needed to talk, to hear your voice."

"Where are you?"

He looked at Steve and tried to buy some time. "Where am I?"

Steve shook his head and mouthed, "No, don't tell her."

"I can't say. I only want you to know I'm going to find Chip. I promise you."

"Win. I know what you're up to. Be careful. I don't know if I could handle losing you and Chip at the same time."

"Really? I mean, I understand about Chip. But . . ."

"I don't want anything to happen to you, Win Bass."

"I'm glad you called. I really needed this."

"Hope and I just left Todd's house."

"What did he say? Did he give you any info?"

"I don't think he had anything to do with this. He's going to resign as pastor of the church tomorrow morning."

"He ought to resign. I still have a hard time believing he doesn't know anything. It's too odd that he met these guys right before Chip was kidnapped."

"I know, but I looked into his eyes. He's a broken man. — broken that he became involved with them. I saw a side of Todd I haven't seen in ten years. It's the Todd I knew when I first opened my life to Christ. He realizes he made a terrible mistake. He's more transparent than I've seen in a very long time, and he's taking responsibility for his actions."

"And what does that do for Chip?"

"Win, remember that people judged you wrongly, so wrongly. You need to give Todd a chance. He wants to talk to you."

"I want to talk to him, but face to face."

"He asked that you call him."

"I'll have to think about it. Meanwhile, Steve and I are back on the road."

"So you're with Steve."

Win gritted his teeth. If the police questioned Grace, they'd ask about his whereabouts.

"All I can say is that I'm okay. Don't worry. And tell Hope her father is going to find her son."

"Okay, and I . . ."

Win waited, but silence followed. "You what?"

"I'll call you tomorrow after the service and let you know what happened."

"Okay. If I don't answer, it's because I can't."

"One more thing. The media hasn't reported on this yet. Be praying. I assume the police haven't released what's happened to the media. Pray that when the media picks this up, it won't hurt the investigation."

"Believe me. If there's one thing I'm doing, it's praying."

Steve smiled when Win finished the call. "Sounds like you have a thing for the little lady."

"Maybe." Win smiled. "What about you? I've never asked. You married? I didn't see any pictures at your house of a wife."

"Nope. Divorced. My fault. I was real stupid when I was younger. Now I'm just stupid."

"I hear ya."

"Take my phone. Find Buddy Thompson in the contacts. The area code should be 337."

"Here it is. You want me to dial it for you?"

"Yeah."

"Hey, Buddy. Steve Joiner here." Steve grinned as he heard his friend's voice.

"Sure, man, it's been a long time. I'm on my way to Leesville and need to talk to you. It's really important." Steve nodded as he listened. "Fried chicken sounds great. Janice makes the best fried chicken I've ever eaten. Look, I have a friend with me. That okay?" Steve looked at Win and nodded. "Give me your address, and I'll punch it into my GPS. We should be there in a couple hours."

"Who's that?" Win asked

"We were together in basic training. He's an outdoorsman and really loved the area when we were at Fort Polk. When he retired a year ago, he moved back. Loves to hunt, and there's great hunting. He lives in a little community, Slagle. It's just outside Leesville. He was a sniper in Afghanistan. He'll have an idea where to start our search."

"I have another question before we get there, and don't get bent out of shape because I'm asking."

"Fire away."

"Does AR-15 stand for 'Assault Rifle-15?'"

"Are you afraid of having an assault rifle?"

"Just wondering."

"No. AR is the trademark for the rifle. It stands for ArmaLite Rifle Model 15. Make you feel better?"

"Maybe."

"Look, I'm not upset, but I know how these things work. I can't have a partner hesitating if we get into a firefight. A one-second delay could get us both killed. That's why I'm so adamant. Maybe it's best if your part of this search-and-rescue mission be the search, and mine, the rescue. You work on helping find where he's located, gathering intelligence, and I'll do the rescue by myself."

"I told you I'm in all the way. Give me some time. I need to process everything."

"The problem is that we're running out of time."

CHAPTER FORTY-THREE

A few minutes before dusk, Steve and Win pulled up to the brick ranch-style house on Slagle Loop, northeast of Leesville. The tops of the pines behind the house waved in the breeze, as if welcoming the visitors.

Buddy, a well-built man in his mid-forties, met them in the driveway and gave Steve a big hug. He extended his hand to Win. "Great to meet you. Any friend of Steve's is a friend of mine. Come on in. Janice is about ready with the best fried chicken you've ever tasted."

"Can't wait. It's great to see you."

Buddy escorted them into the family room where a twelve-point deer head was mounted above the fireplace. The room looked like a wildlife museum, with a bobcat, an elk, and more trophy deer. Buddy turned to Steve. "It's great to see you. What brings you out to this neck of the woods?"

Steve looked down. "My friend here. His grandson was kidnapped this morning, and we have reason to believe the kidnappers brought him somewhere around Leesville."

"Have you contacted the police?"

"That was the first thing we did. But they believe he was taken to Leeville."

Janice stepped into the family room. "Okay, gentlemen. Dinner is served."

"I'll explain over dinner."

After Grace arrived home, she called Jenny. She had been a solid rock for Grace since she'd joined the ladies' prayer group. She always had the right words. When Jenny answered, Grace tried to speak. "Jenny, my grand . . ." A torrent of tears gushed.

"Grace, what's wrong?"

Through her tears, Grace explained the events of the day.

"I'm so sorry," Jenny said. "He's going to be okay. You have to believe that. No matter what happens, you can't lose faith." Grace sniffed as Jenny continued. "I have a list of prayer leaders in the city. I'm going to call them right now, and we're going to muster an army of prayer warriors."

"Jenny, I want to make sure this doesn't get in the media. I don't want to do anything that hinders the police."

"I understand. Let's do this. I know ten women who are great prayer warriors. They know how to keep things confidential. I trust them completely. Is it okay to share with them?"

"Whatever you think. I called you because I want people praying. But I also want to be careful."

"Grace, the Bible says in James chapter five, 'The effective, fervent prayer of a righteous man accomplishes much.' These ladies walk closely with God. When they pray, heaven opens. God works. Things change. God can do more through ten praying people than the FBI, the Baton Rouge Police Department, and the state police combined. I still believe God is up to something big — really big. Somehow He's going to work through this to display His glory."

"I hope so, but I'm going to have to go on your faith. I'm not there yet."

"Let me pray for you."

"I'd really like that."

"Father, You are a good Father. There's no one like You. You love us, and You care about Chip more than we do. I ask You, Father, to surround him with Your love and protection. I ask You to deliver him from these evil men. I ask that You cause things to happen that will let someone know where he's at. I pray for Win and his friend as they search for him. I pray for the police. Give them wisdom and knowledge. I ask for a miracle. And I pray that You would turn this situation from disaster to one that brings You glory and honor. I pray that You would use it to purify Your people. Change Your people through this. Send a mighty revival. And bring

Chip home safely. In Jesus' name, amen."

After Grace hung up, she washed out the Coca-Cola bottle and filled it with more water.

———◇◇◇———

Frankie turned to Bald Eagle. "You got the phone?"

"Yeah. Bruno stole it in the French Quarter from a guy from New York City. Got it yesterday before headin' to Baton Rouge to meet Boss."

Frankie walked to the cage with Bald Eagle, and Bruno followed close behind. "Okay, pretty boy. We're gonna call your grandpa and talk to him. Then we're going to hand you the cell phone. Thirteen is your lucky number. You say only thirteen words. 'Please do what they say. They will let me go if you do.' If you say anything else — or make any other noise — you'll never speak to anybody again. Understand?"

Chip looked down. "Yeah."

"You remember those words?"

"Yeah."

———◇◇◇———

Steve sat at the table with Buddy and Janice. "Pastor Washington is just as convinced that Isaiah heard *Leesville* as the police are convinced that he heard *Leeville*."

"What's your gut tell you?"

"Leesville. I know the detectives are professionals, but I trust Pastor Washington. He's very wise and discerning."

Win's cell phone rang, and he glanced at the number. "Area code 212. Where's that? Don't know anyone from there." He put the phone back in its case.

"Man, what are you doing?" Steve said. "That could be the FBI. No telling who it is."

"Let me check real quick and find the location of the area code," Buddy said. In a minute, he quickly returned to the table. "It's Manhattan. New York City."

"There's a voice message." Win put his phone on speaker.

"If ya want to see your grandson alive again, we need $500,000. Don't go to the police. Don't contact the FBI. Don't talk to anyone. We'll give ya instructions Monday morning. Get the money ready." Then came Chip's voice. "Please do what they say. They will let me go if you do." Click.

Win stared at the table. Tears welled in Janice's eyes. Fire raged in Steve.

Buddy stood and pounded on the table. "This is war. We're going to find these guys." He stared at Win and nodded. "We're going to get them."

Steve looked up at Buddy. "And how are we going to do that?"

"If they're here, someone is going to know something. This isn't a large community, and most of the people are Army. We're like a big family. We'll start with our church tomorrow morning. I'll talk to Pastor Franklin. We'll tell the people at our church. They know people at other churches. By Monday, the word will have spread throughout the base and town."

Win shook his head. "That's too late! We need to do something right now. We need to find them before Monday — or I need to have a half-million dollars ready. That's our only choice."

"You're right. Let me call Pastor Franklin. Steve and I have trained in these woods. He can show you some of the basics. If they're hiding in these forests, you'll need to know some essentials of search and rescue."

Janice grabbed Buddy. "I'll prepare the guest bedroom."

"Thanks," Win said, "but I don't think we'll get much sleep tonight."

"I'll get the gear from the truck."

Win sat with his head in his hands. He knew he needed to help, but he sat limp, feeling drained of every ounce of energy.

Steve placed the AR-15, the magazines, and the ammo on the table.

Win raised his head with a blank stare.

"You're kidding. You're not going to do this again."

"It's not just the guns," Win said. "It's the money."

"What are you talking about?"

"Now we know the motive. Money. Don't you see? This wouldn't have happened if it wasn't for my wealth. A few years ago in Seattle, after one of our runs, we were discussing our net worth.

"Calvin told us to be careful. He said our true worth couldn't be measured by material possessions, but only by our value to God. He read a passage from the Bible that says not to accumulate treasures on earth, where thieves can break in and steal. We all laughed and said we hoped our net worth would be so high, thieves would target us. Calvin just stared at us, looking disappointed."

"Is Calvin poor?"

"He has more wealth than all of us." Win shook his head. "If I hadn't come to Baton Rouge and flaunted my wealth — my car, my house — maybe this wouldn't have happened."

"You can't go there, Win. You can't live with the 'what ifs.' Your focus has to be on finding and freeing Chip. Focus. When you're coming down the final stretch in the 400 meters, you have to maintain focus. You're tired. You don't think you can make it. That's when you have to focus on the finish line. I'm telling you, man. This is the final stretch. We're getting close. I can feel it. Focus."

CHAPTER FORTY-FOUR

When Buddy and Steve were in Basic Training, Buddy had received an Expert rating, the highest in marksmanship. He'd hit thirty-nine out of forty targets at distances of 50 to 300 meters. In Afghanistan he became a sniper. His expertise would be invaluable.

Buddy returned to the room with a wide smile. "I talked to Pastor Franklin. He's ready to help in any way possible. A telephone team from the church will be calling every pastor and church within a thirty-mile radius. They're sharing the description of Chip and the two men. The pastors will tell their congregations what's happened and see if anyone knows anything. They'll tell their people to be on the alert. We're going to find these jokers. He said that tomorrow in our service, we'll call for a prayer meeting. Before we pray, he asked if you could share with the people what's taken place."

"This is great." Steve slapped Buddy on the shoulder. "I knew you'd come through."

Win looked at the floor. "I just hope it's not too late."

"I don't know if these guys are hiding in the woods, in a structure, or even if they're in the area." Buddy said. "But we'd better be prepared."

Steve tilted his head. "We? Does that mean you're in this with us?"

"You think I'm going to sit on the sidelines while you two go into battle by yourselves? If I get my sight on those idiots, it's all over. I don't care what kind of mob they work with. They're history."

Win flinched.

"Win, how much have you hunted or trained in the woods?"

Win looked at Steve.

Steve sighed. "He's never shot a gun. Never hunted. Knows nothing about rescue."

Buddy rolled his eyes. "Okay. Let's start right now. This is good timing. It's dark. Why don't you take him behind the house and help him get used to walking softly in the woods? And give him some basics on handling a gun. Meanwhile, Janice and I have a list of pastors to call."

After dusk, a strange calm engulfed the kidnappers' camp. Chip had never encountered this. He remembered that friends who'd experienced the eye of Hurricane Katrina had told him how eerie it was. They'd said all wind and rain stopped. Everything stood still. There had been complete silence and total calmness. Then a ferocious wind had blown and torrential rain had fallen, bringing flooding, devastation, and death.

He leaned against the iron rods of his cage and gazed at the stars. He sat with his mouth open as he stared at the Big Dipper — experiencing the majesty of God's creation. He'd never seen the stars away from city lights. For the first time, he pondered the greatness of God.

Pit bulls interrupted the silence. They heard something in the woods. His three captors pulled out their rifles and looked in every direction. *Is this the eye of the storm?* A melancholy spirit settled in his heart. *I wonder if Dad saw these stars before he was killed. Will this be 'like father, like son?' Am I destined to die young?* His thoughts grew as dark as the surrounding forest.

The dogs stopped barking and his captors prepared to settle for the night. Chip gazed again at the stars. They were so peaceful, so majestic. Goose bumps rose on his arms. *God is real. He created all this.* Tears flowed. *Oh, God. I'm sorry. I failed You. I've doubted You. But I know You're real. Please, forgive me. Jesus, I believe in You. You are my Savior. I open my heart to You. Come and take control of my life. Help me to live for You.*

Chip felt like a boatload of bricks had been lifted from his shoulders. His eyes closed and every muscle in his body relaxed.

Chip opened his eyes and again gazed upward. *Oh, God. If I die out here, if I don't see the morning sky, I want You to know that I love You. And if You do let me live, I'll live for You. But I'll need Your help. I know how weak I am. I just want You to know that I love You.*

Chip crawled into his sleeping bag. Oddly, the cage gave him a sense of security. The bag warmed his body while God's Spirit enveloped his soul. Life or death — he didn't know what tomorrow would bring, but he knew God held his future. He prayed, *I love You, Lord. If I die tomorrow, I know I'll be with You for eternity. If I wake, then I want to live for You.*

Before heading outside, Steve suggested they put on their boots. "The first thing we need to do is to learn to walk softly. Soft is slow, and slow is swift. We'll find our target before our target finds us — if we're quiet. Let's start by learning to walk softly."

Win was surprised how dark it was. He'd never experienced such deep blackness. Both danger and reverence roamed the forest, causing both fear and awe to flood his emotions. "Steve. You think there are any snakes out here?"

"Probably."

Steve's voice came from behind him, and he turned to look. "Hey, man. You're hard to see."

"My dark skin gives me an advantage. If they're in the forests, I'll be one up."

"And I'll probably be minus fifty."

Win and Steve spent an hour in the forest, with Steve coaching Win on walking softly. He also taught hand signals they could use. "Let's head in and see how it's going with Buddy."

"You go ahead," Win said. "I want to spend some time thinking and praying."

Win walked into the front yard, gazing at the stars. *Oh, God, I know You know where Chip is tonight. I pray that You would make Yourself known to him. Surround him with Your presence. Fill him with Your peace. Oh God, save him.* His prayer turned from silent thoughts to loud cries. "Deliver him. Don't let them hurt him! Somehow, let us find him."

CHAPTER FORTY-FIVE

The dogs barked on and off all night, but those weren't the only sounds. Chip wondered if the howls were wolves or coyotes. The kidnappers set a rotation for sleep and keeping watch, but no one slept much. All were used to the city, and the night noises spooked them. It was nearly 4:30 when Chip's exhaustion took its toll and he fell asleep. He pulled the sleeping bag over his head and crashed. He awakened around 9:00, when the men stirred and started talking about breakfast.

Chip lay on his back, thinking about his experience during the night. *God, You're real. Your presence is still here this morning. I love You.* As he stared at the tarp, it appeared that a branch had fallen on it during the night. It seemed to be three to four feet long. *I wonder what that is.* His question was quickly answered. It began slithering.

Hope and Jenny met at Grace's home at 9:00 to pray before they went to Indian Heights Church. Jenny felt this was a special day and God wanted to work in a mighty way. She hugged Grace and Hope, then stepped back and looked at Hope. She gently asked, "Are you okay?"

Hope's lips trembled. Tears flowed. Her eyes told the story. She hadn't slept all night.

"It's okay," Jenny said. "It's going to be okay."

Grace placed her arm around Hope. "Let's go into the family room and pray."

Before they prayed, Jenny took Hope's hand and offered a weak smile. Grace rubbed her back.

Jenny prayed in a way Grace had never heard. She cried, pled, sought God's presence, and asked God to search their hearts. Then she prayed for Chip. "Oh, Father. You know Chip. You know where he is." Her voice took an authoritative tone. "I'm asking You to work in an unusual manner, to allow something to happen that will reveal where Chip is. I'm asking You for his deliverance. Make Yourself known to Chip. I ask this in Jesus' name."

Grace prayed and claimed some of the promises of the Bible. "Father, You said in Your word that if any two agree that You would answer their prayer. I agree with Jenny. I believe You want to deliver Chip, and I'm asking with Jenny that You work a miracle right now. I pray for Win, wherever he is. Lead him to Chip. Show him where he is."

Hope mustered enough strength to pray. "Oh, God. I wish I had the faith . . ." Tears kept her from continuing.

Grace rubbed Hope's arm.

"Please give me the faith to believe You're going to deliver Chip," Hope prayed. "I love him . . ." She collapsed in tears.

They concluded after several more minutes of prayer, and Hope went to wash her face. Grace took the Coca-Cola bottle and quietly refilled it. "God, You hold my tears. You know them. You know what's going on. If I've ever needed You, it's now."

———◦———◦⋈◦———◦———

Chip gasped as the object moved toward the edge of the tarp. He squirmed out of his sleeping bag and moved to the far side of the cage.

A snake peeked under the tarp. Its broad, brown head looked distinct from its neck. The rim of the top of its head extended ahead of its mouth. The moccasin opened its jaws, displaying its fangs and a white lining. It dropped to the ground, coiled, and stared at Chip. Its eyes and fangs gave the appearance of pure evil.

Chip tried calling for help, but nothing came out. The snake shook its tail, threw its head back, hissed, and charged. Chip finally screamed, "Ahhhhh! Snake! Snake!"

As the snake lunged toward Chip, he threw his sleeping bag to block its strike. The rapid fire of a semiautomatic gun sounded. Chip jumped against the rails. The snake fell limp.

Pandemonium broke out in the campsite. Guys yelled. Chip

stood in one corner of the cage, his breathing so rapid he hyperventilated.

Bald Eagle held his semiautomatic rifle, breathing heavily. He placed the barrel on the belly of the snake. No movement.

Frankie shouted, "What ya doin', man! Somebody's gonna hear those shots and come lookin. You dumb or what?"

"A dead boy won't get us no money. Ya wanted me to let that snake get him? Now, that's dumb."

Frankie grabbed Bald Eagle's muscle shirt. "Ya calling me dumb?"

They stared at one another until Bruno pulled them apart. "Come on, guys. It's not much longer, and we got us a hundred grand. Cool it."

Frankie stared at Bald Eagle. "Your boss man better hurry up. I can't stand much more. No sleep, snakes, a crybaby kid — I've had enough. You tell boss man we need to finish this thing, fast."

The pit bulls began barking and jumping, looking down the trail. Frankie looked at them. "Stupid dogs. I can't believe it."

Bald Eagle lifted his hand. "Listen. Someone's coming. I hear an engine."

Frankie pointed at the rifles. "Put them in the tent. Get your handguns and put them in your pants, under your shirts." He walked to the cage and pointed his finger. "You say anything, and you'll never see another snake — or anything else. I don't want to hear a sound."

An old man with a scraggly beard and baseball cap pulled up on a four-wheeler to within twenty yards of the pit bulls. He had a shotgun strapped around his shoulder. "I heard some screamin' and shootin'. What's goin' on?"

Frankie yelled at the pit bulls, "Quiet!" He turned to the old man. "Don't come too close. Those bulls ain't ate yet. We're camping out, and a snake sneaked up on us. My friend screamed, and we blew it to snake heaven."

The old man strained his neck to see around the trees and thick brush. The clearing and Chip's cage were about fifty feet from the pit bulls and hidden by the trees. "It ain't huntin' season. Why ya campin' here?"

"It's a free country. Ya got a problem?"

"I ain't got no problem. I know what ya up to. But ya just gonna' find more snakes."

"Just what you think we're up to?"

"Ya tryin' to find gold in those holes. But there ain't nothin' there but snakes."

"What ya talkin' about, old man? What gold?"

"Ya ain't foolin' me. I met lots of people lookin' for gold in those holes. Only come after huntin' season. Think ya gonna find the Reverend Devil's loot, do ya? Ain't gonna happen."

"Well, thanks for the warning. We need to get back to breakfast. So best ya leave now."

"Okay. But I don't like those dogs 'round here."

"We don't like you around here. So leave now, while you're able."

The old man put his hand on his shotgun.

"I wouldn't go there," Bald Eagle said, "if ya know what's good for ya."

"Just don't let those dogs loose. You'll regret it if ya do." The old man turned his four-wheeler and headed back to the dirt road.

CHAPTER FORTY-SIX

Before they arrived at the church, Win, Steve, and Buddy discussed what to tell people. The church building was a plain, brick structure. A padded prayer rail stretched across the front of the auditorium just below the platform. The room appeared to hold around 250 people. Before the service, Pastor Franklin led Buddy, Steve, and Win into his office.

Pastor Franklin patted Win's shoulder. "I'm so sorry for what's happened. We'll do everything we can to help. I can't promise we'll find him, but I know our people. They're some of the most loving people on this planet. They'll do everything they can to help you find your grandson." He smiled. "Our church is not a large one, but it's a praying one. We'll turn this morning's service into a prayer meeting. First, I'll ask you to tell everyone what has taken place. Then we'll ask God to intervene. I believe that God is a God who answers prayer. Let's see what He does."

Pastor Franklin looked at Buddy with a smile, then glanced back at Win and Steve. "I don't know what kind of church you men come from, but our church is about sixty percent military, and the rest are locals. In this kind of a situation, some of our people can get very emotional. I thought I ought to prepare you. When they pray, they cry out with desperation. We have one lady, Miss Pearly. When she gets hold of something in her heart, she's like a heavenly bulldog. She won't let it go. Some people say she prays so fervently, the doors rattle." Pastor Franklin chuckled. "Thought I ought to prepare you in case you've never heard anyone pray that way."

"Don't worry about me." Win pointed to his chest. "There's plenty of desperation inside here."

The men had a time of prayer before returning to the sanctuary. Pastor Franklin looked astonished. The church was packed. People stood in the back. "An unusual crowd this morning. Lots of visitors." After a couple of worship songs, Pastor Franklin introduced Steve and Win and asked them to speak. Steve spoke first. He explained what had happened during the kidnapping in Baton Rouge. He described the men, especially the one with an eagle tattoo and why they thought the kidnappers might be in the area.

Win spoke next. As he did, an older man whispered to one of the church members.

Tears flowed down Win's cheeks. "I love my grandson. I didn't even know him until a few months ago. We quickly became friends. Now, I've lost . . ." He wept.

Pastor Franklin had been about to rebuke the two men who kept whispering, but he placed his arm around Win and prayed. The auditorium filled with sobs.

After the pastor prayed, Miss Pearly cried out, "Oh, God. Our hearts break for this child. You, who delivered the Egyptians from their taskmasters; You, who parted the Red Sea; You, who turned the water into wine; You, who raised the dead — we cry to You for this child."

Amens sounded through the congregation.

"Yes, Lord!" she shouted. "Save this boy! Set the captive free!" She stopped and took two deep breaths as though she were listening. "Father, I pray that You would reveal where this boy is being held. In Jesus' name, I pray. In Jesus' name."

A loud chorus of "amen" and "yes, Lord" sounded. People broke into singing: "Amazing grace, how sweet the sound that saved a wretch like me. I once was lost but now am found, was blind but now I see."

Before the second stanza, the two men who'd been whispering made their way to the front. They grabbed Win and Steve and pulled them into a circle with the pastor.

Buddy didn't know what was happening, but he decided he'd better start the second stanza. As the church sang, the young man introduced the older man to the pastor. "This is my father. He and my mom are visiting this weekend. Dad, tell them what you saw."

"Yesterday, my wife and I went to Wendy's to grab a quick bite, and when I turned into the parking lot, a boy ran into my car. My car knocked him to the pavement, and two men in a black SUV grabbed him and yelled that the boy was drunk. They shoved him into the SUV and sped off. One was bald, with a large tattoo covering his head."

Win grabbed Steve, shook his shoulders, and shouted, "He's here! He's here! He's somewhere in Leesville."

Buddy stopped the singing. Silence engulfed the church. Win turned to the congregation. "He's here, somewhere in the area. We have to find him."

A shout of "Hallelujah!" came from the back. The church broke into singing: "Through many dangers, toils and snares, I have already come. 'Twas grace that brought me safe thus far, and grace will lead me home."

A young couple wept and made their way to the front. The young man spoke softly. "We don't attend this church. We really don't go to any church. About five months ago, we lost our . . ." He cleared his throat. "We lost our son when my wife gave birth. We've had . . ." He shook his head. "I've had so much guilt. We started arguing, blaming each other." His wife stood with her head low, weeping. "We decided we couldn't get over this, that divorce was the only option. We planned to file tomorrow. Our last hope was to try church. So we came this morning. As we heard the story and saw the people's love . . ." He looked at his wife.

She glanced back at him. "We need help."

Pastor Franklin placed his hand on the man's shoulder. "Jesus can help you. He can heal the hurt and remove all the feelings of guilt. There's a couple about your age who went through something similar a few years ago. Jesus healed their hurt and removed their guilt. What He did for them, He'll do for you. They're here this morning. I'd like them to talk and pray with you." Pastor Franklin motioned to a couple on the fourth row. They came and escorted the young couple to a private room.

The pastor halted the singing and spoke to the congregation. "God's presence is here in a special way today. He's touching hearts. I don't understand all that's happening, but I know He wants to touch many of you. Maybe you've come with a heavy burden. Maybe you don't have a relationship with God. Or maybe you had one a long time ago, but you left that relationship. We have an altar here. I invite you to come and pour out your heart to Him."

So many people heeded the pastor's words, every space was taken at the prayer rail. People even knelt behind the people kneeling at the rail. The entire front of the church filled with people seeking God. After the front of the church filled, people moved into the aisles and knelt there until there was no room in the aisles. People were everywhere — praying, crying, confessing sin, giving their hearts and lives to Christ. Win had never seen anything like it.

People prayed, then sang. They prayed more and sang more. A lady came out of the office area and approached Pastor Franklin. After she whispered to him, he turned toward Steve and Win with wide eyes. He turned and headed toward the office.

Buddy spoke above the cries and asked those who remained standing to form small circles and pray for Chip. "We now know he is somewhere in the area. Let's ask God to lead us to him." The roar of prayer ascended to heaven.

After a few minutes, Pastor Franklin returned to the auditorium. All the blood had drained from his face. Raising his voice, he pleaded with the people. "Please, give me your attention. Something has happened. It may be dramatic. Please, continue praying. Pray with your whole heart."

He motioned for Steve, Buddy, and Win to follow him into the office. "I just received a call from the pastor of the Pleasant Hill Church. He's headed here now. We need to talk."

CHAPTER FORTY-SEVEN

Grace, Hope, and Jenny slipped into the auditorium of Indian Heights Community Church a few minutes before the service. People were buzzing about an emergency meeting of the deacons, elders, and staff that Pastor Mayo had called at seven that morning. No one knew what it was about, but rumors spread rapidly.

Ten minutes before the start of the worship service, no one had come out of the meeting room. The church had never experienced such an urgent session of its leadership. People speculated it could be anything from moral failure to a diagnosis of cancer.

It wasn't just the leadership meeting that stoked the speculation. That morning there was another unusual element: color. Only a handful of African Americans attended Indian Heights. Yet more than one hundred African Americans sat in small clusters throughout the auditorium. No one knew why such a large group had come that morning. The band normally practiced until ten minutes before the service. No one had seen them.

Grace, Hope, and Jenny found it hard to keep from engaging with others. Everyone wanted to know if they knew what was happening. Todd had asked Hope and Grace to sit on the first or second row. They found a place at the end of the second row of the middle section and waited.

A woman's voice startled the three women. "Excuse me, are you Hope Thibodeaux?" They turned to see who it was. Hope's eyes grew wide. Grace's chin dropped. Jenny murmured, "Oh, no."

A television camera was pointed at them, with a local reporter holding a microphone. Hope covered her face. Grace whispered, "This can't be happening."

Jenny stood and faced the reporter. "This is a worship service. My friend is here to worship God. I think everyone would be better served if you waited until afterward."

An usher came to the rescue. "I'm going to have to ask you to take the camera outside. You're welcome to stay, and your friend is welcome to stay, but we have a policy. No cameras except the ones from the church."

The reporter handed her microphone to the cameraman and motioned for him to leave. "Could I talk to you before the service starts?" she said. "There's a report that's just come out that . . ."

"Hi, Jenny!" A swarm of ten ladies descended upon Jenny, Hope, and Grace. "Sorry we're a little late." The reporter looked dazed.

Jenny stood. "No, you're just in time." She turned to Grace with a smile. "The cavalry has arrived. Three of you sit directly in front of us, three right behind us, two of you on the left side of Hope, and two on the right side of me." The ladies filled the seats surrounding Hope, Grace, and Jenny. With a scowl, the reporter took a seat across the aisle.

Grace turned to Jenny. "Who are these ladies?"

"The ten prayer warriors I told you about. We felt they all needed to be here this morning to pray during the service."

A keyboard player came on the stage and played softly. A spirit of expectancy filled every inch of the auditorium as deacons, elders, and staff appeared. Todd and Elaine Mayo came through a side door, with Pastor Washington and Isaiah at their side.

The worship leader asked the congregation to stand and sing. There was no band of musicians. As they sang a worship chorus about the holiness of God, Grace sensed God's Spirit quietly filling the auditorium. The worship leader asked everyone to sing the great hymn "Holy, Holy, Holy."

As Todd ascended to the platform, silence wrapped its arms around the congregation as a mother would her children when she senses danger. But the hush that swept over the congregation also possessed a mood of reverence. Todd looked at the pulpit, then cleared his throat and gazed across the congregation. Normally he wasn't at a loss for words, but nothing was normal about today.

"It's hard to know where to start. There are two very important things I need to share with you today. The first is a confession. The second, a plea. Let's start with the confession. I've been your pastor and friend for decades. When I came here, the church met in a one-room, wooden building. We've grown. Lives have been changed as God worked among us. When I arrived at Indian Heights, I had a simple devotion to Jesus. I loved Him, and I loved you. My life's passion was to grow in Christlike character and to help you grow in the same way."

He took a long pause, looked down, then around the congregation. Tears shone in his eyes. "About ten years ago, something happened. It was subtle. I can't put a finger on the moment. But I shifted my focus. It was no longer the One from whom all blessings flow. My priority became the blessings that were flowing so freely.

"God not only blessed us spiritually, but also financially. We built buildings and established some wonderful programs. We flew high, ran fast. Somewhere during that time, I lost sight of Jesus. I rationalized my shift in priorities by thinking if our church was growing, then God must be pleased. I forgot that His pleasure is in who we are and who we're becoming.

"I quit becoming what God desired, because I became infatuated with things. I changed from growing in character to growing budgets. I quit seeking God's kingdom and started building my own empire. Of course, this affected my preaching. I had to keep up the appearance that I was God's man because I had His blessings. I violated some of life's most basic principles. I bought cars I couldn't afford, purchased a home that was completely beyond my means. I expected God to provide for my wants rather than meet my needs.

Todd paused again. "It all caught up with me during this economic downturn. I got upside-down in my house note. Instead of confessing what I'd done and repenting, I tried to cover it up. That led to a horrendous nightmare — and the reason I'm standing here today.

"In my attempt to cover my wrong thinking and wrong actions, I tried to get a new loan. As you know in this economic environment, that's very difficult. When we came to the brink of foreclosure, I panicked. I found a shadowy source of financing. I met with these men in Gonzales. God tried to get my attention when I ran into Grace Johnson and she challenged me about what I was doing. By that time, I was blinded by greed. Gold had become more important than God."

Todd began weeping. Pastor Washington came alongside and placed an arm around him. Grace glanced at the prayer warriors. All had their heads bowed in a posture of prayer. The tension in the air multiplied.

Todd continued. "Yesterday, Chip Thibodeaux was working out at Indian Heights High School and was abducted by one of the men I met in Gonzales."

Everyone gasped. Todd hung his head. Grace glanced at the reporter. She was scribbling everything Todd said.

Pastor Washington continued standing with his arm around Todd. Finally he regained his composure. "Because of my failure, and because of what it's done to Chip, I hereby submit my resignation as your pastor, effective today.

"I've asked my new friend, Pastor Thomas Washington, to lead us in a time of prayer for Chip. He and members of his congregation are with us this morning. Chip's mother, Hope, and his grandmother, Grace, are here this morning. I've asked our deacons and elders to encircle them and pray for Chip. This is my plea. Please, pray that God will save Chip from these evil men. Please . . . please pray."

Todd stepped aside so Pastor Washington could stand behind the pulpit.

"Pastor Mayo has done two things this morning," Washington said. "He submitted his resignation. I don't have the authority to do anything about that. Your leaders will have to act upon it. But he asked me to lead us in a time of prayer for Chip Thibodeaux. Chip worked out with a young man from our church, and he witnessed the abduction. He's here this morning. Isaiah, would you come to the pulpit?"

As Isaiah walked toward Pastor Washington, a man stood in the back of the lower section. Waving his hand and walking toward the platform, he shouted, "Pastor, wait a minute. The confession is incomplete."

CHAPTER FORTY-EIGHT

When the man who'd interrupted Pastor Washington reached the platform, tears streamed down his face. Pastor Washington looked to Todd as if to ask, "Should I let him speak?" But Todd stood paralyzed.

The man grabbed Todd and gave him a bear hug. "Thank you, Pastor, for your transparency." Pastor Washington bowed briefly and sighed.

"Your confession is incomplete because there are others here who've done the same thing. We need to confess, because we're also suffering the consequences. I'm one of those. For too many years, I thought my self-worth was found in my position at work. My salary. My home. I worked hard but neglected my family. I said I was doing it for them. The truth is, I was doing it for myself. In the process, I lost my family. My son ran away from home a year ago, and my wife and I . . ." The man sobbed. Pastor Washington put his arm around his shoulders.

"We're getting a divorce. We've been separated for three months, and it's my fault — completely. I've been so self-centered. I wish I could go back . . ."

A well-dressed woman quietly walked from the balcony to the platform. The man's sobs became louder as he saw her approaching.

With tears, she embraced the man. "We're not getting a divorce. This is all I ever wanted. I wanted you to put us first."

Todd asked for some of the church counselors to come and minister to the couple.

The church broke into applause, then a standing ovation. People applauded for the couple, but even more for what God was doing.

It was a divine moment when the eternal collided with the temporal. It was the blessings that flow from God's throne when His people repent and turn to Him.

Pastor Washington smiled. "I think this is getting out of hand."

Todd smiled back. "Out of our hands and into His."

The congregation spontaneously sang "Holy, Holy, Holy." Scores of people left their seats and lined up at the front of the platform. All had two things in common: tears and confessions. For the next several hours, Christians stood and confessed their shortcomings.

A spirit of revival swept the congregation. The entire time, the prayer warriors were on their knees. Young families began leaving around noon to pick up their children. But most people stayed.

After an hour, the reporter left. She placed the report on television, and heaven broke loose in Baton Rouge. People from all over the city poured into the Indian Heights church. By three in the afternoon, there was no more room in the sanctuary. The tech team set up an overflow room with a big-screen television in the gymnasium. It quickly filled.

The stairs to the platform were turned into a makeshift prayer altar. People filled the altar and stood in long lines, telling of how God had spoken to their hearts and changed their lives.

A testimony would incite brokenness in others. Those broken over their failures would come to the altar and pray, then give testimony. The movement of God's Spirit spread like wildfire.

Isaiah asked the young people to meet with him to pray for Chip. Hundreds of youth gathered in small prayer groups. He and Chip's friend Emma led them to seek God.

A spirit of prayer captured everyone from the teens to senior adults. Each of Jenny's ten ladies took a Sunday school room and met with people to pray for Chip's deliverance.

The Spirit of God permeated the Indian Heights Church. Brokenness over sin was the order of the day, and God's grace flowed freely. Broken hearts were healed, shattered lives were put back together, and God's presence rested on the people.

The church in Leesville continued in prayer as Pastor Franklin escorted Buddy, Steve, and Win to his office. "The pastor at Pleasant

Hill just phoned. A ninety-four-year-old lady in his church came to him very upset. She lives north of Hornbeck, close to Florien. She heard gunfire and screaming in the forests.

"Her neighbor came by her house and said he went to see what happened. He told her some angry men were there. One had a shaved head with a tattoo of an eagle. He also said they had pit bulls.

"She's lived there most of her life. Nothing scares her, but she was afraid. The pastor is driving here with her right now."

Win rubbed his face. "Wow. This is coming down fast. We need to move quickly. Can we talk to the lady on the phone?"

"I asked that. The pastor said it would be best for her to sit down and talk to you. He said we'd understand once we met her."

Steve paced and rubbed his hands. "We'd better get ready. Can you bring her to Buddy's house? We'll change and get our gear ready in case we need to go out there right away. Besides, Win needs a little more instruction."

"As soon as they arrive, I'll bring them to you."

———◇◆◇———

At Buddy's home, Win, Steve, and Buddy changed into camouflage outfits. Steve walked Win through the basics of handling the rifle. "After the pastor and old lady leave, we'll have some target practice." Win's stomach churned.

Within forty-five minutes, Pastor Franklin arrived with the Pleasant Hill pastor and the elderly woman. She was surprisingly spry. Pastor Franklin smiled at Buddy. "You have an empty milk carton?"

Buddy rubbed his ear. "Any special reason?"

"Miss Lizzy chews. She needs a place to spit. Said she'd come and tell everything, but she needed an empty milk carton."

"No problem. We'll get her an empty carton."

Everyone sat around the kitchen table, waiting to hear from Miss Lizzy. The pastor from Pleasant Hill spoke first. "Miss Lizzy goes to our church. When our van picked her up this morning, she was really upset. The driver brought her to me, and she told me what happened before the van picked her up. I thought Miss Lizzy ought to tell you."

All eyes stared at Miss Lizzy.

"Well, I'm just so upset. We ain't had none of those gold diggers around here for years. Now they come back and disturb everything."

Win rolled his eyes. *An old lady talking about gold diggers.*

Miss Lizzy spat in the milk carton. "That Reverend Devil just won't go away. Everybody keeps looking for his gold, but I tell ya, they ain't gonna find no gold. I coulda told 'em they'd only find a pit of snakes."

The Pleasant Hill pastor saw the disappointment on the men's faces and interrupted. "Miss Lizzy, these folks aren't from around here. They probably don't know anything about the Reverend Devil. Let me explain."

She spat. "Okay with me."

"The Reverend Devil was the name given to the outlaw John Murrell nearly two hundred years ago. He was the wickedest of wicked men. He told slaves he'd help them escape. When they came to him, he sold them to other slave owners."

"He was the most notorious outlaw ever to come to this part of the country." Miss Lizzy's voice became forceful. "One thing Murrell did was hold revival meetings in these woods. There was a Reverend Joseph Willis, a fine man, who reached many of the people for Christ. Murrell would gather some of Reverend Willis's flock and preach to them in a brush arbor. As he preached, his gang stole everyone's horses. That's how he got the name 'The Reverend Devil.'"

Win's face fell. "Interesting. But what does that have to do with my grandson?"

"That's the problem with you city boys." Miss Lizzy spit. "You gotta learn to wait. Now let me finish.

"The Reverend Devil sold his horses across the Sabine in Spanish territory. But he would hide out in these forests in caves. A lot of people believe that's where he hid his gold, but it ain't so. I grew up in those woods. I played in those caves. There ain't no gold.

"People used to come and dig in those holes, looking for gold. They quit comin' a few years ago because the snakes made their home there. People come lookin' for gold, and all they find is a pit of snakes. Ya know, that's what's wrong with the world. Everybody wants their pot of gold and don't care if it's stolen stuff from a no-good like the Reverend Devil. But the good Lord's gonna let 'em find those slimy snakes."

Win rubbed his face. "Ma'am, I know you think we're impatient, but my grandson is missing. Some very dangerous men have him, and I'm afraid we don't have long. If we don't find him quickly, something really bad might happen."

Miss Lizzy patted Win's hand. "Don't you fret yourself, Sonny. I'm a-gettin' to it. Ya see, since those snakes came, we ain't had nobody diggin' for gold until today."

"Today?" Steve asked.

"That's right. Today. Those gold holes are only about a quarter-mile in the woods from my house. There's a clearing, and they're right behind it. About 9:00 this morning, I heard some screamin'. Sounded like a kid. Then I heard some shots."

Win's eyes darted frantically, and Steve's face twitched.

"There's only one other person lives in those woods. Ole Cotton. He heard the shots, too. So he went back there, and some men met him when he came close. He couldn't see into the clearing because they had pit bulls. He was some mad. But those men had guns, and he was outnumbered.

"He got on his four-wheeler and came to my house and said he was leavin'. Headed to his girlfriend's house over in Texas. He said I should leave, too. He's scared, and I ain't never seen him scared."

Buddy stood and took a deep breath. "Miss Lizzy, did he say how many men or what they looked like?"

"Yep. Three men. One had a bald head with a tattoo all over it."

"Miss Lizzy, this is really important. Did he see a teenage boy?"

"Said he thought somebody else might be in that clearing, but he couldn't see. I tell ya, they just downright dumb. Snakes live in those gold holes, and they'll eat them boys for lunch."

CHAPTER FORTY-NINE

Miss Lizzy decided to stay at the Pleasant Hill pastor's home for a couple of days, until everything settled down. After they left, Buddy turned to Steve and Win. "What do you think? Are these our guys?"

"No doubt," Steve said. "It's them."

Blood drained from Win's face as he looked at the others. "It's them. I just wish I knew if Chip is okay. Or if he's alive."

Win's cell phone rang. It was Grace's number. He slipped outside to talk.

"Win, something's going on at church. I've never experienced anything like this. God has come. His Spirit visited us, and I know Chip is going to be okay. No matter what happens, I know he'll be okay."

"What are you talking about? God visited you?"

"Unless you've been here, it'll be hard to understand. Todd confessed what he did. He resigned — and then the Holy Spirit's presence filled the church in a way I never imagined. People are still here praying, confessing, and seeking God. The news media picked it up, and people are flooding to the church from around the city."

"I . . . I don't know what to say. I mean, that's great." He paused and bit his lip. "The media . . . you didn't tell anyone what I'm doing, did you?"

"Don't worry. No one knows where you are or what you're doing. I just wanted you to know that I'm certain that God is in control of everything. I don't know the outcome, but I know it'll be good. After what I've seen today, I know God is going to do something wonderful. I know I shouldn't have peace right now, but my heart is overflowing with His peace."

"We had something similar happen here in Leesville," Win said. "Really amazing service. Listen, you can't tell anyone, but we may have discovered where Chip is."

"Where? Hope needs to know."

"We don't know for sure yet."

"I have to tell Hope. Her heart is breaking."

"Okay, but listen — and this is extremely important — this can't get out. If we have to go in and rescue him, no one can know."

When Win returned, Steve and Buddy stopped talking. "Win," Steve said. "I'm concerned about you being a part of this operation."

Win stiffened. "What are you talking about?"

"I'm talking about hesitation. A one-second delay, and we're all dead. You have a problem with shooting someone. When the situation breaks, we won't have time for you to figure out if it's right or wrong. It's too risky."

Win pounded the table. "This is my grandson. Did you hear me, Steve? My grandson! Not yours. Not Buddy's. Mine!"

"I realize that, but you've got this problem with guns."

"I don't have a problem with guns. I have a problem with killing someone."

"Even if that someone is trying to kill your grandson?"

"Look, Steve, nothing or nobody is going to keep me from this."

"Hold on guys," Buddy said." There's one thing I know about any mission. We have to be completely united or we're in a heap of trouble. So both of you calm down. I have an idea." Buddy looked at Steve. "Remember how we trained. What about an all-out non-lethal attack?"

Steve shook his head. "I'm not sure what you're talking about."

"When we trained, we used lethal weapons with non-lethal ammo, and those babies put a heap of hurt on our targets. Knocked them over, sometimes out. They gave us enough time to immobilize the enemy and do whatever was needed."

"Yes, but we used things like rubber-pelleted grenades."

"That's right. I can come up with some."

"Where? How?"

"Trust me. I can get them." Buddy looked at Win and smiled. "Legally." He turned back to Steve. "It'll take me a couple of hours, but I can get them." He placed his hand on Win's shoulder. "This can work. But we've got to have lethal backup."

"What do you mean?"

"I'll use a shotgun with rubber pellets. Believe me, I won't miss. It'll put those dudes on their backs. That'll give you and Steve time to cuff them and put them out of operation. But if I have one little thought it's not going to work, I'll use the AR-15. If those guys don't go down with the pellets, they go to their grave. Believe me. I won't miss, and it'll happen very fast."

Steve smiled. "I like it. I can cloverleaf. We can get close enough to their camp to know exactly what to expect."

"I don't think cloverleafing will work," Buddy said. "Remember the dogs. That's my greatest concern. Mafia or no mafia, these guys won't have a chance. The mob doesn't bother me, but it's the dogs — well, that's another story."

Steve paced. "You're right. They can smell or hear us before we ever get our sights on them."

Win frowned. "What do we do?"

"I don't know. You have any ideas, Buddy?"

"Pray."

"Are you serious? That's it. Pray?"

Buddy nodded. "That's it, my friend. Our destiny is in the wind. If the wind is blowing our scent away from them, we're okay. If it blows it toward them, we've got problems. That's when we could get into an all-out firefight."

"Is there some way we could take the dogs out before we get in there?

"We could lace some meat with poison, but how are we going to deliver that? Nope, we need the wind blowing toward us. Dogs' ears and noses are much more sensitive than humans'. That's why they have those pit bulls."

Steve looked to Win. "I'll give you some more training in the woods behind the house while Buddy gets the ammo."

"Win, if I can come up with the grenades, you'll need some instruction on how to use them. Steve tells me you're fast. You may need to chuck one of those babies. Once the guys are knocked to the ground, you and Steve will need to be on top of them immediately. For backup, you and Steve will carry handguns with real ammo. You okay with that?"

With no hesitation, Win nodded. "I'm good. Don't worry about me."

Steve asked Buddy, "When? When does this all come down?"

"After dark. First, there's a more basic question we need to ask. Should we call the police?"

Steve shook his head. "The first thing they'll do is call Baton Rouge. The cops there are convinced my friend Isaiah heard Leeville. We'll have to go through a whole thing of convincing them he said Leesville. And how are we gonna do that? Tell them an old coot saw the kidnappers then left the state? I don't think that's going to fly."

"And we don't have time," Win said. "In about fifteen hours, I'll need to have a half-million dollars ready." He took a deep breath. "If the police delay in any way, we could be in huge trouble. And with everything that happened in Baton Rouge with the police, I don't think anyone will be ready to go into those woods before tomorrow. And that's too late."

"Then, let's do it. Steve, you get the gear ready and work with Win. I'll pick up the grenades and rubber pellet shells. While I'm driving, I'll call the Pleasant Hill pastor and get some more info on the site. Steve, check out Google Earth and get a better feel for the area. See what you can find. When I get back, we'll put together a plan."

Win walked to the edge of the woods and spent time in prayer. He paced through the trees, wringing his hands. "Father, I know I keep telling You how desperate I am, but I'm really desperate this time. Way over my head. Please, help me."

A verse from Exodus he had memorized with Calvin came to mind. *But Moses said to the people, 'Fear not! Stand firm! And see the salvation of the LORD, which He will show you today. For the Egyptians whom you have seen today, you shall never see again.* Win's heart leapt. *Thank You, Lord.*

Win knew what he needed to do. He dialed Grace.

She didn't answer with the normal hello. "Do you have any more information? We're praying."

"That's why I'm calling. Everything is going down tonight, sometime after dark. We'll know for sure if Chip is where we think. But it won't be easy. I'm convinced we need to see God's hand. That's our only hope."

"Do you have any specifics to pray about?"

"Yes. Wind and dogs."

"What?"

"These guys have pit bulls watching for anyone approaching their site. We need the wind to blow our scent away from them."

"Win, have you talked to the police?"

"No. We're going in ourselves."

"Shouldn't you talk to the police?"

"At this point, we don't have time. The kidnappers called. They want money, lots of it. By tomorrow."

"Oh, no!"

"Grace, you can't go to the police. You can't tell anyone what I've told you. Our lives would be in danger." Win paused. "Maybe I shouldn't have called."

"Don't worry. I'm only going to tell Hope and Jenny. The three of us will stay at the church and pray until this is over."

CHAPTER FIFTY

Grace pulled Hope and Jenny into a small room near the sanctuary. "Win thinks they know where Chip is."

"Where?"

"They've located some guys who fit the description of the men who kidnapped Chip. They're somewhere in the woods near Leesville."

Hope burst into tears. Grace held her and rubbed the back of her head. "Chip's coming home. I just know it."

Jenny cleared her throat. "Did he say how they plan to rescue him?"

"No. He asked that we not tell anyone. He said it would put them in danger."

"How do we need to pray?"

"He said to pray for the wind and the dogs. They have watchdogs. He's concerned about the dogs picking up their scent. Pray that they'll know how to deal with the dogs."

"Grace, could I get the ten ladies in a separate room and have them pray until this thing is over? No one would know. They'd have to commit to not leave the room until this is all over. What do you think?"

"I don't know, Jenny. I told Win I wouldn't tell anyone."

"But I know what happens when these ladies pray. There wouldn't be any way for these gals to talk to anyone until everything is over. We need people who know how to pray to go before God's throne."

"Mom," Hope said, "I think she's right. We need people praying."

"Okay," Grace said. "Let's see if they're willing to make that commitment before we tell them anything."

Jenny called the ten ladies into the room and asked if they would be willing to stay in prayer until Chip was freed. She said they would have to hold confidentialities — and would need to let their families know they'd be holed up in the church for the next twenty-four hours. The ladies responded positively. They checked with their families, and all were able to stay.

Grace got permission from the church to set up the all-night prayer vigil in a room near the sanctuary.

Jenny spoke to her prayer team. "Okay, ladies, here's the situation. Win, Steve, and another man may have located Chip. They're going to attempt a rescue. Right now, their greatest concern is dogs. They want us to pray for the wind to blow their scent away from the dogs. Let's do that. But we need to remember the bigger picture. Pray for Chip to be set free. And pray for the men's safety. Then pray whatever God puts on your hearts."

The women formed a circle, knelt, and sought God.

They later learned that people continued to fill the altar in the sanctuary, with no slowing down. Testimonies were given, interspersed with singing. People flooded the altar, and more gave testimonies. Many marriages were restored. Broken relationships were healed.

As people left, new people replaced them. It appeared the service might last all night. There was no order to the service, but complete order in the service.

⸻

Buddy returned with the grenades full of rubber pellets and rubber-filled shotgun shells. "I talked to Miss Lizzy again. Got more details. The SUV is about 200 yards down a grassy trail just past her house. The forest is like what's behind my house. Pine trees. Scrub oaks. A lot of underbrush."

He turned to Steve. "The ground is pretty much what you and I trained on: that gray, clammy clay. The trail turns a little to the right immediately after the SUV and goes for another 200 or so yards. There's another grassy trail that intersects it at that point. That's where the dogs are. About fifty feet to the left is the clearing. The gold holes are directly behind the clearing."

"Great info. I found the Pleasant Hill Church on Google Earth."

"She told me it's right before her house. She said there's an abandoned house near the church. We could hide our vehicle behind it. It's far enough away from the site, we can get there without being heard. Once we're there, we'll cover our faces with camouflage paint and spray our clothing with pine scent. We'll be able to see them much easier than they can see us. We can go the rest of the way by foot."

Buddy turned to Win and pulled out a grenade. "I have several of these you can use for practice. I have a friend who lives northeast of here, deep in the woods. He's got plenty of space for you to chuck a few. He's waiting right now. We don't have a lot of time. It'll be dark in a couple of hours. Steve will instruct you on the basics of throwing these babies. When you get back, we'll all shower down. I have a special soap that will help with our scent. Then we head to Hornbeck."

Win, Steve, and Buddy made it to the abandoned house at sunset. They parked Steve's truck behind the structure, took out their gear, and readied themselves for the assault. They sprayed their camouflage clothing and painted their faces and hands. Buddy had protective vests for each of them. They were fully armed, ready for battle.

They walked quietly past the abandoned church and old cemetery. The only house between there and the grassy trail was Miss Lizzy's. They walked parallel to the road at the edge of the woods until they reached the grassy trail. They only had a quarter-mile left. It was time to engage the enemy.

The three men formed a line. Buddy was fifteen feet inside the woods, off the left side of the trail. Win walked five feet to the left of Buddy, and Steve was five feet to the left of Win.

Everything stood still. There was no wind. Silence and darkness filled every inch of the forest.

Win was used to running four hundred yards. But this felt as if it was a thousand miles. His heart beat so heavily, he feared Steve and Buddy could hear it.

They walked slowly and quietly. The further they moved into the forest, the darker everything became.

Win was surprised by how his eyes adjusted. A slight breeze began to blow. Win knew someone was praying. It was blowing their scent away from the kidnappers.

About fifty yards into the forest, Win stepped on a twig. His heart fluttered. But he felt the twig before it made any noise. He slowly lifted his boot. The pine straw and soft clay ground kept it from snapping. At about one hundred yards, Win sighed. *So far, so good. Help us, Lord.*

The ladies prayed without stopping. They prayed in a group, then alone. They read Scriptures. They sang, then prayed more.

Just after sunset, Jenny asked the ladies to pray in a very specific way. "I feel we need to pray that God would turn what was meant for evil to good. We need to pray that evil would destroy itself. I don't know what that means. But for whatever it's worth, I sense that's how we need to pray."

The ladies immediately asked God to make the evil work for good. One by one, they cried out to God.

Chip lay in his sleeping bag, exhausted. After his encounter with the snake that morning, he'd been unable to sleep.

Neither could the other guys. They were all spooked —and eaten up with chiggers. Everyone was tired, miserable. They rubbed their arms and legs, covered with big, red bumps.

Frankie scowled. "Bald Eagle, ya gotta talk to the boss. We gotta get outta here soon. Ya tell him we gonna bury his boy in the creek if he don't get the money soon."

A lump rose in Chip's throat. *Father, whatever happens, I love You. Please let Mom know how much I love her.* As Chip poured his heart out to God, peace engulfed him and he began to doze.

He awoke to the dogs growling softly — not barking, just growling. The growls slowly became louder. Something was close. Their growls turned to barks. The barks became louder.

The three men jumped up from the big log in front of the tents and picked up their guns. Frankie shone a flashlight at the dogs. One thrust its head back and forth, with something in its mouth. The other jumped back and forth, barking.

"Snakes!" Frankie shouted. "Lots of 'em."

Chaos ensued. The men yelled. The dogs yelped and jumped. The snakes attacked. "Shoot 'em. Shoot 'em."

The fire of semiautomatic weapons crackled through the trees.

Ten, fifteen, twenty, fifty shots. Then silence.

The aroma of death ascended in the darkness. Dead dogs. Dead snakes. Dead silence.

———⟨⟩———

When Buddy, Steve, and Win heard the yelling, they froze. Once the shooting erupted, Win broke into a sweat.

Steve grabbed Win's arm, placed his other hand in front of his face, and slowly brought it down as though he were telling Win, "Stay calm. It's okay."

Buddy signaled to remain still.

No one moved.

When the shooting stopped, the silence grew until it felt like only the darkness existed. Everything in those woods stood still.

Win had never experienced anything even close to it. It felt more like a dream than reality. Darkness. Fear. Silence. His heart pounded like a bass drum in a marching band.

———⟨⟩———

Grace told Jenny she had something she needed to share with the other ladies. "It's heavy on my heart to pray for Chip right now. I feel we need to pray for all fear to be removed, that he would have courage and strength to do whatever he needs to do. I also think we need to pray for wisdom. Ask God to give Chip wisdom and courage. That there won't be any confusion or fear."

One of the ladies prayed with quiet passion. "Oh, Father, I pray for Chip. You said in Your word that perfect love casts out all fear. I ask You to surround him with Your perfect love. That there wouldn't be any room for fear."

"Yes, Lord," another said. "Your word says that You've not given us a spirit of fear or timidity, but of love, power, and a sound mind. I ask You to give all three to Chip. Fill him with Your love, Your power, and a mind that thinks clearly."

"And Father," Hope said. "I pray for Dad." She paused to clear her throat. "I mean Win. I pray that he wouldn't be afraid. I ask that you surround him with Your love. Help him to act quickly and decisively. And, I pray for Chip." Tears gushed.

The ladies gathered and laid hands on her. "Please, Father. Don't let him be afraid. Let him know that everything will be okay."

CHAPTER FIFTY-ONE

After the shock wore off, Frankie yelled at Bald Eagle. "That's it! I've had enough! Get the kid and cuff him."

"What are we gonna do?"

"I don't know, but I ain't staying in these snake-infested woods one more minute. We're goin' to the SUV. We'll figure it out when we get there. I saw a motel on the north side of Leesville. I ain't stayin' here."

"Boss said not to stay in a motel. He said to stay at this campsite."

Frankie pointed his gun at Bald Eagle. "I don't care what boss said! Get the kid!"

Chip locked his hands on the bars, and his face became a mask of terror. Bruno unlocked the cage, and he and Bald Eagle pried Chip's fingers off the bars. They zip-cuffed his hands in front and led him to the edge of the clearing.

Frankie scanned his flashlight across the grass to see if there were any more snakes.

Chip stared at the dead dogs and snakes.

Frankie grabbed Chip and looked at Bald Eagle and Bruno. "Get the ammo and rest of the guns from the tents." When they returned, he told Bruno, "You hold onto him. Watch your step. I'll keep the light in front of us to make sure it's safe."

Buddy, Steve, and Win stood one hundred yards from the SUV, hearing the kidnappers' voices grow louder as they came down the grassy trail.

Steve quietly moved to a position more forward and deeper in the woods. Buddy remained about fifteen feet off the trail, with Win another five feet inside his position.

Buddy had a clear view of the SUV and saw the men turn the curve and head toward the vehicle.

Win's knees trembled. *God, calm me. I need You right now.* His body relaxed. Confidence rose in his heart. He watched Buddy pull out a weapon. It was the AR-15 with real ammo.

Win made a quick check of his grenades. The time had arrived. This wasn't practice. He swallowed and took a deep breath.

When Chip saw the SUV, he knew if he got inside, he would never see another sunrise. Yet with each step he took toward the SUV, the fear that held him in such a tight grip drained away. Chip glanced back at Bruno. It appeared he was more worried about snakes than restraining him.

Chip knew. It was time. He only had one weapon: his feet. He saw a faint trail going into the woods. *I can do this. Now's my chance. Go for it.*

He jerked his arm, bolted from Bruno, and ran.

"Hey!" Bruno took off after him.

Frankie and Bald Eagle stopped dead, not knowing what to do.

"Shoot him!" Frankie yelled. "Kill him."

Chip ran with his cuffed hands lifted in front of his face in case he ran into something. The darkness was so thick and he ran so fast, he had no idea what he might hit. He flew past a scrub oak and almost tripped over a small brush. Behind him, Bruno wheezed and grunted. *Oh, God. Don't let him see me in the darkness.*

Oomph! Chip ran into a pine and fell to the ground. He moaned.

He heard footsteps near his head. "You stupid kid. You're dead!" Chip heard a rifle being readied and Bruno's caustic laugh. He thought they were the last sounds he would ever hear.

They weren't.

The next sounds were a brief scream and the rifle hitting the ground. Then Bruno fell on top of Chip. Someone rolled the body off him and put cuffs on Bruno's hands. Chip squinted to see who it was. The man had his finger over his lips, letting him know not to say anything.

Win's imagination ran wild. *What happened to Chip? I didn't hear gunfire.*

Frankie yelled, "Bruno, what's goin' on? Bruno, answer me."

Two AR-15 bullets whizzed through the darkness.

Frankie fell.

Bald Eagle took off running.

Win took off after him.

As Win began to catch him, Bald Eagle looked back. He slowed, pulled out his pistol, and looked for his target.

Win dove into the trees, rolled on his back, and grabbed a grenade. He placed it at chin level and pulled the pin with his left hand. He hopped to his knees, pointed his left arm toward the man, and launched the grenade with his right hand.

He dropped to the ground on his stomach. Bullets zinged over his head.

An explosion. Dirt and grass flew everywhere.

Win's target was down. Win jumped to his feet and raced to Bald Eagle, who lay in the grass, moaning.

Win zip-cuffed him, stood him up, and pushed him toward the SUV. He kept Bald Eagle directly in front of him, holding his pistol to his back and using him as a shield.

The lights of the SUV came on and spotlighted Win and Bald Eagle. Win flinched and stopped. His heart raced.

"Good job, dude."

Win laughed. Steve's voice had never sounded so good.

"Gramps!" Chip ran to Win, and the two embraced.

Win's eyes moistened. "I've never been so happy to see anyone." He placed his arm around Chip's shoulders.

Steve stood in front of Bald Eagle, pointing his rifle at his face. "Come on, we've got a place for you with your friends."

Buddy had his gun covering the other two. Both were cuffed and sitting on the grass against the SUV. Frankie's thigh and shoulder were bleeding, and Bruno still looked dazed from Steve's knockout blow. Steve assumed the guard position, and Buddy worked on Frankie to stop the bleeding.

Once the kidnappers were secured, Steve slapped Win's chest. "We're gonna sign you up today. Special Ops, here you come."

Win snickered and pointed toward their prisoners. "What are we going to do with them?"

"As soon as Buddy finishes, he'll call the police. I think it's best that he make the call."

———◇◇◇———

The ladies continued with their prayers. They spent much time claiming promises God had made in the Scriptures. Jenny prayed, "Father, You said that as the mountains surround Jerusalem, You would surround Your people. I ask You to surround Chip, Win, and the others who are with them. Draw a circle of protection around them. I ask that they would find You as a shelter, a strong tower of refuge."

Grace stared at her ringing cell phone. It was Win. She looked at the ladies. They looked up and raised their hands. Grace took a deep breath and answered. "Win?"

"Yes. It's me."

Tears welled in Grace's eyes. Hope's mouth dropped open. The others stared in silence.

Grace could tell by Win's voice that everything was okay, but she had to know for certain. "Is everything all right?"

"Everything's great. I have someone here who wants to talk to you and to his mom."

Grace burst into tears and handed the phone to Hope.

CHAPTER FIFTY-TWO

Hope trembled as she took the phone. "Chip?"

He struggled to speak. M . . . — Mo . . . Mom."

It took a long time for Hope to respond. Every time she tried to speak, she cried. Finally she was able to tell him how much she loved him and how they had been praying. "Are you okay?" she asked. "Are you hurt in any way?"

"I'm okay. I can't wait to get home."

After a few minutes, Hope handed the phone to Grace. "Chip, the entire church has been praying for you. The church is packed. They don't know yet that you've been freed, but everyone has been praying."

"Really? Praying for me?"

"When you get here, we'll tell you all about it. Before I go, can I speak to Win?"

She asked him, "Is Chip really okay? He's not just trying to reassure us, is he?"

"He has a few bruises and scrapes, and a lot of chigger bites from being out in the woods. Other than that, he's fine."

"I'm going to let Todd and the church know that Chip's free. Everyone's been praying."

"Give us a little time before you do that. The police are on their way. Let's get these guys formally arrested before we make any announcement. And besides, we still don't know who hired these guys. I'm concerned about Todd."

"You don't still think Todd had anything to do with this?"

"Just a few days before this happened, you saw Todd with this creep I just handcuffed. We know he wanted money, and Todd wanted money from me. So I'm nervous about Todd."

"I know Todd didn't have anything to do with this. If you were here, you'd understand."

"Let's talk about it later. I'd like to see if I can get anything out of these guys before the police arrive."

"Win, thanks. And I . . ." Grace paused. "I appreciate everything you've done."

Win chuckled. "When I get home, I want to talk to you about all these pauses."

Grace smiled. "I'd like that. I'll talk to you later."

Win walked back to the SUV and stooped to look Bald Eagle in the eye. "Who put you up to this? Who's paying you?"

Bald Eagle spit in his face.

Win lost it. He grabbed him by his muscle T-shirt, pulled him a few inches off the ground, and shoved his head against the SUV. "You stupid . . ."

Steve grabbed Win. "He's not worth it. Let the police handle this. They'll be here any minute."

Win stood rigidly and gritted his teeth. He pointed at Bald Eagle and tried to speak.

Steve patted Win's shoulder. "Come on, man. Cool down."

Win opened the SUV to see if he might discover any information. He immediately backed away from the stench of whiskey, cigar smoke, and body odor. But something seemed familiar about the smell. Win looked at Chip. "You rode in this for three hours. How'd you survive?"

Chip laughed. "It wasn't easy. I almost threw up a couple of times."

As Win walked away, two police cars followed Buddy down the grassy trail. Buddy told the police what had happened. Five minutes later, Pastor Franklin arrived with the pastor of the Pleasant Hill Church and a well-known local attorney. More police came. An ambulance. The woods turned into a small village.

An officer told Buddy, "We're going to need you guys to come to Leesville with us. We'll need to get a statement from each of you. We need to talk to the kid. Do you have the names of the detectives in

Baton Rouge handling the case? We need to contact them. We'll talk more when we get back to Leesville."

Buddy, Steve, Win, and Chip hopped in Buddy's double-cab pickup and followed the police. The pastors and attorney followed. On the way, Win's phone rang again. "We're headed to the police station right now. Everything's under control. How's Hope?"

"She's okay. Todd wants to talk to you."

"I don't know. I . . ."

Todd spoke. "Win?"

"Yes."

"You okay, man?"

"I'm okay. And Chip's okay. That's what matters."

"I'm so glad. The reason I asked Grace if I could speak with you is that I need to ask your forgiveness. I was way out of line when I asked you for money. I don't know how it happened, but I lost my focus. Took my eyes off what it's all about and made money my focus. It slowly strangled every ounce of passion I had for Jesus and others. Everything became about me, my blessings. My future.

"That led me to make the biggest mistake of my life," Todd said, "meeting with those thugs. I don't know if that meeting had anything to do with Chip's abduction, but I'm so sorry. Please, forgive me."

Win gritted his teeth. He needed to know if Todd had anything to do with Chip's abduction. "Todd, I'm not ready to talk about this right now. Let's talk about it when I return to Baton Rouge."

"No problem. I'm just thrilled you're okay and Chip's safe. There's one more thing. People here have been praying. The church is packed. We can connect Chip to the PA system, and he could speak to everyone. Is that okay?"

"That's not my decision. You need to ask Hope and Chip."

"Hope is fine with it. Can I speak to Chip?"

"Sure." Win handed him the phone. "Pastor Todd Mayo. He wants to talk to you."

"Pastor?"

"Chip, it's so good to hear your voice." Todd explained the situation and what he wanted to do. "Is that all right with you?"

"Yeah. I'm blown away that all these people have been praying for me. Go ahead. Connect me."

"Okay. Hold on a couple minutes."

Chip looked at Win, shrugged, and smiled. "I can't believe this."

Todd's voice came over the phone as he spoke to the congregation. "We're going to stop the prayer and worship for a few minutes. We have an announcement from a special person. He's on the phone right now. Chip, are you there?"

"Yes, sir. I'm here."

The roar of applause continued for several minutes. Chip's eyes watered.

"The people here have been praying for you. Can you give us a quick report about what's going on and where you are?"

"I'm in a truck with my grandfather right now. We're headed to the police station in Leesville. I'm okay. I want to thank everyone for praying. God answered your prayers. I don't say that lightly. I'll explain later, but it's truly a miracle that I'm in this truck. Thanks so much."

Applause broke out again. After hanging up, he told Win, "That's awesome. I can't believe that all those people were praying for me." Chip smiled, and his body relaxed. "God is real. He really does answer prayer."

"He does." Win stared out the window, then turned back toward Chip. "When we get back to Baton Rouge, I want you to be careful about meeting with Todd. We can talk about it once we're finished at the police station. Just be careful."

Chip tilted his head. With a soft voice, he asked, "Really?"

CHAPTER FIFTY-THREE

It was the busiest Sunday evening in many years for the Leesville police. Chip, Win, Steve, and Buddy were at the station for several hours, occupied with paperwork, questions, and interviews. The three kidnappers were booked and placed behind bars. Chip, Win, and Steve would meet early Monday afternoon with Detective Bourgeois in Baton Rouge.

They arrived at Buddy's home late Sunday evening. Buddy's wife, Janice, fixed a meal that Chip devoured. Then she cleansed Chip's chigger bites with rubbing alcohol and applied calamine lotion. The bites didn't keep him from sleeping. He was exhausted.

After a night's rest, Win, Steve, and Chip headed to Baton Rouge.

No one talked. Win stared out the window, attempting to process all that had taken place. Chip sat quietly in the back. Once they reached Interstate 10, Win asked the inevitable question. "Chip, you have any idea who's behind this?"

"Not really. But if I had to guess, it would be Coach Landon."

Win turned to Chip in the backseat. "Why?"

Chip told Win and Steve about overhearing the conversation between Coach Landon and Jamie, and he described the encounter with the man with a scar.

"Why didn't you tell us this?"

"I was afraid. I didn't know what to do."

"When we get to Baton Rouge, you have to tell Detective Bourgeois everything."

Chip hung his head. "Yeah. I know."

Win sighed. "This sheds a new light on everything. I was thinking it was Todd."

"Pastor Mayo? Why?"

"Your grandmother saw him meeting with the bald tattoo guy a few days before you were kidnapped."

"What?"

"Listen, Chip. Your mom and your grandmother don't think he had anything to do with this. But I want you to be careful. Until we find for sure who is behind this, I don't want you to take any chances. Just make sure you're not alone with him."

"You don't really think he would've done this?"

Win rubbed his forehead. "I don't know what I think. If Coach Landon was supplying the drugs for Jamie, and he was getting them from some unsavory characters, it could be him. We need to find out. Maybe the detectives can get those guys to confess. They'll probably be transferred to Baton Rouge."

Win picked up his car at Steve's and drove Chip home. Grace and Hope ran out and embraced Chip. All three wept while Win watched, grinning. Once they were in the house, Hope and Grace doted on Chip.

Chip smiled at Win. "Maybe I ought to get kidnapped again. I've never had this kind of treatment." He winked. "Hey, Mimi. You ought to have seen Win. He's one superhero."

Grace lifted her chin and smiled. "Oh, really?"

"He knocked out the guy who was chasing me. Then turned and shot the second guy. He hopped up real quick and chased down the third man. This old guy is a real hunk. The woman who gets him is gonna have a big catch."

Win shoved Chip's shoulder, and Chip laughed. Grace walked out of the room.

Win mouthed, "What are you doing?"

"Just trying to help."

Win closed his eyes and smiled. Chip was back to his old self.

Hope and Grace went with Win and Chip for their 2:00 p.m. session at the police station downtown. Win's attorney, Ray Landry, and Steve met them there. Multiple interviews took place simultaneously: one with Chip, another with Win and his attorney.

Grace and Steve were questioned separately.

After a full afternoon, Detective Bourgeois released everyone. He never apologized to Win about his suspicions, though he let Win know he was no longer suspected of any crime. He even expressed appreciation for his part in the rescue.

Win asked the detective about his thoughts.

"I don't know yet. We'll have to follow up on this information. The abductors are being transferred to Baton Rouge. When they get here, we'll put the squeeze on them."

"What do you think about Pastor Todd Mayo? We're headed to a 'praise celebration' this evening at the church. Do you think that's wise in light of the information Grace has provided?"

"I can't tell you what to do. I find his meeting with this Bald Eagle guy interesting. But that doesn't prove anything. We need more information. We've issued an arrest warrant for Coach Landon for the distribution of illegal drugs. He's probably being picked up as we speak. We need to hear what he has to say."

Win, Grace, Chip, and Hope met Todd Mayo a half-hour before the service. Todd embraced Chip, but Chip was stiff.

Todd smiled broadly. "It's so good to see you. We've prayed for you so much. Tonight will be great."

Chip managed to smile. Todd explained what had happened and what he expected this evening. They prayed together then entered the auditorium.

They were surprised to see the sanctuary filled ten minutes before the service. Pastor Washington, Isaiah, and Steve sat on the first row. The altar was packed with people praying and seeking God. Chip embraced Isaiah and thanked him for telling the police what he'd seen and heard.

Pastor Washington stepped to the platform and asked everyone to stand for prayer. God's Spirit gently descended upon the congregation. It was as though yesterday's worship service had never ended.

A man stood and walked to Pastor Washington. With tears, he confessed, "I've struggled with pornography for years. It's ruined my marriage. I want to be free." Pastor Washington prayed for him and called counselors to minister to him.

A lady came weeping from the altar to the pulpit. She confessed anger she'd held for years toward her parents. She said God had just forgiven her, and she wanted to live free from bitterness. Three ladies walked out of the crowd and knelt to pray with her at the altar. Testimonies continued for an hour.

Todd whispered to Win, "This is what's been happening since yesterday morning. We're trying not to control what God is doing. We want His leadership in everything."

After the first testimony, Chip's jaw dropped. He sat in awe of what he was seeing.

After an hour Todd slowly made his way to the platform. He announced that this night was very special, not just because of the move of God's Spirit, but because Chip Thibodeaux was with them. The crowd stood and applauded as Chip made his way to the platform.

Win watched everything carefully. He recalled Jamie's funeral, when three men had stood on the same platform. He remembered those feelings he'd experienced. The darkness. Again three men stood on the platform: Todd Mayo, Thomas Washington, and Chip Thibodeaux. This time, the platform was filled with light.

How different, Win thought. *When God's presence fills a place, everything becomes transparent.* Win recalled 1 Corinthians 4:5, which he had learned with Calvin: "Therefore judge nothing before the appointed time until the Lord comes. He will bring to light the hidden things of darkness and will reveal the purposes of the hearts. Then everyone will have commendation from God."

As Win thought about the verse, Chip thanked the people for their prayers. Win gasped. He knew.

Grace put her arm on his. "Are you okay?"

Win nodded. "I know who's behind the kidnapping."

CHAPTER FIFTY-FOUR

After the service, Grace grabbed Win. "What's going on?"

"I know who did this. When I was at Jamie's memorial service, Coach Landon, Todd, and Eric Braun stood on the stage together. Everything was dark. I felt the presence of evil. Tonight light filled the church, and especially the platform. The entire sanctuary was filled with God's presence, and it exposed the darkness."

"What are you talking about?"

"Remember when we were at the track meet, and Eric Braun came up and blew cigar smoke in my face?"

"What does that have to do with tonight?"

"Don't you see? Two of the men on the platform at Jamie's funeral were exposed when God's presence came and filled the church. The darkness in Todd and Coach Landon's hearts was exposed."

"You're still not making sense. What does that have to do with Eric Braun and the track meet?"

Win shook his head as though waking from a deep sleep. "As I listened to the transparency of the testimonies tonight and I looked at Todd, I realized that only one person on the platform at the funeral hasn't had the darkness in his heart exposed. That's when I remembered the cigar smoke. When I opened the kidnapper's SUV in the forest, it was filled with the smell of alcohol and cigar smoke. I nearly gagged. But the smoke was familiar. Tonight I realized it was the same smell as Eric's expensive cigar."

"Do you really think Eric is guilty, based on a smell in an SUV?"

"I'm sure."

But is that enough evidence for the police?"

"I need more information. I'm headed to my house to do some research." He grabbed Grace's arms, looked into her eyes, and kissed her on the forehead. "I'll call you tomorrow."

———⬥———

Grace blew out a breath.

"Mom, what's going on?"

"I'm not sure. Win thinks he knows who is behind Chip's kidnapping. He's headed to his house to do some research."

"He does? Should we get police protection for Chip until this is over?"

"I don't know what we need to do. This is all new territory."

Chip walked up. "I'm telling you, Mimi. Win's a catch."

Grace smiled and slapped his shoulder.

———⬥———

Win searched the Internet. He found people associated with Eric Braun, the name of his present company, and others associated with it. Once he had enough information, he called his PI friend, who said he'd get back to him in a couple hours.

The news came in ninety minutes. "This Braun guy went to work about six years ago for some guys in New Orleans. Pretty bad dudes. Mafioso types. Some guys associated with the Colombo family in New York moved down there. Law enforcement believes they've been involved with human trafficking. When they came to New Orleans, they also became involved in real estate. Developed some properties.

"This Eric Braun guy worked for them. His company is a subsidiary of theirs. He's part owner and runs the Baton Rouge development arm. Nothing illegal has been pinned on any of them, but from what I hear, they can be ruthless when collecting money."

"Thanks. Do you think the mob would have been a part of my grandson's kidnapping?"

"Don't know. They have a history of kidnapping people who've betrayed them."

"What if someone found a kid they'd kidnapped and returned her? Would they consider that betrayal?"

"No question. My guess is that a perfect storm occurred when you arrived in town. The mob wanted to know who'd crossed them when the kid was taken from the truck stop in Houston. Braun may have had an idea that you were the guy. He saw a way to get even and make money, then used some of the street thugs he'd met to carry this out."

"Why do you think that?"

"Braun's company has taken a major hit through this downturn in the economy. Money's dried up. Nobody can get loans. He's way over his head. And get this: he owes a half-million dollars to the big boys. He needs quick cash. I'm sure he knew you had the money. He found a way to raid your kingdom and also make some points with his bosses."

"Do you think this was revenge from the traffickers or Braun's need for money?"

"Could be both."

"Can you email me any documents? I'd like to give them to the police."

"You'll have them in a half hour."

Win met with Detective Bourgeois the next day and gave him the documents.

Bourgeois scanned them. "I'm impressed. If you ever need a job, check with us." He smiled. "This will help us with our interviews. When we find out anything, I'll let you know."

"What about Coach Landon? Has he said anything?"

"He confessed to selling drugs to the Braun kid. But he's adamant he didn't have anything to do with kidnapping your grandson."

"Do you believe him?"

"I do. His sources were completely different from the New Orleans guys. His suppliers were out of Lafayette and Lake Charles."

"Any thoughts on Todd Mayo?"

"Now that we have this information about Braun, let's see what pans out with our interviews with the kidnappers. My hunch is that Mayo is not involved. Maybe we could pressure him to talk. But here's what I think. He probably made a foolish decision, and it caught up with him. I doubt he's involved in this kind of crime. But, rest assured, we'll find out."

The arrest of Coach Landon devastated the Indian Heights track team, but the team still competed at the District finals, two weeks after Chip's abduction. Assistant coaches did everything possible to have the team ready. Chip felt good about his conditioning and readiness. Isaiah finished well in his competition and qualified for the finals. Chip and Isaiah looked forward to running against each other at Catholic High in the district games.

Win took Grace to the meet. He surprised her when he picked her up.

"What's this?" she said.

Win smiled. "My new car. You like it?"

Grace looked puzzled. "It's just so . . . not like you. She hesitated. "It's so different from your sports car. An SUV. That's a family car."

Win's eyes twinkled. "I sold my sports car and bought this. Came out of the deal with twenty grand."

"This is nice," Grace said. "You really did what you said you'd do."

"As I told you earlier, I could sell my sports car, scale back a little, and still have a really nice vehicle. I could take the extra cash and help put together a computer center for Pastor Washington's after-school training. Help teach them to stay safe when they go online. That's way more important than any status symbol."

"It's great." Grace shook her head. "I've never heard of anyone doing that."

Win laughed. "Me, either. For most of my life, I found my value in the things I possessed. After I gave my life to Christ, my perspective changed. I discovered I had value because of who I am in Him. But I didn't know how to let that truth guide my life. Through everything that's happened, I realized it's okay to have things, just not be married to them. So I said goodbye to the sports car and hello to the SUV. And hello to a computer center for the kids."

Grace hugged him.

"Hop in. Let's head to Catholic High and see how this baby rides."

The crowd at Catholic High seemed like a family reunion. Hope, Steve, Pastor Washington, Todd, and Elaine were there to watch Chip and Isaiah run.

Win thought, *This is where it all began a few months ago. I just wish Jamie could be here.*

The announcer made the last call for the 400 meters. This was the first time for Chip and Isaiah to run against one another in a meet. Isaiah had lane five and Chip, lane two. Chip walked to Isaiah and gave him a fist bump. "Let's take these guys. Me first, you second."

Isaiah smiled. "Don't think so. Me first and you second."

Back at his starting position, Chip smiled and pointed at Isaiah. "Next time you see me will be at the end of the second curve. After that, you'll be in my rearview mirror."

"Runners, take your marks." Chip stretched and took his position.

"Get set." A two-second count. *Boom.*

Chip and Isaiah got off to a good start. They immediately pulled ahead of the other runners. Isaiah had the lead down the straightaway. Chip moved up on him.

Everyone was behind them when they entered the second curve. Isaiah was in the lead, with Chip not far behind.

They were dead even when they came out of the final curve.

Chip took the lead and kept it until the finish — just as he'd told Isaiah.

Both qualified for state.

They gave one another a hug. Both had run their best times ever.

Isaiah's coach came to him. "Great run, son. That's the fastest time any junior has ever run the 400 meters in the history of this state."

Chip looked at Isaiah. "Wow. A record."

As he caught his breath. Isaiah smiled. "You're good, man. Real good."

———◇◇———

As Win and Grace walked out of the stands at Catholic High, they saw Detective Bourgeois. Win extended his hand to the detective. "I didn't know you liked track."

"It's not often I get to see a crime victim perform. Thought I'd check it out. Besides, I have some news."

Detective Bourgeois smiled. "Thought you might like to hear it firsthand. We used the info you gave us to squeeze those guys. They spilled everything. It was Braun. We also were able to get information about the trafficking ring. We've turned it over to the FBI. I'm pretty sure they worked with Braun to kidnap Chip because of revenge and money. We've talked to the girl, LaKeisha, and she's identified two of the guys as having taken part in her kidnapping. "

Win's mouth fell open. "Are you sure? How do you know the men are telling the truth?"

"They gave us enough details to corroborate their stories. We've got a case. Rock-solid."

"What happens next?"

"We arrested Braun this morning. I think the FBI has broken the interstate trafficking ring." Bourgeois extended his hand. "Just wanted to let you know."

CHAPTER FIFTY-FIVE

The state championship came two weeks after district. Chip and Isaiah were thrilled to run at LSU. For both boys, it was a dream come true.

Going into the championship, Chip was ranked first in the 400 meters and Isaiah fifth. A couple of guys from New Orleans and Shreveport could give them a run for their money. Both Chip and Isaiah said they were ready — running for different schools, yet teammates.

Win was so excited that Grace kept having to tell him to slow down as they walked to the stands.

Win had made big plans for today. He'd invited family and friends to a large get-together at his home after the meet. On the agenda were several surprises.

He felt confident it would be a celebration of Chip and Isaiah's victories. He had invested much in their training, and today was payday.

Steve brought Isaiah's mom. It was the first time she'd been able to take time off from work to watch her son run.

Expectation filled the section where Hope, Grace, and Win sat.

Chip had lane four and Isaiah, lane five — the perfect setup. The boys could push each other. Before they went on the track Chip grabbed Isaiah. "Let's pray before we run."

Isaiah let out a deep breath. "I need it. I've never been this nervous."

"Me either."

Both said a brief but passionate prayer. Neither asked to win. Both asked that God enable them to do their best.

They took their places. The gun went off.

Chip and Isaiah came out of the blocks strong. So did the runner from Shreveport. He was in lane one.

Chip was hot on Isaiah's tail as they came into the second curve. He overtook him in the curve, but he heard the Shreveport runner catching him.

Chip started to panic. He then remembered what Win had told him. *Focus. Keep your focus, and you'll keep your form.*

As they came out of the final curve, the lactic acid buildup was huge. Every muscle in his body felt like it moved in slow motion.

Focus. Focus. Use your arms. Keep your form.

Chip's eyes were fixed on the finish line.

He saw the runner from Shreveport on his left. They were neck and neck.

Something happened inside Chip's body. His legs gained strength. He moved ahead of the other runner in the last forty meters.

Chip crossed the finish line the new Louisiana 400-meter state champion. Then came the runner from Shreveport, then Isaiah, beating the time he'd run at district.

While the runners regained their composure, Chip and Isaiah's friends and family cheered. Grace repeatedly jumped, then turned and kissed Win. She blushed.

Win smiled. *Today's a really good day.*

Late that afternoon, everyone gathered at Win's home. The smell of victory filled the house. Win had a Cajun meal catered: plenty of jambalaya, crawfish etouffee, boiled shrimp, dirty rice, seasoned sausage, potatoes, and corn on the cob.

Win and Grace made it to the house before the others. Steve brought Isaiah's mom, and Pastor Washington picked up not only Isaiah, but also LaKeisha.

LaKeisha hugged Win and thanked him for caring enough to help her. "I know God sent you to rescue me."

Win was thrilled to see LaKeisha. "I need to thank you. I wouldn't be here with my friends and family if I hadn't seen you that night. I think God sent you to rescue me. Now come on in."

Hope and Chip came a little later. Todd and Elaine were the last to arrive. Laughter flowed as freely as the sodas.

After people finished eating, Win gathered everyone. "I'd like to have a time of thanksgiving tonight. God has been good to all of us. Chip won the state championship, and Isaiah set a new record for a junior. It's a great day. But first, I have a few things to say. And I have an announcement."

Win looked directly at Todd. "Thanks for your friendship. I'm sorry I doubted you."

Todd nodded and smiled.

Win then turned his words to the entire group.

Grace leaned closer and listened. Everyone quieted, curious what this announcement might be.

"You probably all saw the *For Sale* sign in the front yard. I put the house up for sale a couple of weeks ago. But it's no longer for sale. I received a call from my Realtor, and she said a buyer signed a contract today."

Everyone wanted to congratulate Win, but they weren't sure where his comments were headed.

"I've found a place on a small lake near Indian Heights. I know you're wondering why I'm telling you this." He turned to Pastor Washington. "Pastor, could you come here for a minute?

"Working with the kids at your church has been an incredible blessing. It caused me to reexamine my priorities. I want the profit I'm making on this house to expand the center for the girls' home in Denham Springs, and I want it to be used to offer education to the community about trafficking. I want to attack this problem until we've removed it from Baton Rouge. I'm going to talk with my friends at Dresdtech to see how they might help."

Everyone applauded.

Thomas Washington shook his head. "I'm speechless."

"Don't say anything, because I have more. I've talked to the Dresdtech Foundation, and they're donating thirty new computers, fully loaded with software. I found some guys from LSU who have donated their time to build a website for the center."

"Wow. I, I . . ."

"Thomas, wait a minute," Todd said. "First, I have something to say." He put his arm around Washington. "For too long, our communities have been separated. Many of our people grew up in Istrouma, and many have computer skills. If you're willing, I'd like to challenge them to get involved. To help your kids develop computer skills."

Thomas Washington smiled and shook his head. "I think we've got a real training center."

Everyone cheered.

Hope broke up the celebration. "Can I say something?" Everyone's eyes fixed on her.

"When Win showed up, I didn't know what to think. I doubted his sincerity — even became angry. I thought he was trying to replace my dad. But God changed my heart. God gave me a dad, and no one can ever replace him. He will always be that special person to me. But . . ." She paused. "Win is my dad, too." She walked to Win and kissed him on the cheek. "I love you, Dad."

Isaiah lifted his hands. "Hey, people. If this is gift-giving time, Steve and I brought gifts from the 'hood."

Pastor Washington rolled his eyes.

"Just a minute. Steve is getting them out of the car. I just want to congratulate Chip. He's the new 400-meter state champion. That's really cool. I figured he'd win. So I bought this." Steve handed Isaiah a nicely wrapped gift. "So, my friend, my running partner, here's to the new state champion."

Chip smiled and bumped fists with Isaiah.

Steve shouted, "Open it!"

Chip tore into the wrapping paper and broke the tape. He opened the box and threw it in the air, screaming.

A four-foot black rubber snake bounced out of the box.

Isaiah fell to the floor laughing. Pastor Washington shouted, "Isaiah!" and Isaiah's mother hid her face.

Chip jumped on Isaiah and put him in a headlock. "You're crazy, man. Crazy." They laughed so hard, they had to stop wrestling.

Once everyone calmed, Steve brought out another wrapped present. "And I have a gift for my friend Win Bass."

Win shook his head. "I'm afraid to open it." Everybody prepared for the worst.

"No, man. I'm your friend." Steve smiled. "We've been in battle together. You don't develop closer friendships than when you've been in battle with someone. Trust me."

Win smiled back. "I trust you like I trust that snake." He slowly opened the gift, testing to see what might jump out. When nothing moved, he lifted the top of the box about an inch. He looked up at Steve and smiled.

He laughed and pulled out a bright red water pistol. Steve pulled another from his back pocket and started squirting. Win returned fire. Everyone else ran for cover.

Everyone finally gathered back in the room. "You have to start somewhere," Steve said. "I thought a baby step was the place to start learning."

Thomas Washington shook his head and patted Win on the shoulder. "I apologize for my flock."

Win's eyes moistened. "You guys are great friends." He hugged Todd. "Thanks for being my friend." He turned back to the group. "I never knew what it meant to have family, but now I do. I'm home. I'm finally home."

Everyone left around nine o'clock. Grace stayed to help Win clean up. After a few minutes, Win said, "Let's go out by the old oak tree."

Grace flashed a skeptical look. "At night. Just you and me. I don't know."

⎯⎯⎯◇◇⎯⎯⎯

Hope and Chip were halfway home when she realized she'd left her purse at Win's. "We've got to go back."

"Why?"

"I left my purse."

Chip sighed. "Okay."

Hope took the next exit and headed back.

⎯⎯⎯◇◇⎯⎯⎯

Win took Grace's hand and walked her across the street. "We were in a car. There weren't any houses back then." He smiled. "I think you'll be safe."

A twinkle filled her eyes. "Okay, but I want you to know ahead of time that I said yes then. But if the question is asked tonight, the answer is no."

"You are so distrusting. You don't even know the question."

"Well, Mr. Bass, what's the question?"

"The question is, 'Will you dance with me?'"

"Here? Where's the music?"

Win pulled out his phone. He reached around the back of the old oak and pulled out a battery-operated docking station. He placed his phone in the station and selected a song. As "Chapel of Love" began, he gently took Grace's hand.

Win smiled as he twirled her and sang about going to the chapel to get married. He bent his body forward, rotated his shoulders, and moved backward. With his finger, he motioned her to follow.

Grace followed. Her eyes sparkled in the moonlight.

Win continued to sing with the music, about loving until the end of time.

Win sang so loudly, they didn't hear Hope and Chip pull into the driveway.

Grace smiled. "You still have the moves — for an old man."

"And you still have the magic — for a . . ."

"Watch it."

"For a beautiful lady."

Win stopped the music. He pulled out a small box and dropped to one knee. He opened the box with a diamond ring inside. "Here's the real question. Will you marry me?"

Blood rushed to Grace's face. Time stood still.

Then a voice bellowed. "Mom, Dad, what's going on?"

Win and Grace burst into laughter.

With tears in her eyes, Grace whispered. "Before they get across the street, the answer is yes."

Win stood to embrace and kiss Grace.

Chip and Hope stood speechless.

Win turned toward them and extended his arm. The four formed a circle with their arms around one another, and Grace broke the news. "Your father, and your grandfather . . ." A delighted gleam appeared in her eyes. "We're going to get married. We're going to be a family."

"God is so good. I'm finally home." Win took a deep breath. "Maybe life will be normal now."

Grace gently placed her hand on his chest. "Knowing Win Bass like I've come to know you these past few months, I have a feeling you've only ended *this* adventure."

She placed her finger on his lips. "I don't think normal is a part of our future."

INFORMATION ABOUT SAMMY TIPPIT

Discover more of Sammy Tippit's books:
www.sammytippitbooks.com
Learn more about Sammy Tippit's international ministry and receive
materials that help you to grow in Christ:
www.sammytippit.org

ACKNOWLEDGEMENTS

Writing *Running Home* has truly been a team effort. The journey began when I attended a "Fiction Boot Camp" led by Jerry B. Jenkins. He assembled an incredible team of mentor/teachers. It was at the boot camp that God birthed this story in my heart. I'm so thankful to the novelists who poured into me and the other students. Jerry B. Jenkins, DiAnn Mills, James Scott Bell, and Dr. Dennis Hensley provided an understanding of what it takes to write a captivating story.

My wife, Debe "Tex" Tippit and my daughter Renee Tippit Barker spent countless hours reading, critiquing, and counseling me during the writing process. I was blessed to have a group of Beta Readers, who gave tremendous input after I completed the manuscript: Dot Dickinson, Marilea Spedale, Karen Nolan, Tim Grissom, Darleen Honc, Larry and Ann Spence, Jesse and Mary Hellums, Karen Fillis, Terie LaField, and Beth Thomas.

It's difficult to describe how much I appreciate Andy Scheer's editing. He did an outstanding job! Kylla Lanier made sure I was accurate in my portrayal of human trafficking. Darlene Maroney did a great job of proofreading the manuscript. There were so many who helped with my research questions — too many to mention. Bob Arndt was so persistent in developing the book's website and helping with all the technical details of this work. I am especially appreciative to my cousin, Curt Isles, who brought me to the area where Chip was portrayed as being held in captivity.

HUMAN TRAFFICKING

I recommend anyone interested in halting the darkness of human trafficking to visit the Truckers Against Trafficking website:
http://www.truckersagainsttrafficking.org

www.ingramcontent.com/pod-product-compliance
Lightning Source LLC
Chambersburg PA
CBHW071135260626
47162CB00003B/796